LOCK & KEY

LOCK & KEY

TRACI HUNTER ABRAMSON

Covenant Communications, Inc.

Published by Covenant Communications, Inc.
American Fork, Utah

Printed in the United States of America
First Printing: September 2013

19 18 17 16 15 14 13   10 9 8 7 6 5 4 3 2 1

ISBN 978-1-62108-539-3

For Laura Cwick

Thank you for making swim season such a joy.

ACKNOWLEDGMENTS

My continued thanks and appreciation to Samantha Millburn and Rebecca Cummings for your tireless efforts in helping me in all of my writing efforts and for your invaluable feedback. Thank you to the wonderful people at Covenant for your support and encouragement and for supporting my addiction to the written word.

Thank you to Jen Leigh, Amber Green, and Chrisi Fisher for picking up the slack for me when writing deadlines and Church obligations collide, to John, Melodee, and Sarah Garvin for providing such wonderful examples of what's really important in life, and to my family for loving and supporting me even when life is completely insane.

Finally, thank you to the many readers who have been so supportive of my writing and who motivate me to keep going even when my characters don't want to cooperate.

CHAPTER 1

CARINA CHANNING SET THE HOUSE key on the kitchen table, still not sure why the ordinary item had turned her life upside down. Logically, she understood the key was a link to her past, a time she was fighting hard to forget. She shuddered. She wanted to tuck it away in a drawer somewhere and forget about it, but she couldn't suppress the driving need to understand, to know why it had been sent to her and why someone would try to kill to get it. She needed to know why someone would die for it.

She glanced around her new apartment, trying to distract herself. She could make a home here and had already begun to. A sand-colored sofa and matching chair dominated the living room, and design sketches littered the kitchen table. Her dream of starting her own clothing line was within reach; she had her first client already under contract.

Just as she was pulling one of the designs toward her to examine, the door to her apartment swung open. A smile immediately lit Carina's face when Jay Wellman, the man who had become such a huge part of her happiness, walked in, followed by Bianca. Seeing that Bianca's long red hair was wet, Carina guessed they had come straight from the swimming pool.

Bianca was the tallest of the Channing sisters, even though she was the youngest, but people rarely saw any resemblance between her and Carina anyway. Carina's Italian ancestry was evident in her dark hair, dark eyes, and olive complexion. Bianca, on the other hand, had inherited their mother's fair skin as well as her height.

But even with Bianca's height advantage, Jay towered over both girls as he looked down at Bianca. "That didn't count."

"You just can't accept that a girl beat you," Bianca countered, her voice laced with humor.

"You cheated." Jay turned to Carina and jerked a thumb toward Bianca. "You didn't tell me she cheats."

"I improvised." Bianca grinned up at him. "You're the one who told me Navy SEALs have to adapt to any situation. You're a SEAL. You should have adapted."

"What's going on?" Carina asked before the bantering could continue.

"I challenged him to a race; he lost." Bianca shrugged. "Your boyfriend isn't a very good loser."

"You grabbed my ankle, pulled me underwater, and then you beat me."

Bianca looked at Carina innocently and shrugged again. "He said he was up to the challenge."

"I'll bet he did." Carina bit back a smile.

"I'm going to go change." Bianca tossed a carefree look over her shoulder. "Jay, let me know if you want a rematch."

Jay smiled darkly. "Oh, I will."

Carina couldn't stop the chuckle that escaped when Bianca disappeared into her bedroom. Jay's eyebrows rose, and he turned to look at her. "You think this is funny? Do you know the kind of ribbing I'm going to take from my squad when they find out about this?"

"What makes you think they'll find out about it?"

"You know Bianca's going to tell them the first chance she gets."

Carina felt that little lift in her heart when she thought of Jay's four teammates and the way they had been so accepting of both her and Bianca. She also acknowledged that her youngest sister was treating Jay like the older brother she'd never had. "You're probably right."

He gave her a look of disbelief, and Carina could see the flash of humor in his eyes. "Probably?"

Bianca's bedroom door opened, and she poked her head out. "Hey, Jay. What's Tristan's number?"

"I'm not telling you."

"Fine." She rolled her eyes. "I'll just get it from Seth."

Jay shook his head and plopped himself down on Carina's couch. "What have I gotten myself into?"

"I often ask myself that same question." She sat down beside him and reached for his hand. "Personally, I think you're crazy to have fallen for me."

"Not crazy. Lucky." Jay settled back and swung his arm around her shoulders. "Are you all set for our trip?"

Her stomach clutched uncomfortably at the thought of visiting her estranged father. For so long, she had believed he was the person responsible for taking her mother's life, but the events of the past few months had proven he'd been innocent all along. Unfortunately, the only person who could prove his innocence was dead.

"I have everything worked out to take next week off from work, if that's what you mean." Her shoulders rose and fell as she drew a deep breath. "I'm just so nervous about seeing him. I have no idea what I'm supposed to say."

"You'll figure it out," Jay reassured her. "You have too many unresolved questions in your past that you need answers to."

"I know you're right." She looked up at him. "Are you sure you can juggle things to come with me?"

"My leave is already approved," Jay told her. "With everything we've been through lately, I don't want you traveling all the way to Colorado alone."

Jay glanced over his shoulder toward Bianca's bedroom door before he continued. "Besides, this was a great way to get my parents to come to my baptism on Saturday. If we didn't need them to look after Bianca, I'm not sure they would have agreed to make the trip."

"I really appreciate them being willing to stay with her next week." Carina lowered her voice. "She doesn't let on, but she is still struggling with the fact that someone in our own family tried to kill us."

"She looks like she's adjusting pretty well so far."

"I'm just glad Gianna has been away at college; I'd hate for both of my sisters to have to deal with this." Not wanting to dwell on the past, she asked, "Are you ready for your baptism?"

"Honestly, I'll be glad when it's over."

"How come?" Carina asked.

"Once I'm Mormon, my dad will stop asking me if I'm sure about this."

"I gather he isn't crazy about you converting."

"I think it's more that he doesn't get it," Jay told her. "I mean, I get where he's coming from. I used to think the same way he did, that religion was no big deal."

Carina nodded in understanding. She thought of Jay's father, the giant of a man who had a heart like a marshmallow if you could chip through the gruff exterior to find it. Immediately, she compared him to her own father. Giovanni Perelli had lived his life committing one crime after another but had ultimately tried to protect his immediate family by sending them away and having her mother pretend she had taken them away.

Her voice was a little wistful when she said, "At least you know your dad will support you no matter what. He's a great guy."

As though he could read her thoughts, Jay gave her shoulder a comforting squeeze. "It's not going to help to worry about seeing your dad. We just need to enjoy our time away. Hopefully, by the time we get back from Colorado, you'll have the answers you've been looking for."

The familiar sensation of excitement and dread fluttered in her stomach. "I sure hope so."

* * *

Jay Wellman walked to the front of the chapel and took the seat the bishop offered him. Then the bishop and five of Jay's fellow Navy SEALs encircled him and laid their hands on his head.

He closed his eyes and listened to Seth Johnson perform the priesthood ordinance confirming him a member of The Church of Jesus Christ of Latter-day Saints. A sense of peace and acceptance washed over him as Seth continued to speak, offering him a blessing filled with promise.

When the prayer ended, Jay stood and shook hands with Bishop Zimmerman. Then each of his teammates and his team commander embraced him before they filed back to their seats.

As soon as he took his seat on the pew beside Carina, she reached over and took his hand. He felt that familiar tug deep in his gut, the one that confirmed his love for this incredible woman. She amazed him in so many ways—her talents, her strength, her sensitivity, and her tendency to put others' needs before her own.

The sacrament hymn began, and he glanced over at Carina's sisters. Gianna had arrived home from college to spend some time with them and would leave tomorrow to go back to BYU. In another week, Bianca would start her junior year of high school. He felt bad that her sixteenth birthday had come and gone months ago and the poor kid still didn't have her driver's license.

The entire summer had been so crazy that neither he nor Carina had been able to carve out any time to teach her how to drive. He had gone on several missions that had taken him away from Virginia Beach, and Carina's days had been dominated with work and settling into her new apartment.

Even though Bianca hid it well, he had to imagine she was struggling with all of the changes in her life. A new apartment, a new job, a new swim team, a new school.

Unfortunately, friends weren't yet on her "new" list. Yesterday at his baptism, she had been the only person there under the age of eighteen, except for the bishop's son. Jay couldn't imagine what it must be like for Bianca, always surrounded by adults, always the only person in the room who didn't have control of her own life.

The priesthood holders passed the sacrament, and Jay's thoughts continued to wander. When the meeting concluded, he found himself surrounded by his friends as they crowded in to congratulate him on his new Church membership.

His teammates had already started filtering out of the chapel to go to Sunday School by the time Bianca reached him. She gave him a congratulatory hug and then turned from him to greet Pete Wellman, Jay's father and her former swim coach.

"Well, don't you clean up nice." Pete reached out and tugged at one of her red curls.

"She could say the same about you," Jay commented.

Bianca's smile was automatic, as was the amusement in her voice when she told Jay, "I hardly recognized him without his clipboard."

"You know you miss me," Pete said with a hint of sarcasm.

"I do miss you." Bianca's smile faltered. "It's different here than I thought it would be."

Pete's eyes darkened, and he looked at her intently. "Is everything okay with the new team?"

"I guess." She shrugged. "It's nothing like swimming for you."

"That's because I'm one of a kind," Pete said with a healthy dose of arrogance.

Humor filled Jay's voice. "Dad, you are definitely one of a kind."

"You know it," Pete agreed easily. He turned his attention back to Bianca. "You hang in there. I'm sure you'll do great."

"I'll try."

Jay noticed the bishop's son Jonah coming toward them, his dark hair sun-bleached, his body long and lean.

He stopped when he reached Bianca, then shifted his weight awkwardly before he asked, "Bianca, are you coming to class?"

"Yeah." She reached up and gave Pete a quick kiss on his cheek. "I'll see you later."

"Yes, you will." Pete looked over at Jonah as though he was sending a warning shot across his bow.

Jay smothered a grin. Of all people, Pete should know guys weren't high on Bianca's priority list. Swimming definitely came first with her, and so far, Jay hadn't seen any indication of that changing anytime soon.

As Bianca and Jonah started to walk away, Jay heard Jonah ask, "Who was that guy?"

"Jay Wellman's dad."

"He's kind of scary."

Jay chuckled to himself when Bianca turned to Jonah and said, "You have no idea."

CHAPTER 2

SHE SAT BENEATH AN UMBRELLA on the flagstone patio, the water of the swimming pool lapping quietly in the warm Chicago breeze. Birds chirped from somewhere in the distance, and the bright sun hung in the clear blue sky, shining down on the peaceful setting. But she didn't feel peaceful.

She didn't have to look at the newspaper articles about Raymond Alexander's death to remember every detail, nor did she have to look at the photographs she had obtained of Carina and Bianca Channing to know what they looked like. All she cared about now was making them pay.

Together, the two sisters had been responsible for killing the most important man in her life. Raymond had taught her everything. He had given her a family heritage, a thirst for power, and a need to be part of the business that had been rightfully theirs. Together, they were the Perelli family, even though they didn't carry the name.

Raymond was gone now, but she could still follow his dreams. He had given her the tools, and she knew exactly what she had to do. She would find Carina Channing, and after she retrieved the key to her future, she would make sure Carina and her precious little sister would never again see the light of another day.

* * *

Jay leaned against the wall in Seth Johnson's living room and let himself absorb the scene. All four of his teammates from the Saint Squad were present, along with their wives. His parents had also joined them, as well as Carina and her sisters.

Seth's wife, Vanessa, had been the instigator of this particular gathering, insisting they needed to celebrate Jay's baptism and confirmation. Seeing his parents in this LDS environment was oddly revealing. While his father grumbled about being surrounded by Mormons, he fit in surprisingly well.

As a former athlete and now renowned coach, Pete Wellman had never been much of a drinker—an occasional beer watching a ball game maybe, but even then he was more likely to reach for a tall glass of water. Jay had followed in his father's footsteps in that regard, and he was grateful for that now. Giving up the occasional drink had been an easy transition. The challenge for his conversion had been that he hadn't felt a need for religion in his life. After all, he had the career he wanted, and generally, his life was good.

His teammates had given him nearly a dozen copies of the Book of Mormon during his first year with the squad. They had invited him to their various Church activities and prayed with him at the beginning of each workday and at the start of each mission. None of that had inspired him to change his life.

But then everything had changed in a matter of seconds.

A helicopter crash, one he had walked away from, had shaken him to the core. Then meeting Carina and helping her through her own struggles had forced him to take a hard look at his priorities. The experiences left him searching for something he hadn't immediately been able to identify. Little by little, his life had been touched by the gospel, and his exposure had intensified.

Ultimately, he had broken down and prayed about this religion he had been exposed to so much during his time with the Saint Squad. The minute he had opened his heart completely to the gospel, he'd found clarity he hadn't even known he was searching for.

Now he was Mormon. Now he was really one of them.

Across the room, he heard his father ribbing Bianca about being short, a fact that couldn't be further from the truth. Bianca was nearly five foot eleven now, but next to Jay's father, who was six foot three, she definitely was on the shorter side.

Jay barely resisted pointing out that six foot three wasn't exactly tall in this crowd. Jay had several inches on his father, as did his teammate Seth and his commanding officer, Brent Miller.

Good-natured bantering continued in various conversations around the room while Carina helped Seth and Vanessa put food out on the dining room table.

Pete crossed to stand beside him. "So you're really one of them now, huh?"

"I am," Jay said, recognizing the chiding tone and the humor that hummed beneath it. "I really appreciate Mom and you coming up for my baptism."

"It wasn't a problem. This was a good time for a training break for my swimmers since the summer season is wrapping up." Pete motioned toward Carina and changed the subject. "Are you sure it's safe for Carina to visit her father?"

"I sure hope so." Jay's shoulders lifted. "As far as we know, her father hasn't been in contact with anyone from his past since the FBI moved him again."

"Just be careful. There's no guarantee there isn't someone else in the Chicago mob looking for her."

"I think it's Carina's father who would be the likely target if the family sends someone else. The FBI is trying to convince him to testify against the rest of his family."

Sarcasm laced Pete's voice. "Good luck with that."

"Yeah, I doubt it's going to happen," Jay agreed. "But at least I'll know Carina isn't traveling there alone."

"You let me know if there's anything else I can do to help out. I know things haven't been easy for the past few months."

"I appreciate it, Dad," Jay told him. "Too bad you don't live closer."

"At least we're both on the East Coast."

Jay thought of his last deployment and said, "Right now, I'm just grateful we're in the same country."

A former Marine, Pete nodded in understanding. "I hear you. You've got to appreciate these moments when you've got them."

* * *

Carina shifted uncomfortably in the hard plastic chair, feeling completely out of place. She had tried to visualize what to expect during her flight from Norfolk, Virginia, to Colorado Springs and during her drive to the prison, but her efforts hadn't prepared her for the reality of actually being there. The smell of disinfectant, stale tobacco, and the lingering scents of some kind of meat from lunchtime assaulted her senses.

Prison guards stood in the corners of the wide, windowless room, and more than a dozen narrow metal tables were lined up neatly in three rows. Carina had been placed at the table in the far corner, the one that would afford her the most privacy, but she found herself feeling very much like a prisoner herself.

She wished Jay could have come inside with her, but they both knew her father would never talk openly in front of a stranger. Personally, Carina wasn't sure he would talk to her either. After all, they had been strangers to one another for more than ten years, ever since her mother had run away from Chicago with her sisters and her in tow.

She stared at the harsh white walls, afraid to make eye contact with the other people in the room. Other criminals visiting with various family members. She could hear the couple closest to her speaking rapidly in Spanish, their voices lowered enough that the words were difficult to make out. Two tables beyond them, a large man covered in tattoos spoke to an even larger man.

When the metal door along the far wall opened, Carina looked up to see her father, Giovanni Perelli, walk in, escorted by a single guard. Her father looked older, much older than when she had seen him at the trial for her mother's murder. His dark hair had begun to gray at some point over the past few years, and he had added a few pounds around his middle.

Giovanni's eyes swept over the room before landing on Carina. Then those dark eyes narrowed. He controlled the surprise on his face so quickly that Carina wondered if perhaps she had imagined it.

The guard led her father to her, and Giovanni took the seat across from her but didn't speak until the guard stepped back to give them a little privacy, or as much privacy as they could manage within the walls of this prison.

"What are you doing here?" he asked in English, a language that had rarely been spoken between them. "You shouldn't be here. It's too dangerous."

"I have questions," Carina said, automatically shifting into Italian. "And you have the answers."

His expression was serious and a little wary. "I don't have the answers you're looking for."

"I think you do." Carina leaned forward and lowered her voice. "You didn't kill Mama, did you?"

Pain and grief flashed into his eyes. "I loved your mother with all my heart."

Carina didn't miss the way he avoided giving her a direct answer, but the expression on his face confirmed what she had learned several months ago. "You need to tell the authorities the truth."

"There is much you don't understand, things I can't tell you." His eyes shifted to look at the guard in the corner. "These walls have ears, even when you think you're alone."

"Uncle Alexander is dead. You don't have to protect us from him anymore."

"Raymond . . . Things are never as simple as they appear."

"Then explain them to me. Help me understand."

"Just know that I tried to protect you from all of this. Now I need you to protect your sisters. Help them live a normal life, a life away from the family."

"I am, but I still need to understand. You sent me a key. What does it go to?"

"It's insurance. Hold on to it, and don't give it to anyone." He leaned forward and lowered his voice. "I mean it. No one can be trusted. If anything happens to me, you'll receive the information you need to protect yourself and your sisters."

The concern Carina felt for her father, for the man who hadn't been part of her life for the past decade, surprised her. "You sound like you expect something to happen to you."

"The possibility always exists," he said. "Tell me how you are. Tell me about my little ones."

Carina couldn't help her lips from turning upward. "They aren't so little. In fact, they're both taller than me."

A wistful expression flitted across his face. "Are they happy?"

"I think so. They still miss Mama. We all do."

"I know." His voice wavered slightly. "I'm sorry she was taken from you. It should never have happened."

"Papa, tell me what I can do to help you get out of here. If you didn't kill Mama, you shouldn't be in here."

"Justice has a funny way of getting even."

Carina noticed the guard moving toward them, indicating that their precious few minutes together were coming to an end. Urgency filled her voice. "Tell me about the key."

"You're a smart girl," Giovanni said cryptically. Then he lowered his voice to a whisper. "You already have everything you need, but be careful. There is more danger out there than you can possibly know."

"I don't understand."

Then all too quickly, the guard reached them and her father pushed back from the table. "I love you, Caramia. Please tell your sisters I love them too."

Emotions clogged her throat, and she swallowed hard. "I will, Papa." Then Carina stood and watched helplessly as her father was led away.

CHAPTER 3

JAY SENSED CARINA'S TENSION THE moment she walked back into the waiting room, her shoulders rigid, her face a bit too pale. She already looked completely out of place here, like a rose surrounded by thorns. She had dressed down for her visit, wearing jeans and a scoop-necked shirt she had designed and made herself.

It wasn't the clothes that made her look so out of place but rather the air she carried with her. She might have come from a criminal family and been forced to scrape by for the past few years since her mom died, but those teenage years she had spent living in Denver's high society and her college experience at NYU had clearly helped mold her into the woman she was today. Simply put, she had class.

Even though he was eager to learn about the source of her current tension, he wasn't about to start any kind of discussion with her in a public place. He rose at her entrance and wordlessly waited for her to check out and reclaim her identification from the guard at the main desk. Then Jay escorted her outside.

As they walked to the parking lot, he remained alert for anyone who might be waiting for them. Or, more specifically, waiting for Carina. He zeroed in on a stocky man standing in a guardlike stance beside a silver sedan. The man looked them over and then shifted his attention to the woman walking right behind them. Apparently, the man was looking for someone, but it didn't appear to be them.

Another man lingered across the lot, but this one looked more the type to try to score drugs than to be an employee of the well-dressed and reportedly drug-free Perelli family. Dismissing him, Jay continued to where their rental car was parked at the edge of the lot.

He opened the car door for Carina and then circled around to get behind the wheel. It wasn't until they had cleared the lot and he was sure they didn't have a tail that he glanced over at her and said, "Tell me what happened. Did your father tell you anything?"

"Not really." Carina shook her head, and Jay could hear the tears threatening in her voice. She took a moment to steady her emotions before she continued. "He was pretty cryptic about everything, but we were right that he wasn't responsible for my mother's death."

"Is he willing to fight to prove that?"

"I doubt it. He seems to think he's keeping us safe by staying in prison."

"If he's willing to deal, he might be able to get out of there and get extra protection for all of you."

"I wasn't about to bring that topic up, especially not in an open room like that." She shifted in her seat, angling toward him. "Do you think it's possible that the visitation room is bugged?"

"I don't know. Why?"

"He said something about how there are ears everywhere. It's like he was sure someone was listening to our conversation, and he was afraid to say too much."

"Your family has demonstrated in the past that their reach was longer than the authorities thought it was, but it could also be that he's just being paranoid," Jay said.

"Maybe. Regardless, he wouldn't talk about the key. All he said was that it was an insurance policy in case anything happened to him. He said if something did happen, I would receive the information I need to protect my sisters and me."

"Did he say anything else about it?"

"Only that I already had all the information I needed." Carina's eyebrows drew together. "He has to be talking about the card I got, the one of Central Park with the numbers written on it."

"We'll figure it out," Jay promised her. "It may take some time, but we'll find out what that key goes to and why it was so important."

"What if it's still important to someone?" Carina asked hesitantly. "What if this isn't really over?"

Jay stiffened. "Did your dad say something that made you think you might still be in danger?"

"He just said something about protecting my sisters."

"We've been really careful about not doing anything that would let your family trace you to Virginia Beach."

"I know," Carina said. "Honestly, I thought you were being overprotective when you insisted I sublet an apartment so nobody could find me through my lease. Now I'm starting to wonder."

"You've been in Virginia for over a month now, and we haven't seen any sign of trouble," Jay reminded her. "For now, I think we just keep taking precautions, and we'll keep looking for the lock that your key opens."

"I know you're right," Carina said. "I'm just glad you're supposed to stay in Virginia for the next little while. I think it's going to take some time before we really feel safe."

Jay's hands tightened on the steering wheel, and he sent up a silent prayer that his squad wouldn't be called into action anytime soon.

* * *

Pete stood on the pool deck and watched Bianca's new coach run his team through a set of useless drills. The drills might have been of some value if the coach had taken the time to correct his swimmers' strokes, but instead, he seemed content to sit on the side of the deck until it was time to give the team the next portion of the workout.

Pete could already see some of Bianca's bad habits reemerging, habits he'd spent several long months correcting. He wished he had his clipboard so he could make some notes on what she needed to work on and then reminded himself he wasn't Bianca's coach anymore.

He had to admit that he was a little surprised at how much he missed having her around. He supposed part of that was because two of his other swimmers had left for college the week before, leaving him with only four swimmers under his tutelage.

He had decided years before to only coach six swimmers at a time so he could give them the attention they deserved. When one of his former swimmers, a woman he had coached to the Olympics, had asked for a special favor, Pete had made an exception and taken Bianca on as the seventh.

Her departure from the team last May had been kept low-key, but word had apparently spread that his team had openings. For months, he had been receiving tapes on swimmers who wanted him to coach them, but so far he hadn't felt like dealing with auditioning any new additions.

He noticed Bianca come to a stop at the wall behind the boy she had been talking to at church on Sunday. When the boy pushed off on the next interval and did a breaststroke pull out, Pete watched him, automatically analyzing his stroke.

The boy had potential, Pete decided. If he were coaching him, he would definitely lengthen his glide and deepen his pull, but it wouldn't take much to increase his efficiency.

Pete watched him the length of the pool and then looked out over the rest of the swimmers. Another boy stood out, and it didn't take long for Pete to recognize the type. This boy was the star of the team. His strokes were classic and efficient. He was fast and had power, but unlike Bianca's friend, Pete didn't see the same potential for improvement.

Pete continued to look over the athletes in the pool, entertaining himself by checking practice times and analyzing the potential of Bianca and the two boys who had caught his attention.

When the coach called out their cooldown, Pete saw Bianca ask her coach something. He couldn't hear the words that were said, but he noticed the way Bianca bristled.

As soon as the swimmers finished their cooldown and headed for the locker room, Pete crossed to the coach. He knew he shouldn't get involved, but he didn't let that stop him.

Without introducing himself, Pete stepped in front of the coach and asked, "Bianca isn't giving you a hard time, is she?"

"You must be her dad," the coach said and then continued without waiting for Pete to correct his assumption. "I was starting to wonder if she had any family besides her sister."

"She's got me," Pete said. "Is she doing okay? It looks like she's shortening her reach on her freestyle again."

The coach tensed. "Maybe you should leave the coaching to me."

Pete cringed inwardly. Apparently, this wasn't only an inadequate coach but also one with an ego. "You do realize Bianca has the potential to get a division-one scholarship with the right training."

"All parents think their child is capable of getting a full ride. The reality is that swimming scholarships are hard to come by."

Rather than continue debating, Pete changed tactics. "Then let me ask your opinion. Do you think Bianca is capable of swimming in college?"

"It's hard to say. She's only sixteen. We'll have to see how much she improves this year."

"I see." Pete took a step back. "Well, thanks for your time."

Without waiting for a response, Pete walked over to the entrance and waited for Bianca. As soon as she came out of the locker room and crossed to him, he asked, "What was the problem with your coach at the end of practice?"

"Nothing." Bianca pushed the door open and led the way out to the parking lot.

Pete waited until they were in the car before he pressed the issue. "Spill it. What did you say that irritated him?"

Bianca rolled her eyes. "I just asked if he noticed if my reach on my freestyle was too short."

"And what was his response?"

"He said I should stop asking him that, and he said he'd tell me if there was a problem."

"The answer to your question is yes, you are shortening your reach again," Pete told her. "Are there any other teams around here you might be able to join?"

Bianca shook her head. "The one I liked the most is closed. That coach isn't taking new swimmers. The other two we looked at are way too expensive. Not that I think those coaches are much better than Russell."

"We'll figure something out," Pete told her. "But for this week, I think you should swim for me instead of your regular team."

"You'd be willing to coach me while you're here?" she asked incredulously.

Sarcasm laced Pete's voice. "Someone's got to fix your freestyle."

Bianca let out a squeal and gave him an impulsive kiss on the cheek. With a grin, she told him, "I know you miss coaching me."

"Now you're getting delusions of grandeur."

"Hey, I did beat Jay last week."

"Oh, really?" Pete arched a brow. "I've got to hear about that."

CHAPTER 4

BIANCA STOOD ON THE POOL deck and watched her little five- and six-year-olds work their way through the water. She had started coaching the beginning swimmers on her team right after moving to Virginia Beach, and she had already come to enjoy the kids and their vibrant personalities.

When they came to a stop at the end of the pool, she squatted down so she could talk to the kids on their level. "That was really good, everyone. Now this time, I want you to concentrate on reaching those arms out." She stood up and demonstrated the form. "Let's do it again."

Bianca propped one foot on the starting block in front of her, a ripple of satisfaction spreading through her when one of the boys managed to translate what she had asked for into action. She was so focused on the kids and how she might explain what she wanted that she didn't notice the head coach approaching until he was almost beside her.

"You are spending way too much time talking to the kids about technique. They need to put in more yards."

"Doesn't it make more sense to fine-tune the technique now? If they keep doing it wrong, it will be that much harder to break them of their bad habits later."

"Their strokes will smooth out as they put in the yards," Russell insisted. "I outlined the program I want you to follow. I expect you to follow it to the letter."

"You don't want me to teach them how to improve?" Bianca asked incredulously. "Why not?"

"Some of your techniques still need some work. I don't want you to pass your bad habits on to these kids."

"You mean like how my reach is too short on my freestyle?"

Russell's eyes narrowed. "Either do it my way, or I'll find someone else who will."

Bianca felt her temper surge, and she didn't bother to hold it back. Nothing she did was good enough for this man. "In that case, I quit."

"What?" The coach looked at her as though he had never considered her resignation as a possibility.

"I'll finish today's practice, but after that, I'm done coaching for this team."

Clearly annoyed, he glared at her. "Since you clearly can't follow simple directions, maybe that would be best."

* * *

Carina gripped her hands in her lap as Jay drove through the middle-class neighborhood. Over a month before, pop singer Kendra Blake had chosen one of Carina's designs to use for her wedding dress. When she said she wanted to meet to discuss options for the bridesmaids' dresses, Carina and Jay had decided to fly to Nashville before heading home to Virginia.

Up until today, most of her correspondence with Kendra had been through e-mail and through her friend Amy Miller. Amy, the wife of Jay's commanding officer, was also Kendra's future sister-in-law. She had been instrumental in introducing Kendra to Carina's designs.

The fact that Carina had lucked into such a situation was surreal. Now faced with the prospect of meeting the woman who was one of the most well-known singers of her generation and the daughter of a famous actor, Carina felt as if she was about to enter some kind of alternate universe.

When Jay stopped at a traditional colonial that looked very much like the others in the Nashville neighborhood, Carina looked at him skeptically. "Are you sure this is it?"

"This is the address Amy gave us," Jay told her. "Come on. Let's go see if we're in the right place."

Carina grabbed her tote that contained a thick file of her design sketches and gathered up a garment bag that held the wedding dress she had spent countless hours making for Kendra. She joined Jay on the sidewalk, and together they approached the front door. She was convinced they were at the wrong house right up until Kendra Blake herself opened the door. Her blonde hair was pulled back in a ponytail, her feet were bare, and she wore a T-shirt with faded blue jeans.

Her smile was instant and genuine. "You must be Carina and Jay."

Carina nodded, desperately trying not to be intimidated by this woman's accomplishments. Kendra was barely twenty-six, just a year older than Carina, yet she had already won several Grammys and countless other music awards.

"Please, come in." Kendra stepped back and waved them inside. "I really appreciate you coming here. My schedule has been insane for the past few months."

"It's not a problem," Carina managed to say. She held up the garment bag. "Did you want to try on the dress first, or would you rather look at sketches?"

Her eyes lit up. "The dress, definitely."

"I haven't done the adornments yet. I wanted to make sure the size was okay first." Carina handed her the bag.

"I'm going to go try it on." Kendra motioned to the living room. "Please make yourselves comfortable."

"Thanks," Jay said and walked over to the long leather couch. Carina followed him and sat down, her stomach jumping with nerves.

What if Kendra didn't like the finished product? What if she changed her mind? What if Carina wasn't good enough to do this for a living?

Jay reached over and gave her hand a squeeze. Lowering his voice, he said, "It will be fine."

A moment later, Kendra walked into the room, her hands lifting up the skirt of the princess-style gown to keep it from dragging on the floor. Her eyes were alight with excitement. "Carina, it's beautiful." Kendra lowered the skirt and ran a hand down the shimmering material. "You are a genius."

Carina sighed. "I'm so relieved that you like it."

"I love it."

Carina reminded herself that she needed to check the fitting of the gown. "It looks like it's a little long."

"Actually, I have my shoes in my room." Kendra motioned toward the hall. "Come on. We can do the fitting back there." She glanced over at Jay. "Jay, feel free to watch TV, or if you want, there's a pool table in the game room through there."

"I'll be fine. Thanks."

Kendra led the way back to her room, and Carina was struck again by how surreal this moment was. Here she was, the daughter of a convicted criminal, the person responsible for the care of her two younger sisters, standing in Kendra Blake's bedroom while Kendra tried on her wedding dress.

"Are you still trying to keep the wedding a secret?" Carina asked. She knew one of the reasons Kendra had agreed to consider her as her designer was that Amy had convinced Kendra that Carina could be trusted.

"We are. So far, only Charlie's family and my sister know what's really going on."

"What about your parents?"

"My dad can't keep a secret," Kendra said with a hint of humor. "That's why we're pretending we're holding a formal party when we get married. Even though we're getting married in the temple, we won't exchange our rings until the party so my dad will get the chance to walk me down the aisle."

Kendra slipped her shoes on and looked in the full-length mirror on the wall. "This dress is perfect. It's exactly what I've always dreamed of."

"I'm so glad."

Kendra turned and smiled at her. "You realize what this means, don't you?"

Worried, Carina shook her head.

"If everyone else loves this dress as much as I do, you're about to be in very high demand."

Relief washed over her, and she broke into a smile. "I hope you're right."

"I have little doubt."

* * *

"Hey, Bianca. Where have you been?" Jonah asked when Bianca walked into the pool area. "I haven't seen you all week."

"My old coach was in town, so I was working out with him."

Before Jonah could respond, Todd approached. "Nice to see you decided to show up."

Bianca just rolled her eyes. She couldn't say exactly what it was about Todd that irritated her, but she figured his overinflated ego was likely the culprit. "I'm surprised you even noticed I was gone."

Todd ignored her comment and continued. "Coach thought maybe your dad decided to pull you out of swimming."

"What?"

"I guess your dad thought you were good enough to pull a college scholarship. When coach said it was a long shot, I guess he was pretty annoyed."

It only took a second for Bianca to realize the man their coach thought was her father was really Pete.

Before she could come up with a response, Jonah asked, "How would you know what Coach said to her dad?"

"Russell told me." Todd gave Bianca a cocky look. "Don't tell me you really thought you were that fast."

Refusing to be baited, she turned to Jonah. "I'm going to go get some water."

"I'll come with you," Jonah said and started toward the drinking fountain on the other side of the pool. As soon as they were away from Todd, Jonah lowered his voice. "Don't let him get to you. He's just being a jerk."

"Is he ever not a jerk?"

"Not really." Jonah shrugged. "He just doesn't think before he speaks."

"I think I'm going to have to find a new team. This coach hates me."

"He doesn't hate you. If he did, he wouldn't have hired you to coach the little kids."

"Yeah, well, I'm not doing that anymore."

"What happened?"

"Like I said, this coach hates me."

"I think you just intimidate him."

Surprised, she stopped walking and turned to look at him. "Why would he be intimidated by me?"

"Because you ask questions that I'm not sure he knows how to answer."

"Considering he's the head coach, he really should know the answers."

"I know." Jonah lowered his voice even more. "But until you got here, we all thought he knew what he was talking about."

Russell stepped onto the deck. Bianca tried to remind herself that she liked swimming. "It looks like that's our cue."

Bianca noted the surprise on Russell's face when she approached, and she was relieved he didn't speak to her. She hadn't really considered that he might think she had quit the team entirely when she quit her coaching job. She had just been grateful she had Pete to coach her for the past week.

They had opted for the community pool located a little closer to her apartment, both for convenience and because Bianca had wanted to avoid running into anyone from her team. Now that Carina was home and Pete was gone, she didn't have much of a choice but to swim with Russell again until she could find a new team.

She stepped into the pool and started her warm up. She hadn't told Carina yet that she had quit her job. Carina was already so stressed out with starting on the bridesmaid dresses for the wedding she was working on that Bianca hadn't found any time to really talk to her.

Besides, Jay and his parents had been at their apartment last night so they could all spend some time together before Pete and his wife, Sandra, went back home to Miami.

When the coach gave them the next part of the workout, Bianca cut through the water, her thoughts scattering in a dozen directions. One corner of her mind instructed her body, relaying the workout her coach had given her, but competing with his words were the echoes of Pete's most recent instruction. *Tighten up that left hand. You're pulling wide.* Overshadowing it all were her overriding concerns about tomorrow. Her first day of school.

It was hard to believe she was about to attend her fourth school in three years. She had wanted to move from their home in Phoenix to Miami. She'd been so excited to swim for Pete that she had looked at the move as an adventure. This move was anything but.

Most of the swimmers on this team went to a different high school. Jonah was one of only three people on the team who also went to her school. The only others were Todd and his friend Keshawn, who was nearly as conceited as Todd.

Bianca finished the first set and stopped at the wall. When the coach gave them the next set, she noticed the way he looked at everyone but her. She gripped the wall, her tension rising. This coach was clearly as ready to get rid of her as she was ready to leave. The question was, where else could she go?

CHAPTER 5

CARINA SAT AT THE KITCHEN table, stacks of papers covering nearly every available inch of space. She had returned home from Kendra's with the wedding dress in hand, as well as a list of alterations, an order for six bridesmaids' dresses, and a check with five figures on it.

She still couldn't believe the amount of money Kendra had insisted on paying her for her designs. The publicity she would generate for Carina was worth more than any amount she could pay her. But Kendra had insisted.

Carina still felt like she was walking on air after seeing the delight on the soon-to-be bride's face after she tried on her dress.

Now, with Kendra's check in hand, she was faced with the reality that it was time to deal with the red tape required to set up her company, Eleganza. She nearly had the paperwork complete when the front door opened and Bianca walked inside.

Carina glanced over at her. "How was practice?"

"Fine," Bianca said shortly, barely looking at her as she passed by the kitchen.

"Bianca?" Carina waited for her sister to turn before continuing. "What's wrong?"

"Nothing. I'm just tired."

"No, really, is everything okay with you?" Carina stood and closed the distance between them.

"Yeah. I'm fine."

"Hey." Carina grabbed Bianca's arm before Bianca could rush past her. "Talk to me. What's going on?"

"I just miss Miami." She shrugged casually, but Carina didn't miss the sadness in her eyes. "A lot has changed lately."

"I know. I'm sorry for that." Carina pulled her into a hug. "Are you worried about starting at a new school tomorrow?"

"A little nervous," Bianca admitted.

"It'll be fine. You've never had any trouble making friends. I'm sure your phone will be ringing off the hook by the end of the week."

Bianca's shoulders came up again, and she seemed to muster her courage. "There's something else."

"What?"

"I quit my job."

Carina took a step back. She thought of the check from Kendra, her hopes of using those funds to build her company, but the look on her sister's face took priority. "Why did you quit? Did something happen?"

"Russell didn't trust me to do the job my way, and I can't coach like he does." Bianca looked at her hopefully. "I was actually hoping we could figure out a way for me to switch teams."

"Pete said he wasn't impressed with your coach." Carina glanced over at the kitchen table, wondering if she could hold off on creating her website for a while longer. That might help her pay for a new team for Bianca. "I don't mind you switching, but we didn't find a lot of options here that were close enough for me to drive you to."

"If I had my license, I could drive myself," Bianca pointed out.

"If you had your own car. I'm sorry, but I don't think I can pull that off right now."

"I know." Bianca let out a sigh. "My fees are paid for this month. I guess I'll stick it out with Russell for now."

"That's probably a good idea. It would give you time to check out some other teams and figure out what team fits you the best."

"Yeah," Bianca said, her voice still subdued. Then she asked, "Are you mad that I quit?"

"No, I'm not mad," Carina assured her. "I don't want you to be in a situation that's going to make you miserable. Don't worry. We'll figure something out."

Bianca nodded, then slowly walked down the hall toward her room.

* * *

He stepped into the room unseen, music and chatter from the party downstairs drowning out the subtle sound of his footsteps padding across the carpet. His gloved hands ensured that he'd leave no fingerprints behind; no evidence would indicate that he had ever been there.

After closing the door behind him, he clicked on the small flashlight in his left hand and slowly spun in a circle until the beam landed on the Renoir painting hanging behind the desk. Soundlessly, he crossed the home office and checked to make sure the painting wasn't wired with an alarm.

He knew enough about art to recognize the value of the painting, but that wasn't what he was after tonight. He lifted the artwork from its mounting and gently set it aside to reveal a safe recessed into the wall behind it.

This was more like it. His skill in bypassing such obstacles was the reason he had been chosen for this job, and he had no intention of failing. Too much was riding on tonight.

He retrieved his tools from his jacket pocket and went to work on the lock. Seconds ticked by, turning into minutes. Sweat dripped down his back as he turned the tumbler slowly and waited for the magic numbers to reveal themselves to him.

Finally, he conquered the sequence and pulled the handle to open the safe. His palms started sweating as he stared at the contents. He had expected to find the files he had been sent after, and even the stacks of hundred-dollar bills weren't a surprise. What he hadn't anticipated was discovering plastic bags filled with white powder. He could only guess it was heroin or cocaine.

Ignoring the cash and drugs, he retrieved the files tucked on the left side and took them over to the desk. He then pulled the compact hand-held scanner from his inside jacket pocket and went to work. One by one, he scanned each document, pleased to find he had indeed discovered what his employer was looking for.

He used the wireless attachment to transmit the file contents to the designated e-mail address and then proceeded to put everything back the way he'd found it. Before closing the safe, he snapped a photo of the contents with his cell phone and sent a picture mail to the man who had hired him. He had just secured the lock when the door cracked open and light spilled into the room.

He froze, his mind racing for a reason he would be standing in the dark.

A woman stepped through the doorway and flipped on the light. Her dark eyes sized him up, and then her gaze shifted to the painting perched against the wall. Though she appeared to be Italian, her voice was honey smooth and carried the ring of the South. "It seems we have a problem."

"It's not what you think."

Her hand disappeared into her handbag and came out with a compact pistol. "It never is."

* * *

Bianca wandered through the unfamiliar halls at her new school, searching for the elusive classroom where she was supposed to start her day. Hopelessly lost, she looked around for someone to ask for directions. That's when she saw Todd walking toward her.

She realized she must be desperate when seeing him was a welcome experience. She took a step toward him, intending to see if he could point her in the right direction, but he gave her a disinterested glance and turned his attention to the guy walking beside him.

Bianca stared after him for a moment, both disgusted and annoyed that he hadn't even acknowledged her.

"Did you need some help finding your class?" someone behind her asked.

"What?" Bianca turned to see a girl with mousy brown hair and a warm smile. "Actually, yeah."

She pointed at Bianca's schedule. "Let me see that."

Bianca handed the paper to her.

"Oh, that classroom is down the hall over there. I'll show you." She started across the hall. "I'm Allison, by the way."

"Bianca."

"So, do you know Todd?" Allison asked, her voice a little wistful. "I saw you watching him."

"Not really. Why?"

"I was just wondering. He's pretty much the most popular guy in school. He and his girlfriend have been together since freshman year."

"He has a girlfriend?"

"Margot Adams." Allison pointed down the hall at a slender blonde. "That's her over there."

"Poor girl."

Allison's eyebrows furrowed. "I thought you didn't know Todd."

"I guess I should rephrase. I know him. I'm just not a fan."

"Really?" Allison asked, surprise evident in her voice. "Why? Everyone here likes him."

Bianca shrugged noncommittally.

Allison waited a moment, but when she realized Bianca wasn't going to answer her question, she pointed down a short hallway. "That's your classroom over there. I'll see you later."

"Yeah. Thanks."

Allison nodded, then disappeared down the hall. Bianca turned and walked into her classroom and practically ran right into Todd.

"So you're not one of my fans, huh?"

Bianca's eyebrows lifted. "Please don't tell me that surprises you."

"Actually, yeah."

"Then you have more ego than I realized." Bianca moved past him and took a seat. When Todd slid into the desk beside her, she let out a sigh of annoyance. "I wasn't good enough to say hi to in the hall, and now you want to sit next to me?"

"Oh, so you were hoping I'd talk to you in the hall?"

Bianca pointed across the room. "Why don't you go sit over there? I can't think of any reason why you would really want to sit with me."

His eyes sparked with amusement. "Maybe I like a challenge."

"I doubt your girlfriend would appreciate that." Bianca looked at him pointedly. "And I'm not interested."

"I doubt that."

Bianca was spared having to come up with a response when the bell rang and the teacher stepped in front of the class.

"Okay, everyone. Take your seats." The woman, who appeared to be around forty, handed a clipboard to the boy at the far corner of the room. "Please write your names on this seating chart. For the first few weeks, these will be your assigned seats."

Bianca groaned inwardly. This day was not starting out the way she had hoped.

CHAPTER 6

PETE WALKED THROUGH THE FRONT door and dropped his coaching bag on the chair in the living room. Things were not going the way he had planned. He had auditioned four swimmers today for his small, elite team, all of whom had the potential to become world-class athletes. And every one of them had demonstrated that he wasn't the right coach for them.

One had started the day by guzzling an energy drink, a substance Pete had banned his athletes from using years ago. Two others clearly had too much ego to be coachable. The other had shown a lot of potential and seemed eager enough to learn; he was just too darned annoying.

The day had gone downhill from there.

Sandra walked into the room, her eyes narrowing. "Is something wrong?"

Pete dropped into his favorite chair. "I'm starting to wonder why I even bother."

"You do this because you love coaching."

"I love coaching people who will listen," Pete corrected.

"Who's giving you a hard time today? Adam or Dillan?"

Pete's eyes narrowed. He should have known his wife would see right through his complaints and cut straight to the heart of the matter. "Adam."

"Is it time to cut him loose?" Sandra asked. "You've been having problems with him for a while. Maybe you should look into picking up someone else. Let another coach deal with Adam and his temper tantrums."

"I already did," Pete admitted.

"So spill it. What else is bothering you? I gather your tryouts didn't go well this morning."

"It's not just that. Eric told me today that his wife just got a job offer in Norfolk. They're seriously thinking about moving. Apparently, I'm the only thing really holding them here."

"Honey, that's a tough decision, one they'll have to make on their own."

"Maybe." Pete shrugged. "I was actually thinking . . ."

"About?"

"With all of our kids scattered around the country, there really isn't anything holding us here."

Sandra's eyebrows lifted. "You want to move?"

"Thinking about it." His shoulders lifted again. "Two of my swimmers just left for college. Now that I've dropped Adam, I only have three left. If Eric really does move, I'll be down to two, and both of them are only living in Miami so I'll coach them."

"You want to move to Virginia?"

"It would be a better situation for Eric. Of the swimmers I have left, he's the one who has the most chances at the next Olympic games," Pete said. "And one of our sons does live in Virginia Beach."

"That's true," she said and seemed to consider. "It would be nice to be closer to at least one of our kids."

"I was hoping you might think that."

"And you have always talked about wanting to build your own aquatics facility," Sandra added thoughtfully.

"I don't know if we'll ever have the money to fund that dream, but I do think it might be time to start fresh somewhere," Pete said, trying to keep his voice casual. When she didn't answer right away, his impatience pushed him to ask, "What do you think?"

A wave of appreciation washed through him when she gave a definite nod. "I'll call the Realtor in the morning."

"I'm going to look into pool space." He headed for the phone.

"How soon were you thinking about moving?"

"Nathan and Dillan are still rooming together. When I talked to them about the possibility of a move, they said they thought they could sublet their apartment without a problem." He hesitated before he broke the news he knew would get a rise out of her. "I figure if everything falls into place, I could be there coaching within two weeks."

"Two weeks to move?" Her jaw dropped. She stared at him and slowly shook her head. "You never have been one to move slowly."

"You knew that about me when you married me," Pete reminded her. He circled her waist with his hands and leaned down to kiss her. "Of course, we both know I was the lucky one on our wedding day."

"True," she said with humor in her voice. "Very true."

* * *

Bianca felt an arm wrap around her shoulder and cringed. She stepped away, turning to see that, indeed, it was Todd stalking her again. "What do you want?"

"Just thought you might want to hang out tonight after practice."

"Thanks, but no thanks."

"Oh, come on." Todd reached for her hand, and his voice was both teasing and persuasive. "It's time you start living a little."

Bianca pulled her hand free. "In case you missed it the first ten times I told you, I'm not interested."

Annoyance flashed in his eyes. "This playing hard-to-get is starting to get old."

"I'm not playing," Bianca told him and took a step back. "I wish you would get a clue."

Frustrated that she shared three classes with Todd, she turned away and started down the hall. She had only made it a few steps before she felt the arm wrap around her shoulders again.

Bianca stopped long enough to turn away from him so she could wiggle out of his grasp. "Todd, back off. I mean it."

"No you don't. Trust me. Every girl in school would like to be in your shoes."

"Then go pick on one of them," Bianca shot back. "Or better yet, why don't you just pay attention to your girlfriend?"

"Jealous, are we?" Todd smirked and gave her a knowing smile. "I'll see you tonight."

Bianca gritted her teeth and tried to shake off the sickening feeling she always got when Todd played these stupid games. She knew he was referring to practice, but he seemed to deliberately be trying to make it sound like they had a date planned. She slid into her seat next to Lynette, one of the few girls she had met at her new school.

"I can't believe you would go behind Margot's back like this," Lynette whispered, leaning closer.

"I'm not going out with Todd," Bianca insisted, frustration vibrating through her voice.

"It sure looks like you are," Lynette said. "And Margot is steaming."

"I don't even know Margot, and I wish I didn't know Todd."

"Well, believe me, Margot and everyone else at school knows who you are now."

"Great." Bianca blew out a breath. So much for fitting in at her new school.

* * *

"Something's going on with Bianca." Carina sat across the table from Jay, her frustration and concern evident in her voice.

"You said she wasn't happy with her team," Jay reminded her.

"Yeah, but I think it's more than that. I think something's going on at school, and she's not talking."

"It's been a tough few months for her," Jay said.

"I know, but before we moved here, she used to talk to me about everything. Now she hardly talks to me at all."

Jay reached over and squeezed her hand. "Do you think she resents having me around so much?"

"She adores you."

"Yeah, but she isn't used to having to share you with anyone," Jay said. "And I know she misses Lou."

"I know," Carina said, grief washing over her as she thought of her former bodyguard. "We both do."

"Has Bianca been talking to Gianna at all? Maybe Gianna knows what's bothering her."

"Gianna hasn't said anything. I'll try to call her later." Carina picked up the card her father had sent her and looked at it for the thousandth time. The scene on the cover was common enough, a simple photo of Central Park in New York City.

She had memorized the words on the inside, *Remember who you really are*, but she and Jay both suspected that the string of numbers at the bottom was the real clue. She read them out loud, hoping for some inspiration. "*995 5*."

"I think we have to look beyond what's written on the card," Jay told her. "Why did he choose to send you a card from New York? Did he ever take you there for a vacation? Do you have a family friend there?"

Carina shook her head. "The first time I went to New York was when I had my campus visit at NYU during my senior year of high school."

The door opened, and Carina heard Bianca walk in.

"And you're sure your mom didn't close on the condo she was buying there?" Jay asked.

Carina shook her head. Her mother had been in the process of purchasing a condominium in New York for her so she would have her own place while she attended graduate school. Those plans had come to a screeching halt when her mom was murdered. "I checked with the Realtor, and he assured me the sale didn't go through."

Bianca walked in and dropped her backpack on the floor. "Still trying to figure this out?"

"Yeah." Carina looked up at her sister. "But we don't have a clue what Dad was trying to tell us."

Bianca seemed to waver between wanting to stay in the kitchen with them and wanting to go to her room.

"Maybe you should come help us. It never hurts to have a fresh perspective," Jay said.

"Okay." Apparently pleased to be included, Bianca dropped onto a chair between them. "What have you tried so far?"

Carina's heart lifted a little as she watched Bianca interact with Jay as he explained all of the research they had already attempted and the failures that had resulted.

"I still wonder if maybe it's part of a zip code," Carina commented. "You said one of the possibilities was El Paso, Texas. Raymond was from Texas."

"I can't find any evidence that he or his family has ever been to El Paso." Jay shook his head. "I get the feeling this is just one half of the puzzle. You said your dad mentioned that if anything happened to him, you would get more information, right?"

"Yeah, but he also said I already had everything I needed to figure this out."

"Could the words be some kind of code to tell us where to look?" Bianca asked.

"If it is, I have to think they're meant to make you think of someplace where the rest of your family wouldn't know to look," Jay said. "I think we need to focus on Central Park. Your father might have chosen this card completely at random, or that might be the piece of the puzzle we're missing."

"You know, my team is supposed to be traveling to New York for a swim meet in December," Bianca said. "If you guys are cool with me competing in it, maybe you could come too and we can check out Central Park in person."

"That might not be a bad idea," Jay considered.

Carina watched Bianca come to life as she and Jay talked over the possibilities. She leaned back in her chair, a little of her earlier tension easing. Maybe Jay was right. Maybe Bianca just needed more attention and time to adjust to their new life here.

* * *

Three days was all it took for Bianca to realize there was no way she was going to survive a whole year of sitting next to Todd Layton. She hadn't thought he could be more obnoxious than he had been that first day of class, but every time she saw him, he proved her wrong.

She felt his hands grip her shoulders from behind, and he leaned forward to rest his chin on her shoulder. The crude suggestion he whispered in her ear reddened her cheeks, and she jerked away from him.

"Leave me alone."

His response was a low chuckle.

Bianca counted the seconds until the bell rang and then immediately sprang out of her seat. Instead of heading for the door, she walked straight to the teacher's desk, where Mrs. Farnsby had sat down and appeared to be logging into her e-mail.

"Mrs. Farnsby, may I please switch seats?"

"Why?" The teacher looked up at her as though her attention was still more on the computer screen than on Bianca.

Bianca glanced at the door to make sure the other students had all left. Then she lowered her voice slightly. "I just don't want to be near Todd."

Surprise flittered across the teacher's face, but when she spoke, her voice was firm. "I'm sorry, Bianca, but I can't rearrange seating charts every time someone can't get along. I know you're new here, but if you give yourself a little time, I'm sure everything will work out."

"I seriously doubt that."

"Well, I'm afraid you'll have to adapt. The seating chart will remain the same until the end of the first quarter."

Annoyed, Bianca turned and headed for the door with every intention of going to the principal's office. If her teacher didn't want to deal with the problem, maybe Mr. Smythe would. She was only two steps out the door when she looked down the hall and saw Todd with a huge grin on his face. Standing right beside him with a mirroring grin was none other than her new principal, Mr. Smythe.

CHAPTER 7

EVERYTHING WAS READY. TONIGHT JAY was going to do it. He was going to ask Carina to marry him.

He couldn't ever remember wanting anything more. And he couldn't remember ever being more scared. They hadn't been together for that long, only five months, but he was starting to feel like they were both dancing around what would come next. He was ready to start planning for that next stage in his life. He just prayed that Carina was ready too and that she wanted to spend the rest of eternity with him.

He still hadn't picked out a ring for her, but knowing Carina's eye for fashion, he thought she would prefer to choose her own. His mind was so focused on his plans for the evening that he barely noticed Seth walking toward him. "Hey, Jay. Change of plans. Our dive for this morning was canceled."

"Do you know why?"

"I don't know yet." Seth motioned down the hall. "But Brent wants to meet with us right now."

Jay fell into step with Seth and started down the hall.

"Are you all set for tonight?" Seth asked. He was the one person Jay had confided in about his plans.

"I've never been so scared of anything in my life."

"I remember," Seth said with understanding. "It's amazing how one woman can be more terrifying than a dozen armed men."

Jay drew a deep breath and blew it out. "What am I going to do if she says no?"

Seth responded without missing a beat. "You'll die a slow and painful death."

Jay looked over at him, horrified. "Thanks a lot."

"You asked," Seth reminded him with a grin. Then he slapped a hand on Jay's back. "Relax. Carina isn't going to say no. She loves you. Everyone can see it."

"I hope you're right."

They reached Commander Brent Miller's office and took their seats beside Tristan and Quinn, who were already inside.

"I just got word from Kel," Brent began, referring to Kel Bennett, the commander of SEAL Team Ten. "He's scrapped our training schedule for the rest of the week. Instead, he's asked for us to go through a readiness exercise."

Jay listened to Brent go through the details, his heart sinking. The words hadn't been spoken yet, but the implications were clear. They were shipping out. And the fact that their dive had been canceled meant it was likely going to be within the next forty-eight hours.

They had been home for only a few weeks, but the loss of thirty-one fellow SEALs in a helicopter crash the month before had hit the teams hard. They all knew they might have to rotate out sooner than planned, but Jay had been praying that sooner would come a whole lot later. And he had certainly hoped to have a ring on Carina's finger before he had to step back on a plane.

He couldn't quite imagine what their future together would hold, especially knowing what kind of family she came from. Even though the FBI was convinced that Carina was safe from the Chicago mob, the mystery of the key and the veiled warnings Carina's father had given her were enough to make Jay wonder.

He had taken every precaution he could think of when she moved to Virginia Beach. GPS blockers on her cell phone and car, an apartment lease that wasn't in her name, one that included utilities. Realistically, he doubted she was in mortal danger any longer, but the fact remained that the mysterious key held great importance to her family, and until they could uncover its purpose, he wasn't going to feel that Carina was really safe.

The last thing he wanted right now was to ship out to who knew where for who knew how long.

"You okay?" Seth asked as they headed out of their meeting and down the hall.

"Yeah. Just worried about leaving Carina right now."

"The timing really stinks," Seth said sympathetically. "Hopefully you'll at least get to take her out tonight like you planned."

"It's not just that," Jay admitted. "I'm worried that this thing with her family isn't really over."

"Still no clue what that key goes to, huh?"

Jay shook his head. "We're sure the numbers on the card she received are the clue, but we haven't been able to decipher it."

"One of you will figure it out."

Jay's cell phone rang, and Seth took a step toward their office. "I'll go get started on our readiness reports."

"I'll catch up with you in a minute." Jay pulled his phone from his pocket. His mood brightened slightly when he saw his father's phone number illuminated on the screen. "Hey, Dad. What's up?"

"Any chance you'd be willing to let your old man crash at your place for a couple of weeks?"

"Sure, but I may be heading out soon," Jay told him. "Why are you coming to Virginia Beach?"

"Actually, your mom and I are moving to Virginia Beach," Pete said. He went on to explain Eric's situation and the plans to relocate his team.

"This is great," Jay said enthusiastically. "Just use your key and make yourself at home at my place if I'm not there."

"I appreciate it."

"And Dad, can I ask a favor?"

"Name it."

"Can you keep an eye on Carina and Bianca while I'm gone? I'm still uneasy about their whole family thing."

"You got it," Pete said without hesitation. "Besides being closer to you, Bianca's one of the reasons I'm looking forward to the move. She's not in a good spot with that new coach of hers. It's about time she starts swimming for someone who believes in her again."

"She'll be thrilled to hear you're coming." Jay looked up to see Seth motioning for him to come into their office. "Dad, I've got to go. I'll talk to you later."

"Be safe."

"I will. Thanks."

* * *

"Gianna, have you talked to Bianca lately?"

"We texted last night. Why?"

"Something's not right with her, but I don't know what's going on. She's stopped talking to me about things."

"Is she still mad that you wouldn't let her go with you to see Dad?"

"I don't think so." Carina heard the edginess in Gianna's voice. "Are you still mad I didn't let you guys come?"

"I understand why you didn't want me to go, but it's frustrating. I really want the chance to get to know our father instead of just remembering bits and pieces from my childhood."

"I don't want anything to happen to you or Bianca."

"I know, and she does too, but at some point, you're going to have to let us grow up. You don't have to protect us forever."

Carina sighed. Gianna had been on this "I'm an adult" kick since graduating high school. "At least promise me you won't try to see him until we're sure it's safe."

"Carina, you're not ever going to think it's safe."

"Maybe not," Carina agreed. "But someone's already tried to kill for that key. Until we figure out what it goes to, we can't take the chance that someone else will be able to find one of us and try again."

"You don't have to worry about me for now. I'm too busy with school to do anything but study."

"And date."

"How would you know that?" Gianna asked suspiciously.

"I just know you," Carina said and felt herself relax enough to smile. "You've never been able to stand staying home every night. Is there a boyfriend I should know about?"

"No. I'd tell you if there was."

"I hope so," Carina said. "And if you get a minute, would you please call Bianca? Maybe she'll tell you what's bothering her."

"Okay. I'll try."

"I really need you to do more than try," Carina said gently. "I know this move hasn't been easy on her, and she really misses you."

"Okay, okay. I'll talk to her."

"Thanks, Gianna. I appreciate it."

* * *

Bianca stepped out of the girls' locker room at the pool and looked around, instantly relieved when she saw that Todd wasn't there yet. The boy didn't get that her answer was never going to change. No meant exactly that: no.

At first he had seemed to see her resistance as a challenge. Now he was getting mean. This morning he had knocked her homework off of her desk, deliberately stepping on it so it ripped. Then at lunch he had "accidentally" run into her when she was carrying her tray to the table. Bianca had ended up wearing most of her food rather than eating it.

All she wanted was for Todd to leave her alone. Was that too much to ask? She noticed Jonah talking to their coach across the pool and realized she wasn't the only one having a bad day. Russell appeared to be in lecture mode, and Jonah definitely didn't look happy.

When the conversation ended, Jonah headed for the far side of the pool. Bianca swam toward him, a little surprised to see the dejected look on his face. One thing she liked about Jonah was that nothing ever seemed to bother him, but something clearly was. "Is something wrong?"

He tried to gloss over the question. "Just the same old stuff."

"Since I'm new here, maybe you can tell me what that means," Bianca suggested.

"Coach is mad because I won't compete on Sundays. He kicked me off of the relay."

"But you're one of our fastest hundred freestylers." Bianca looked at where Russell stood, disgusted. "He could at least let you swim in the preliminaries on Saturday."

"He said if I won't swim in the finals, I can't swim at all."

"What a jerk."

Jonah's only response was another shrug.

"Well, I'm sorry you can't swim in the relay. He'll probably tell me the same thing when he realizes I don't compete on Sundays either."

Jonah's eyes met hers, and concern sounded in his voice. "You haven't told him yet?"

Bianca shook her head. "I'm already on his bad side. I didn't think it was worth it to rock the boat until right before he puts our entries in." She noticed Todd heading toward them and muttered under her breath. "Great."

"Is something going on between you and Todd? I've seen him hanging around you at school all week."

"He thinks he likes me."

"I thought he had a girlfriend."

"Exactly," Bianca said emphatically. "Like I would want to date a guy like that."

Bianca cringed when Todd stepped in front of her, excitement in his eyes.

"Did you hear the news?" Todd asked. Then he rushed on without waiting for a response. "Pete Wellman is moving here. He's having tryouts for his new team two weeks from Saturday."

Bianca stared at him, stunned. Pete? Moving here? Before she could manage to ask for details, Jonah asked, "Who?"

"Pete Wellman," Todd repeated and looked at him disdainfully. "Eric Mattinson and Dillan White's coach. Swimming for him practically guarantees you can make it to the Olympic team."

Despite the excitement Todd's announcement caused, Bianca rolled her eyes. "Pete's good, but he's not a miracle worker."

"How would you know?" Todd sneered. Apparently her repeated rejections had finally sunk into his thick skull. "It's not like you'd ever be good enough to swim for him."

"Gee, thanks." Sarcasm dripped from her voice. She quickly decided it wasn't worth her effort to inform him that Pete had indeed already coached her.

"That was harsh," Jonah said.

"Yeah, well, your friend here is more full of herself than I realized."

Bianca straightened her shoulders. "Then maybe you'll finally leave me alone."

"Like you're worth my time." Todd shook his head. "Besides, once I start swimming for Pete, I won't have to deal with you losers anymore."

Bianca watched him swagger off, her heart sinking a little. What would she do if Pete agreed to coach Todd? He was the fastest on the team, and this was supposedly the best year-round team in the area. Looking over at the coach, she found herself wondering how that could be. "I really hope Todd doesn't end up swimming for Pete."

"At least we wouldn't have to deal with him."

"Personally, I'm praying that he stays here and we can go swim for Pete. It would be the best of both worlds."

"I'm not good enough to swim for someone like that."

"You're better than you think you are," Bianca told him. "Besides, Pete gets the whole Mormon thing. He doesn't like it, but he does get it."

"Even if that's true, I wouldn't have a clue how to get a tryout with him."

"You just leave that to me." Bianca gave him a cryptic smile and leaned closer. "Did I ever mention that the old coach I was working out with a few weeks ago was Pete Wellman?"

Jonah looked at her with disbelief. "No way!"

Bianca's smile widened. "Way."

CHAPTER 8

CARINA HUNG UP THE PHONE, a sense of dread settling in her stomach. She had known the day would come when Jay would ship out again, but she truly hadn't expected it for another few months.

As had happened the last time he left, Jay hadn't been able to tell her where he was going or when he was coming back. Carina could only hope this trip would be for a few days rather than weeks or months.

Carina walked out to her car, wondering how Bianca would feel about the news that Jay had left town today. She still wasn't sure what to think of her sister's uncharacteristic moodiness. Gianna had followed up on her promise to talk to Bianca but reported that Bianca hadn't mentioned anything worrisome.

As much as Carina wanted to believe everything was fine with Bianca, something still wasn't quite right. When she had dropped her off at practice earlier, Bianca had acted like she didn't even want to go inside.

Carina was starting to think she would have to find a way to adjust her work schedule so she could stay with Bianca during practice. It was possible that her frustration with her current coach was the source of the problem, but it still wasn't like Bianca to let situations like this get to her. Carina had never known anyone as capable of letting things roll off her back as Bianca.

When Carina drove into the parking lot, Bianca was already waiting outside. Carina pulled up to the curb and waited for her to climb in before asking, "Have you been waiting long?"

Bianca shook her head, and Carina was surprised to see the huge smile on her face. "You'll never guess what I heard today."

"What?"

"Pete is moving here to Virginia Beach."

"Are you sure?"

"Positive." Bianca clicked her seat belt in place. "I called him right after I got out of the pool. He said he'll be here sometime next week."

"What about his team down in Miami?"

"They're coming with him," Bianca said. "Eric's wife got a job in Norfolk. They're moving here this week, and Dillan and Nathan will be here a week or two after that."

"What about Adam?"

"He's not coming," Bianca said. She gave Carina a speculative look. "Pete didn't say why, but I got the impression that Adam isn't swimming for him anymore."

"Adam was a bit demanding."

"True," Bianca agreed. "I assume you're cool if I swim for Pete again."

"Absolutely." Carina said, trying to be excited for her sister instead of concentrating on the dollar signs involved in paying Pete's coaching fees.

"I'm surprised Jay didn't say anything to us about his dad moving here. I guess he's been working on the details for the last week or so."

"Maybe he didn't know," Carina suggested. "He's been pretty busy at work lately."

"I'll definitely have to razz him about it tonight." Bianca settled back in her seat. "I assume he'll be over for dinner."

"We had actually planned to go out for dinner, but he had to leave today."

"Leave where?"

"I don't know."

"Oh. That kind of leaving." Bianca gave her a sympathetic look. "Sorry."

Carina tried to think positively. "At least we'll have more time together."

Bianca looked over, a devilish light in her eyes. "We could start that time together with going out to dinner. Maybe Cheesecake Factory."

"You know I can't afford that."

"Okay, I'll settle for McDonalds."

"Nice try." Carina shook her head. "You know Pete doesn't like you eating french fries."

"He's not my coach yet."

Carina grinned at her. "I'm not sure he ever stopped being your coach."

Bianca gave her a sorrowful look. "I really do like french fries."

* * *

Pete surveyed the twenty-five-meter pool in the Virginia Beach recreation center, where he would host his early-morning and afternoon practices.

He thought of the fifty-meter pool he was used to training at in Miami and found himself a little wistful. The move to Virginia Beach would leave him fighting for pool space and force him to split his time between two facilities.

The second location, a fifty-meter pool in Norfolk, would house his midday practices. If nothing else, his swimmers would have to learn to be adaptable. His wife would remain in Miami for a few more weeks to get their house ready to rent. They had decided to hold on to it for now in case this move didn't work out. Until she was ready to join him, he was content to stay at Jay's apartment.

Word about his move had spread faster than he had expected. Dropping Adam had come to the media's attention, since he was the defending world champion in the 200 IM. When a reporter had contacted him for a statement, Pete refused to comment on the specific reasons Adam no longer swam for him, but he'd let the reporter believe Pete's decision to move to Virginia Beach might have factored in. An article had appeared on the swimming magazine's website the next day.

The phone calls had started within an hour: an overexuberant parent from Richmond, a world-class athlete from Georgia, even a girl who was currently training all the way across the country in Portland, Oregon. And, of course, he had received dozens of calls and e-mails from parents of high-school swimmers in the Virginia Beach and Norfolk area.

Pete was glad he had given himself a couple of weeks to sort through the possibilities before holding a tryout. He had already decided, after watching Bianca's practice in Virginia Beach, that he wanted to consider the local talent as well as the swimmers who were in a position to follow him to wherever he chose to coach.

Bianca had asked the favor that he look at one of her new teammates. He would see soon enough if she had an eye for talent or if she was just hoping for a favor for someone who had more dreams than ability. Jonah Zimmerman was one of a dozen athletes he would evaluate today during his afternoon workout.

Pete had deliberately waited until Eric could be here so he could get his input on his potential new teammates. Knowing money was still tight for the Channing girls, he had already decided he would be willing to stretch his self-imposed cap from six to seven so he could scholarship Bianca. She would never be the most talented swimmer on the team, but he knew from experience that her attitude and work ethic made a huge difference in how the rest of his athletes performed.

The effect of her innate cheerfulness hadn't been that obvious until she had been forced to move from Miami last May. Within days, the trouble with Adam had started. Even Pete's other two high-school swimmers, Danny and Amber, had seemed to struggle more with his demands after Bianca left.

Eric was the first to arrive. "So this is our new home, huh?"

"One of them," Pete motioned toward the pool. "I was able to reserve some extra lanes for this afternoon. We have a dozen kids trying out today, and then Bethany Jackson will be here Monday."

"She's looking for a new coach?"

Pete nodded. "I can't blame her. She should have been the top seed in the 200 fly at the last Olympics, and she didn't even make the team."

"Yeah, her first turn at the trials probably cost her at least two places, if not three."

"I agree."

"What exactly do you want me to do during these tryouts?" Eric asked.

"We have six lanes. I want you in the middle lane, and I want you to push your workout speed. Let's see if anyone is able to keep up."

"Okay." Eric motioned to the locker room. "It looks like the first of your victims has arrived."

* * *

Bianca couldn't believe she was running late to her first practice with Pete. She had hoped to be there early to introduce Pete to Jonah, even though they had seen each other before at Jay's baptism and again at his confirmation.

Instead, Carina had been caught up with something at work, and now Bianca would have to walk into Pete's tryouts ten minutes late. Definitely not a good start, since Pete considered ten minutes early to be on time.

She hurried into the pool area, dropped her towel on the bleachers, and started for the closest lane. That's when she saw him. Todd had come to a stop at the wall right behind Eric.

Her heart dropped into her stomach. She couldn't believe he was one of the swimmers Pete was considering. She stared at him for a moment and could feel her face pale.

Pete's voice broke into her thoughts. "You're late."

"Sorry," she mumbled and headed for the lane where Jonah and another boy were waiting for the next part of the workout.

"Are you okay?" Jonah asked quietly when she slid into the water.

"I didn't know Todd was going to be here."

"You had to figure he would be. He's the one who told us Pete was moving here."

Bianca didn't bother to respond. She could already tell Pete was about to send them onto the next set.

When she pushed off the wall, she let her mind wander. Of course she knew that swimming for Pete would be different here in Virginia Beach than it had been in Miami. Half of her former teammates were now gone, and the facilities were different. But she had so hoped to get away from Todd and all of his constant verbal jabs. It was bad enough that half of the school thought Todd had cheated on his girlfriend with her, but dealing with him for so many hours outside of school only made the rumors seem more true.

What would she do, she wondered, if Pete really took Todd as one of his swimmers? She couldn't swim with him anymore. That was one thing she was already certain of. But what would Pete say if she told him he would have to choose between Todd and her? And what would she do if Pete chose Todd?

He had a good chance of being selected. His times were excellent, and he already had great form. But he was such a jerk. Bianca prayed Pete would see that for himself.

CHAPTER 9

CARINA HURRIED OUT OF HER apartment, determined to run a few errands before picking up Bianca from practice. She slid into the Mercedes that had once belonged to her mother and dropped her purse in the passenger seat. When she pulled out of the parking lot, she noticed another car fall into place behind her, and her eyebrows furrowed in concentration. Had she seen the silver SUV somewhere else before?

She shook her head. She was probably just imagining things. She was still paranoid because her uncle Raymond had tried to kill her a couple of months ago in his attempt to gain possession of the key her father had sent her. Ultimately, Raymond had died in the struggle, but knowing he was gone hadn't chased away the uneasiness that had followed her since that day.

Carina took a right and headed for the nearest fabric store. If she was lucky, she would be able to find a few of the notions she needed for the bridesmaid dresses before picking up Bianca.

Mentally, she made a list of what she needed. When she parked and climbed out of her car, she noticed that the SUV pulled in behind her. Her unease intensified. She reminded herself of the FBI's assurances that she was no longer in danger, but with the possibility of this car following her, those promises weren't terribly comforting at the moment.

Carina settled her right hand on her bag, where her handgun lay concealed. She quickened her step toward the store and the safety a public place could provide. Then she dared to look back at the suspicious vehicle.

When she saw her uncle Marciano step out of the SUV, flanked by the men who were clearly his bodyguards, she didn't know whether to face him or flee. She stared at him, noting the grim expression on his face and the way his hair had grayed over the past few years. At the moment, he wasn't anything like the fun-loving uncle who had gone with her and her father the first time she went to see the Chicago Cubs play at Wrigley Field. Instead, Marciano looked just like he had the day someone in her family had shot and killed the man who had been feeding information to the feds.

Despite the pounding in her chest, she stood her ground and waited for Marciano to close the distance between them.

"You've grown up," Marciano said in Italian.

Carina responded in his language. "Why are you here?"

"We need to talk."

"Clearly you know where I live. Why are you following me around? You could have just knocked on my door."

"I wanted to make sure no one else was following you. I also didn't want your sisters to see me."

A ripple of uneasiness swept through her. "Why not?"

"Your father doesn't want them involved in any family business."

"He doesn't want me involved either," Carina countered.

"You're right, but unfortunately, this matter involves you whether we like it or not." He motioned to his car. "Please, Carina. We need to speak privately."

"I have to be somewhere in a few minutes."

"It's important," Marciano insisted.

Carina didn't try to speculate on what was important enough to prompt this unlikely visit, and she couldn't deny that she was curious. "Fine, but first I need to make a phone call."

"Calling the FBI will only complicate matters."

"That's not who I'm calling." Carina took a step away from her uncle. "Will you excuse me for just a minute? Then we can talk."

He nodded his assent. Carina stepped a few yards away and dialed Pete's number. She knew she was interrupting his practice, and she could hear Pete's impatience in the gruffness of his voice. Without giving an explanation as to why she needed the favor, she asked if he could give Bianca a ride home. When he agreed and she ended the call, she turned back to Marciano. "Now, what do you want to talk to me about?"

"Not here." He motioned to his vehicle. "Come with me. It's a nice day to go for a walk on the beach."

"The beach?" Carina looked at him suspiciously. "Why would you want to take me to the beach?"

"It's a good place to talk. Plenty of background noise and not a lot of people this time of year."

"Fine, but if you want me to go with you, I'm driving." Then she jerked a thumb at his bodyguards. "And they can follow."

He was silent for a moment, and then he nodded. "Fine."

Carina climbed into the driver's seat, waited for Marciano to sit beside her, and wondered what in the world she was getting herself into.

* * *

By the time she was halfway through the practice, Bianca could feel her muscles protesting from the increased pace Pete was demanding today. Thank goodness she had worked out with him only a few weeks ago to remind her exactly how tough he could be. And all in all, she'd rather deal with him any day over Russell.

Throughout the two-hour practice, Pete largely ignored her and instead took the time to give pointers to the various new swimmers. When practice ended, Pete motioned for all of the swimmers to gather in the two center lanes so he could talk to them.

"I still have a few more swimmers to look at, but I will let you all know in the next few days if I feel you will be a good fit for this team," Pete said, his voice gruff. "As most of you already know, I only have three slots open."

Bianca pulled her cap off and dipped back in the water to smooth out her hair. She climbed out of the pool with the intent of making it to the locker room before Todd could corner her again.

She was within four yards of her destination when she felt an arm come down around her shoulders. She stiffened, bracing for another confrontation. When she turned her head, her body relaxed instantly when she saw it was Eric rather than Todd who had snuck up behind her.

"It's so good to see you." Bianca reached out and gave him a hug. "I understand you're the one I have to thank for Pete moving down here."

"I think it was a combination of the both of us." His eyes narrowed. "Are you okay? For a second, I thought you might turn around and punch me."

"Sorry. I thought you were someone else."

Bianca didn't miss the way Eric's posture instantly became defensive, like a big brother ready to strike. "Who?"

"Just one of the guys trying out for the team."

"He's been giving you a hard time?"

Bianca wanted to deny it, but quite simply, Todd had worn her down, and she was tired of pretending everything was okay. "Yeah."

"Which one is he?"

Bianca turned and saw Todd walking toward her. Self-preservation had her taking a step toward the locker room. "I'll talk to you later."

"Yeah, later," Eric said, but Bianca didn't miss the way he shifted so she could escape before Todd could catch up with her.

She walked into the changing area and lowered herself onto one of the benches. She looked down at her hands to see them shaking. Her stomach was in knots. She couldn't keep living like this, always wanting to run and hide, but she had no idea how to deal with someone like Todd. In truth, this was the first time she'd ever had to.

Bianca checked her cell phone to see if Carina had texted her yet to tell her she was here. When she saw that there weren't any new messages, a sense of relief washed over her. If Carina was running late again, Bianca could hide out in the locker room, where there was no chance of running into Todd. Hopefully he would be long gone before her sister arrived.

* * *

Pete studied the notes he'd made on his clipboard, pleasantly surprised by the potential he had seen in the pool today. The quick workout pace of the day had helped him whittle his list down to five, and a conversation with one overly ambitious mother had cut another one off the list. He could understand parents wanting to be present at the tryouts, but it was obvious after talking to the mother and son that the mom wanted her eighteen-year-old to be in the pool a whole lot more than the kid wanted to be there. Pete didn't have any interest in investing his time in a swimmer who didn't love the sport.

Another parent helped him further. Pete saw a great deal of potential in thirteen-year-old Katia but had been worried about her age. Katia's father expressed concern that the demanding workouts and heavy practice schedule might backfire and cause the girl to burn out before she could reach her full potential.

Pete had agreed, promising to give the girl another tryout in a year or two if she decided the Olympics was a dream worth sacrificing for.

Now he looked at his remaining possibilities. Pete had been pleased to find out Jonah was one of the swimmers he had noticed at Bianca's team practice a few weeks ago. Todd, the other standout from her team, had come too. Today had confirmed that he did have definite potential, and he was a bit more polished than Jonah. Robin was a sophomore at Christopher Newport University and had already told Pete she was willing to take a lighter course load and go to school year-round if he agreed to coach her.

Jonah, Todd, and Robin. Assuming he did pick up Bethany Jackson, he would have to trim this list down to two. Otherwise, he could keep all three of these swimmers.

He noticed Eric approaching and held up his clipboard. "I've got it narrowed down to three from today's workout. After I see Bethany swim this afternoon, I should be able to make a final decision."

"I think we have a problem," Eric said. "One of the boys is giving Bianca a hard time."

Pete's eyes darkened. "Define 'giving Bianca a hard time.'"

"I'm not sure exactly, but I walked up to her after practice and put my arm around her, and she practically jumped out of her skin until she realized it was me."

"That's not like her."

"I know."

"Any idea who it was?"

"Since she all but ran into the locker room when Todd started walking toward us, I think he's a pretty good bet."

Pete shook his head. "That's too bad. The kid has talent."

"He was one of the swimmers you were considering?"

"Yeah, but we don't need a bully on the team."

"I'm not positive that it was him. I asked her who it was, but I didn't get an answer. I thought maybe she'd talk to you."

"Carina asked me to give her a ride home. I'll see if I can get her to talk," Pete said with a nod. "Tell me what you think of these two: Robin Hansen and Jonah Zimmerman."

"Robin reminds me a lot of Amber. Good technique, kind of quiet, and the faster someone is swimming behind her, the faster she goes."

"What about Jonah?"

"He has quite a few stroke flaws, but nothing you couldn't fix. I got the impression he doesn't have a lot of confidence in his abilities, and he looked intimidated by Todd."

"They're currently teammates."

"That would make sense, then. Obviously, Todd is faster than Jonah is at this point. Personally, I think if Jonah fixes the crossover on his freestyle and lengthens his stroke, he'll be the stronger swimmer of the two. I also think he's more versatile."

"I was thinking the same thing," Pete agreed. "Plus, the fact that Bianca asked me to give him a tryout weighs in his favor. She wouldn't have asked if she didn't think he would fit in here."

"Sounds like you have two of the three spots filled."

"It does. I'm going to go see if I can find Bianca and figure out what's bothering her."

"Let me know if there's anything I can do."

"Thanks, Eric. I'll see you this afternoon."

CHAPTER 10

THE LOCKER ROOM DOOR OPENED, and a young mother walked in with two small children. Bianca looked up, embarrassed.

She leaned down and gathered her things, praying that the coast was clear now. Nearly ten minutes had passed since she had seen Todd heading her direction. Surely he wouldn't wait around for her today.

She peeked out the locker room door and was surprised to see Pete standing right outside.

"Bianca, I told your sister I would give you a ride home."

"Oh, okay." Bianca shifted the bag on her shoulder and fell into step with Pete as she followed him out to the parking lot, her shoulders tensing when she noticed Todd outside, leaning against his car a short distance away.

"What's the deal between you and Todd?"

"Nothing."

Pete gave her a withering look. "Spill."

Bianca looked wary. "Can we talk about this later?"

Pete didn't respond until after they were both safely in his car. "He can't hear us now. Tell me what the problem is."

"He goes to my school, and he's been following me around and acting like I'm going out with him. Now everyone at school hates me."

"Why would everyone hate you, even if you were going out with him?"

"Because he already has a girlfriend. From what I hear, she's supposedly really nice, although I have no idea why a nice girl would go out with a jerk like him." Bianca stared at Pete and forced herself to ask the question burning in her mind. "Are you going to coach him?"

"I thought about it, but I don't think he's a good fit. Your friend Jonah, on the other hand, has potential."

"Really?" Bianca's eyes lit up. She wasn't sure what excited her more, the fact that she wouldn't have to swim with Todd anymore or that Jonah would be free of dealing with Russell too. "He would be thrilled. Our other coach has been really tough on him lately."

Pete arched a brow. "And you think I'll go easy?"

Bianca felt herself relax enough to smile. "Not tough with workouts. Tough with attitude. He's been punishing Jonah because he doesn't swim on Sundays either."

"That's right. He's Mormon too, isn't he?"

"Yeah." Bianca looked at him skeptically. "You're okay with that, right?"

"Mormons." He blew out a breath and shook his head. "It appears I'm destined to be surrounded by them."

"Yeah, but you love us anyway."

"Let's just say you tend to grow on me," Pete said. "Now, what are we going to do about this bully problem?"

"He's not really a bully." Bianca shifted uncomfortably in her seat.

"When you go to school, do you worry about running into him?" Pete asked perceptively.

"I guess."

"Bianca, bullies can come in a lot of forms. This guy clearly has homed in on you for some reason, and it's time to stop it."

"How?"

"Have you talked to any of your teachers or your principal?"

"I tried talking to one of my teachers, but that didn't work," Bianca said. "I'm afraid tattling on him is only going to make it worse."

"That's what he wants you to think." Pete shook his head. "He only has power over you if you let him. It's time to stand up for yourself."

Bianca wanted to tell him he didn't understand, but she knew something had to change. Her voice was both quiet and sincere when she asked, "What do you suggest?"

"First, we're going to talk to the principal before school to tell him what's been going on."

"Pete, Todd is one of the most popular kids in school. Mr. Smythe isn't going to believe that he's been harassing me."

"He doesn't have to believe you. He just has to have the chance to fix the problem. If he doesn't and you're forced to defend yourself, we'll have it on record that there's a problem."

"How would I defend myself?"

"First of all, if he tries to put his hands on you, a good slap across the face would likely put him in his place."

"If I slap him at school, I'll get suspended."

"Which is why we're going to talk to the principal first," Pete told her. "Hopefully it won't come to that. The other thing we need to do is enlist some help. You said Jonah goes to school with you, right?"

"Yeah. Why?"

"Because I think Jonah is about to become your new best friend."

"He's pretty much my only friend right now at school."

"Does he know that?"

She shook her head. "I never really see him except at practice and church."

"But he's a friend."

"Yeah, I guess."

"Good. Let's go talk to your friend."

"Now?"

"Absolutely," Pete said. "I need to talk to him about our practice schedule anyway."

"I think he was expecting a phone call to let him know if he made the team, not a personal visit."

"If you don't want to drop by unannounced, then call him and tell him we're coming. Or text him or whatever it is you kids do these days to communicate."

"I'll text him." Bianca pulled her phone from her swim bag and relayed the message. She gave Pete directions, shifting uncomfortably in her seat when they pulled up in front of Jonah's house. "This is weird."

"It's weird to stop by a friend's house?"

"I don't usually go to friends' houses. I don't really have friends here."

"That's about to change," Pete said with confidence. "Come on."

Bianca followed him up the front walk and then stood awkwardly beside Pete on Jonah's doorstep. The door swung open to reveal the bishop standing on the other side.

"Hi, Bianca. How are you?"

"Fine, Bishop." She motioned to Pete. "I don't know if you've met Pete Wellman. He's Jay Wellman's dad."

"Yes, of course. And you're the swim coach." Bishop Zimmerman reached out and shook Pete's hand. "Good to see you again."

"Sorry to just drop by like this, but I have some things I'd like to talk to you about."

"Absolutely." Bishop Zimmerman waved them inside and then led the way into the living room, where Jonah was sitting on the couch watching television.

At their entrance, Jonah clicked off the TV and stood. "Hi, Bianca," he said and then greeted Pete. "Mr. Wellman."

"It's Pete, especially since I expect you'll be swimming for me."

Jonah's eyes lit up. "I made it?"

"Congratulations." Pete reached out and shook his hand.

"Thank you so much!"

"Just remember you wanted this when the exhaustion starts catching up with you." Pete turned to face the bishop. "I have some details I would like to discuss with you. Would you mind terribly having Jonah drive Bianca home?"

Bianca noticed the way the bishop's eyes sharpened, like he suspected there was more to the request than met the eye, but he turned to his son. "Would you mind doing that, Jonah?"

"No problem." Jonah crossed the room to the rack on the wall, where key chains hung from the various pegs. He plucked a chain off of the rack and started for the front door.

Bianca followed him outside, not sure how she felt about Pete pawning her off on Jonah. "Sorry about this."

"It's no problem." Jonah said, excitement still humming through his voice. "I owe you for getting me the tryout with Pete."

"All I did was make a call. You got on the team by yourself."

Jonah unlocked the passenger-side door of his car. As soon as Bianca climbed in, he closed the door for her and circled to the other side.

Bianca clipped her seat belt and said, "You know, Pete wasn't kidding about how exhausted you're going to be after a few days of his practices."

"Since you used to swim for him, I'm going to assume you know what you're talking about," Jonah said. "One thing I don't understand though: I thought you said you moved here from North Carolina."

"I did, but I lived in Miami before that."

Jonah gave her a speculative look. "Why do I get the feeling there's a lot more to your story than what you let on?"

Bianca shrugged. "Maybe because you know me better than I thought you did."

CHAPTER 11

CARINA PARKED AT ONE OF the public parking lots near a community beach. Marciano didn't speak until they reached the sand. "It's good to see you again. You and your sisters have been missed."

Carina looked down the beach. A man jogged along the surf with two dogs trailing behind him, and she could see an older man in his backyard, which backed up to the beach. Other than that, the beach was empty.

She turned to face her uncle. "Tell me what is so important that you would travel all the way to Virginia." She hesitated and then added, "And how did you find me here?"

"It wasn't wise to go visit your father."

"Someone followed me here?"

"I was afraid you would visit, and you are in more danger than you realize."

Instantly, she stiffened, and her eyes whipped up to meet his. "What kind of danger?"

"The kind that comes when someone wants power and is willing to go through anyone and anything to get it."

"Who?"

Marciano stopped at the edge of the waves and stared out at the horizon but didn't answer her question. "You did me a favor when you killed Raymond. He was using you girls as a way to control your father."

"I didn't kill him to help out the family. I was protecting myself. I was protecting Bianca."

"And now you both need protection again."

"From whom?"

"I'm not entirely sure. Raymond's son, Levi, perhaps. Or his widow, Linda."

"What makes you think one of them would have any interest in Bianca or me? And what about Gianna?"

"Gianna's safe. You have hidden her well, and she wasn't there when Raymond was killed." Marciano continued to stare at the surf. "You, on the other hand, are of great interest to Raymond's family."

"How do you know this?"

"After Raymond's death, the family was able to reclaim some of the assets your grandfather left to Raymond. We also discovered evidence that Raymond had been involved in more than just the family business. He had started smuggling drugs as well."

Carina looked at him, confused. She remembered the illegal gambling from her childhood and various other illegal activities, but drugs had been taboo as far as the family business was concerned. "The family never deals drugs."

"Yes, but Raymond did. Someone close to him still does."

"But what does that have to do with me?"

"In the paperwork we recovered in a recent visit to Raymond's home, we found a reward notice for the key you have. There are many people out there who will stop at nothing to get the key and the reward that comes with it. I don't want to see you and your sisters hurt, or worse, because of this."

"It could have been Raymond offering the reward before he died."

Marciano shook his head. "I'm afraid that's not the case. We're sure it didn't start circulating until after Raymond's death."

"What do you know about the key? And why did my father send it to me if it would put us in danger?"

"Your father didn't think anyone would find out about the key. He thought he was taking care of you." He fell silent for a moment as though gathering his thoughts. "Your grandfather realized he was starting to lose his mental abilities several years ago. Even though the family tradition is to pass the reins down to the oldest son, he worried about giving complete control to Raymond, since his contact with the rest of us, his contact with our culture, was so limited."

"But I thought Grandfather did give control to Raymond."

"He gave him control, but not all of it. Your father and I were given most of the assets. We think that's why Raymond made an alliance with one of the drug cartels."

"To make more money?"

"To make enough money that he could take over the family business entirely."

"How could he possibly do that? Having more money wouldn't give him the rest of the business."

"Not unless he hurt us enough that we were willing to hand everything over to him."

Awareness lit her eyes. "He killed my mother so my father would cooperate?"

Marciano nodded. "Your father was too smart to just hand over everything to our half brother, but to protect you girls, he agreed to work with him. He convinced me to fall in line too."

"And the key?"

"An insurance policy to keep the rest of the family safe," he told her. "If you give me the key, I can make sure Raymond Alexander's family can't hurt you anymore."

Part of Carina wanted to hand the key over, to put the past behind her once and for all. Another part of her knew he wasn't telling her everything and that there was a reason the key had been sent to her and not to her uncle. "I'm not giving anyone the key, not without knowing what's behind the door it unlocks."

"Don't be foolish, Carina. I don't need the key. I'm only offering to take it from you to help keep you safe."

"I'm not being foolish. My father told me I should keep the key in a safe place and shouldn't give it to anyone." Carina looked Marciano in the eye. "I'm following his advice. The key is in a safe place, and I'm not handing it over to you or anyone else."

She saw Marciano's eyes go dark and his muscles tense. Instinct and memory made her take a step back. She remembered all too well the times the back of Marciano's hand had connected with her aunt's face.

She took another step back. "My father wanted to keep us away from you and the family. Please honor his wishes and let us live our lives without interference."

"Whether you want it or not, a time may come when you need the family's protection. I already lost one man in this battle for control. I can't be certain what he might have told the Alexander family." Marciano pulled a business card from his pocket and held it out to her. "I promised your father I would keep you and your sisters safe. It's a promise I intend to keep. The easiest way for me to protect you is to take possession of the key."

"If you want a copy of the key, talk to my father."

"I told you. The key doesn't mean anything to me, but it is of great value to the Alexander family." He shook his head disdainfully. "I had hoped you would be reasonable, but I can see your time away from Chicago has dimmed your memory."

Carina shook her head. "I remember just fine, and I know I never want to go back there."

"Don't forget your place, Caramia," he said, his voice low. "You may have been gone a long time, but I am still the head of this family."

"Only because my father is in jail for a crime he didn't commit."

"Your father is hardly innocent."

"Neither are you."

The speed and force with which Marciano's hand connected with Carina's cheek knocked her to the ground. A yelp of surprise and pain escaped her, and she lifted a hand to where the slap left her face stinging.

The fear and trepidation she had felt throughout her childhood came flooding back, and she tried to keep them from showing in her eyes. Instead, she gritted her teeth and forced herself to look up at him, allowing him to see only her contempt and disgust.

Marciano took a step forward and leaned down so their faces were close. "Don't ever forget your place again. Your father may have trusted you, but it's me you have to deal with now."

Her voice wasn't quite steady when she spoke. "Just leave us alone."

"You can't change where you come from, Carina," he said without remorse before turning away.

Carina stayed where she was until Marciano walked away and disappeared between the dunes on the edge of the beach. Then, slowly, she pushed herself up off of the cooling sand and wondered what she was going to do now that her worlds were again colliding.

* * *

Bianca looked around the apartment complex parking lot, surprised that Carina's car wasn't there yet. "That's weird."

"What?"

"I thought Carina would be home by now."

Jonah pulled into one of the visitor spots. "Do you want me to walk you up?"

Bianca started to say no, but an uneasy feeling made her reconsider. "Actually, that would be great, if you don't mind. I'm still not sure why she asked Pete to give me a ride home."

Jonah turned off the engine and climbed out of the car. Bianca led the way up the stairs and unlocked the door to her apartment. Cautiously, she walked inside, with Jonah right behind her.

She looked around, not noticing anything out of place. The apartment smelled like it always did, a combination of potpourri, Carina's perfume, and chlorine. A few of Carina's latest designs lay on the kitchen table, along with the postcard their father had sent her and the salt and pepper shakers.

"Is everything okay?" Jonah asked her.

"I guess so." Bianca shrugged.

Jonah reached down and picked the postcard up off the table. He tapped a finger on the picture. "That's Central Park. My aunt and uncle live in this building here."

"Do you get to go visit there much?"

"A couple of times a year."

Bianca looked around the living room, her uneasiness increasing.

"Are you sure you're okay?"

"I just have this weird feeling, like something's not quite right."

"Maybe you should call your sister and check in with her."

"Probably." Bianca pulled her phone out of her bag and dialed her sister's number. As soon as she answered, Bianca asked, "Carina, is everything okay?"

Carina didn't answer her question but rather asked one of her own. "Where are you?"

"I'm at home."

"Is Pete with you?"

"No, he's over at Bishop Zimmerman's house. Jonah drove me home."

"I'm on my way home now. Do you think Jonah would mind staying with you until I get there?"

"I don't think so. Is everything all right?"

"I hope so. I just don't want you to be alone right now."

"Do I need to order some pizza?" Bianca asked nervously. They had been out eating pizza the day their mother was murdered, and since then, the word *pizza* had become their personal code word for danger.

"No. I'll explain when I get there."

"Okay." Bianca hung up and looked over at Jonah, who was looking on, curiosity showing on his face.

"What did she say?"

"She asked if you could hang out until she gets home."

"Sure, no problem." Jonah motioned to the kitchen table and pulled out a chair for her. "Why don't we sit down, and you can tell me more about yourself."

Bianca lowered herself into the chair Jonah held and looked over at him as he sat down beside her. For the first time since leaving her childhood home in Denver, she found herself wondering if she could trust someone with the truth. Admittedly, she didn't know Jonah all that well, but she did know he stood up for what he believed in and she certainly trusted his father.

She leaned back in her chair. "What do you want to know?"

"I want to know everything," Jonah said with a sincerity that surprised her. "But why don't you start with telling me why you live with your sister."

"This may take awhile."

"I've got time."

CHAPTER 12

As soon as Jonah and Bianca were out the door, Pete got right to the point with Jonah's dad. "Bianca is having some trouble, and I'm hoping your son can help her out."

"Have a seat." Mr. Zimmerman motioned to the couch and sat across from him. "What's the problem?"

Pete explained his concerns that Todd was bullying Bianca.

"I've seen Todd at Jonah's swim meets, but I really don't know him or his family well," Mr. Zimmerman admitted. "What can I do to help?"

"I have a couple of ideas, one of which is to see if Jonah would be willing to spend some time with Bianca at school," Pete told him. "It's not an easy favor I'm asking, especially if Bianca's right about how badly her reputation has been damaged."

"I'm afraid she's right about the rumors. Jonah came home a few weeks ago pretty discouraged when he heard Bianca was going out with Todd."

"Obviously, if Jonah believed it, everyone else believes it too," Pete said. "Bianca has been through a lot in the past couple of years. If it comes down to it, I'll try to convince her sister to petition to change schools, but I'd prefer to see if we can fix the problem first."

"I'll talk to Jonah," Mr. Zimmerman said with an air of optimism. "I think he'll want to help out when he realizes what's really going on."

"I appreciate anything he's willing to do," Pete said. "I'm sure Todd's not going to be too happy when I tell him he won't be swimming for me. It won't take long for him to find out Jonah was chosen over him."

"Was Jonah selected over him because of the situation with Bianca or because of his abilities?"

"Jonah was chosen because he has the potential to become a world-class athlete. My job is to give him the skills to live up to that potential. Your job is to help me convince him to believe in himself."

"I will certainly do my best." Mr. Zimmerman hesitated and then asked, "Will it be a problem that he doesn't practice or compete on Sundays?"

"I stopped practicing on Sundays years ago." Pete stood up and held out his hands as though in surrender. "I seem to attract Mormons."

Mr. Zimmerman chuckled and shook Pete's hand. "I think I'm going to enjoy watching my son's progress under your tutelage."

"That makes two of us."

* * *

Jonah stared at Bianca in amazement. When he had first met her, he had found her interesting but had assumed her family life was pretty much like everyone else's in the ward. Then he had noticed her parents were never around. When his dad had dragged him to Jay Wellman's baptism, he'd realized her life was definitely not the norm.

He had thought about asking her out as they started the school year. Then he'd found out she was going out with Todd. That tidbit of information had surprised him. He never would have thought Bianca, of all people, would go out with such an arrogant jerk. Over the past few weeks, he had started to suspect that whatever had been going on between them had ended and had probably ended badly. Now he knew that nothing had ever even begun.

More surprising than that was this newest information that Bianca's mother had been murdered and that her father was in prison. He never would have guessed that she came from such a past.

"So your dad is in prison for killing your mom, but you don't think he really did it?"

"We know he didn't do it," Bianca told him. "At least, we know that now."

"Then why is he still in prison?"

"Because the person who really killed my mom is dead. We don't have any way to prove that my dad isn't guilty."

"Wow. I can't believe you've been dealing with all of this. That's tough."

"Compared to dealing with Todd, my family stuff is easy."

The realization struck Jonah that if he made Pete's team, Todd likely made it too. "Is Pete coaching him too?"

"No. Thank goodness."

"Seriously?" Jonah's eyes widened. Since eight years old, Jonah had swam with Todd, always falling second to him both in races and their coaches' attention. "How come?"

"He only had three slots open. Todd wasn't good enough."

Jonah's voice was incredulous. "And I was?"

"You really need to give yourself more credit. You're better than you think you are. If you weren't, Pete wouldn't have decided to coach you."

"I just can't remember the last time I beat Todd at anything."

"Get used to it," Bianca told him. "With Pete coaching you, I doubt it will take long before you're beating him in the pool too."

"I hope so," Jonah said. "You know, I'm starting to understand why Russell was so intimidated by you. After swimming for Pete, you probably do know more about swimming than he does."

Bianca just shrugged. "I know I'm looking forward to the first time we get to square off against our old team in competition."

"I have to say, I'm kind of looking forward to *not* swimming against Todd."

"Trust me on this one," Bianca told him, a look of confidence on her face. "You will beat Todd. You just need to believe in yourself. I know Pete believes in you, and so do I."

Jonah stared at her, both surprised and touched by the simplicity and directness of her words. He felt his confidence lift a notch and found himself wanting to believe.

* * *

Carina took the long way home. Clearly, Marciano already knew where she lived, but she hoped the few extra minutes would give the red mark on her cheek time to fade.

She pulled up to a stoplight and indulged herself by closing her eyes for several long seconds. Her father had obviously sent her that key for a reason.

The way he talked, it seemed like it was supposed to protect her, but ever since it had come into her life, it had done nothing but cause her grief and pain. All she wanted now was to move forward with the assurance that her past would stay firmly where it belonged: behind her.

Her cell phone rang, and her spirits instantly lifted when she saw that it was Jay calling. She hadn't heard from him at all since he left two weeks ago. "Hi, where are you?"

"Just got back," Jay said, his voice thick with fatigue.

"I know you must be tired, but is there any way you could meet me at my apartment? I could really use your advice on something."

"Sure. Is everything okay?"

"That's what I'm hoping you can help me figure out."

"I'll be there in a few minutes."

"Thanks, Jay. I really appreciate it."

* * *

Jay had expected to find Carina home alone when he arrived, but instead, it appeared that everyone they knew had decided to converge on her apartment at the same time. Bianca opened the door to reveal Carina inside, along with Jay's father and the bishop's son, Jonah.

"Dad, I didn't expect to see you here."

"Actually, I only got here a minute ago." Pete crossed to give him a bear hug. "Welcome home."

"Thanks." He waved toward the kitchen, where Bianca and Jonah were sitting. "What's going on here?"

"I was trying to help Bianca sort out a problem, but I think Carina has more pressing matters we need to deal with."

Jay stepped away from his father and turned into Carina's outstretched arms.

"I'm so glad you're here," Carina said.

"What's going on?"

Carina glanced over at Bianca and Jonah. "Maybe we should talk out on the balcony."

Bianca stood up and shook her head. "I want to know what's going on too."

Jonah also stood and shifted his weight, looking around the room awkwardly. "Bianca, I guess I'd better get going."

Bianca looked like she wanted to protest, but instead, she said, "Thanks for the ride. I really appreciate it."

"Anytime." Jonah crossed to the door. "See you all later."

As soon as the door closed behind Jonah, Carina dropped onto the couch and announced in a shaky voice, "I saw my uncle Marciano today. He said something about how I shouldn't have gone to see my father. I got the impression that he had someone waiting at the prison to follow me home. Either that, or he's figured out how to trace our flights."

Jay's weariness from the last mission was instantly replaced by concern. He lowered himself onto the couch beside her. "What did he want?"

"He said he thinks we might be in danger from someone in Raymond Alexander's family, but I'm not sure if he really came to warn me or if he only wanted the key."

"He asked for the key?" Jay asked.

Carina rubbed her hand over her cheek. "He was pretty indignant when I refused to give it to him."

"I'm surprised he didn't send someone into your apartment to search for it."

"Maybe he did," Bianca interrupted.

"What makes you say that?" Jay asked.

Her shoulders lifted. "I don't know, but something didn't feel right when I got home today."

Pete looked at her skeptically. "What do you mean it didn't feel right?"

"It just didn't feel right. It was like there was someone else here."

"Did you check the other rooms?" Jay asked.

Bianca shook her head. She pressed her lips together and admitted, "I was too scared."

Jay pushed off the couch and pulled his gun out of the holster at the back of his waistband. Hopefully Bianca's imagination was playing tricks on her, but after their other uncle tried to kill them, he wasn't taking any chances.

His father fell into position behind him and then signaled toward the door for the hall closet. Pete gave him a nod and then yanked the door open for Jay. That closet was empty, as were the bathroom and both bedrooms. But the window to Carina's room was wide open, the curtains billowing in the breeze.

Jay checked her room a second time but didn't find anything out of place, except for the open window.

When he led the way back into the living room, Carina asked, "Is everything okay?"

Jay holstered his weapon. "I don't suppose you left your bedroom window open today, did you?"

Slowly, Carina shook her head. "Someone was here?"

"It looks that way." Jay looked over at Bianca. "Did you hear anything when you got here?"

"No."

"What are you thinking?" Pete asked.

"I'm wondering if Bianca got here before our visitor had the chance to search the place or if she arrived after he finished looking around."

"Before," Bianca said with an unexpected certainty. "Whoever it was didn't make it as far as the kitchen."

"How can you be so sure?" Jay asked.

"Because the card from our father was lying out in plain sight on the kitchen table. It hadn't been touched. I would think whoever was here was probably looking for that and the key."

"They might not have known about the card," Jay countered.

"Or they left it so you wouldn't know they'd been here. They could have taken a picture of it or copied down the information," Pete suggested.

"I don't think so," Carina said now. "The last time someone from the family came searching for something, they trashed our apartment."

"Which means Bianca probably got home right as this guy was entering your bedroom," Pete concluded. "She and Jonah must have scared him off."

"I didn't think our family got scared off," Bianca said.

"They don't," Carina agreed.

"Maybe the break-in didn't have anything to do with your family," Jay suggested.

"That's not very likely," Carina told him. "What are the odds that my uncle would show up and we'd have a break-in on the same day?"

"But you said your uncle asked for the key. The break-in happened while you were with him, right?"

Carina nodded.

"Why would he have someone break in if there was a chance you would just hand over what he wanted?"

"He might have known I wouldn't hand it over and sent someone while he knew I wasn't home."

"It's possible. Either way, we should probably call the cops. Let's see if we can get them to dust for prints," Jay said. "Maybe you should both pack a bag and come stay at my place for a few days until we're sure it's safe here."

Bianca looked at him warily. "Is this going to be like last time?"

Jay remembered the last time vividly. A shooting outside the girls' apartment in Miami had ultimately resulted in them leaving Florida, hiding in North Carolina for several months, and then resettling here. He didn't want to think about the possibility that they might not be safe here in Virginia Beach, but at the moment, he wasn't sure about anything.

Jay gave her an apologetic look. "I'm not sure how long it might be before you come back here."

Bianca sighed heavily, but she didn't argue. Instead, she turned away and headed for her bedroom while Carina pulled out her phone to call the police.

CHAPTER 13

"WHAT DO YOU MEAN YOU didn't get it?" Marciano stood on the edge of the tarmac near the private plane that would take him back to Chicago and stared at his son Silvio, the person he had entrusted with much of his future. "I thought you understood how vital it was for you to get the instructions my brother sent Carina. That was our only purpose for coming here."

Silvio forced himself to keep his voice calm. "I was only able to search Carina's bedroom before someone walked in."

"Who? Carina was with me."

"It must have been Bianca, but I heard someone else with her. I couldn't be sure if it was one of those Navy SEALs."

"You're afraid of Carina's friends?"

Silvio straightened. "You said you didn't want me to be seen."

"I also said I need that information." Marciano's voice vibrated with fury. "Carina's birthday is only six weeks away. If we don't gain access to those documents before then, this family will be ruined."

"There has to be a way to stop the transfer of assets, even if we can't find where Giovanni hid all his papers."

"We don't even know what state he registered everything in."

"Do you really think Raymond's family is still looking for Carina?"

Marciano gave him a knowing look. "They've been trying to find out where Giovanni's being held ever since their last attempt to kill him. Now that Alexander is gone, their only chance at regaining control of the family's business is if they can find those papers before we do."

"I'll find them."

"See that you do. I'm not going to spend the rest of my life trying to rebuild what is rightfully mine," Marciano insisted. "Get back to Carina's apartment and find a way to get that information."

* * *

Jay's apartment wasn't intended to house four people at the same time. The only bedroom had a queen-sized bed, which Jay offered to let Carina and Bianca share. The long, narrow living room had a single couch that Pete would use to sleep on, while Jay opted for a bedroll and the floor. Carina hoped she didn't have to try to leave the apartment in the middle of the night, or someone was likely to get stepped on or tackled.

The police had already come and gone at Carina's apartment. She wasn't surprised by the news that they hadn't found any fingerprints that didn't belong. Her family was too clever to leave that kind of evidence behind. The thought that they were also too smart to leave a window open pricked the corner of her mind, leaving an uneasy feeling.

Realizing Jay had passed the exhaustion point some time ago, she insisted he go into his room to grab a nap while he had the chance. She doubted he would sleep well until they sorted out what she was going to do now.

Bianca was in Pete's care at the moment. He had taken her to his afternoon workout in Norfolk. Realizing Bianca needed to expend some energy, Carina hadn't objected to Pete's suggestion that she go.

Carina had spent the last two hours trying to organize the suitcases and supplies she and Bianca had brought with them. She had set up a folding table in the corner of the room by the front door, with her laptop and her designs organized neatly on top of it. She placed the stack of towels Bianca had brought with her in the linen closet in the hall, and Bianca's extra swim gear occupied floor space next to Jay's go-bag in the hall closet.

Carina crossed to the kitchen counter that separated the living area from the small kitchen. She picked up the card her father had sent her, willing it to give her the answers she was looking for. She had memorized every detail on the card, from the photograph of the buildings surrounding Central Park to the words written inside, *Remember who you really are*, to the numbers scribbled beside them: *995 5.*

She assumed the words were her father's way of telling her that the note was from him, but she didn't know what the numbers represented, nor did she know if he had chosen the card depicting Central Park for a reason or if it was just a coincidence. She reached for the salt shaker on the counter. Unscrewing the lid, she reached inside, pushing the grains of salt aside until she felt metal.

Plucking the key from its hiding spot, she leaned over the counter and turned on the sink to rinse it off and then used a paper towel to dry it.

"Making sure it's still there?" Jay asked from the hallway.

Carina turned to look at him. He had showered and shaved and appeared infinitely more rested than when they had first arrived at his apartment a few hours ago. She stared at him for a moment, amazed that amid all of the chaos in her life over the past few months, she had fallen in love. Sometimes she still couldn't believe he loved her too.

"I was just wondering why everyone is so anxious to get it." Carina's brow furrowed. "I have to think that it isn't the key itself that's so important. My family must not know where my father's hidden apartment is either."

"I was thinking the same thing," Jay agreed. "If Alexander or your uncle Marciano knew where the lock was, they could just call a locksmith. Your father had to have given you some other clue they're hoping to get from you."

"Is there any chance there's some clue etched into the key somewhere? I saw that on TV once, where an address was engraved into the key."

Jay shook his head. "We had the lab check that out when we first found it."

"Then it all comes back to this." Carina held up the card.

"How would you feel about making a trip to New York for Veterans Day weekend? I know it's a few weeks away, but I thought maybe we could go up that Saturday to check things out. Maybe we can even go out and see a show or something to celebrate your birthday."

"My birthday is the week after Veterans Day."

"So we'll celebrate a few days early. What do you say?"

"Do you still think my dad's apartment is in Central Park?"

"It's the only thing that makes sense." Jay slid into the seat beside her. "If he said you have all of the clues you need, then we have to assume this card is giving you the location."

"And the numbers?"

"I don't know. When I tried running it as part of an address, I couldn't find anything that matched," Jay said. "I think we've done as much as we can long distance. It's time to go see if we can make some sense of this when we're actually standing in Central Park."

"I'd like that," Carina said. "The real question is what do I do now that my family has found me again?"

"I was just thinking about that."

"And?"

"I know you've spent a lot of time working on Kendra's wedding dress. Have you given any thought as to what you want *your* wedding dress to look like?"

Carina looked at him, dumbfounded. "What does a wedding dress have to do with hiding from my family?"

"I thought maybe you'd consider changing your last name."

Still not quite able to keep up with the quick turn in the conversation, she thought of the paperwork and hassle her mother had gone through when they had changed their names from Perelli to Channing. Then she caught the hint of vulnerability in Jay's expression, and two and two started to equal four. "Are you saying . . . ?"

Jay drew a breath. "I'm saying I want you to marry me."

Carina could only stare at him. He had first mentioned marriage two months before. That had been when he had first told her he was joining the Church. It had also been at a time when they both thought she was finally free of her family. As much as she wanted to follow her heart, she found herself asking, "Why would you want to marry me?"

"You're kidding, right?" He took her hands in his and leaned down for a lingering kiss. His eyes were dark and serious when he spoke to her in a low voice. "I love you. You're everything to me."

Emotions conflicted inside of her, dreams and possibilities warring with the reality that she was first and foremost a Perelli, a fact she would never be able to completely escape. "I'm serious. Look at what happened today. This may never end."

"Carina, it is going to end." He slid his hands up to her shoulders and stared down at her intently. "We've talked about our future. We've prayed about it. This thing with us, it's just right."

"I don't want anything to happen to you because of me."

"Nothing's going to happen to either of us," Jay assured her. "We're going to figure this puzzle out, and then we'll deal with your family."

"And then we'll get married, and I'll change my name."

"Exactly." Jay nodded. Then a look of doubt showed on his face. "Is that a yes?"

A smile bloomed on her face. "Yes."

Jay swept her up in a hug, lifting her so her feet were dangling three inches off the floor. Then his lips met hers, and Carina was overcome with that warm feeling of home she had spent so long searching for. The kiss lingered, and slowly, Jay lowered her back down to the ground. "I love you."

"I love you too."

* * *

Bianca considered the possibility of another move. This wouldn't be like leaving Miami, where she had made some great friends, or like leaving her childhood home in Denver while she was still trying to come to grips with the loss of her mother. She had lived in Virginia for only a couple of months, just long enough to make a lot of enemies and no real friends. Except Jonah, of course.

But Pete was here now. Since leaving Miami, she had missed swimming for him. Now, with the possibility of losing him as her coach for a second time in less than six months, she dreaded the thought of starting over. And what about Carina and Jay? They were meant for each other.

"What's going on in that pretty little head of yours?" Pete asked as he drove toward Jay's apartment.

"I don't want to start over again."

"I thought you might want the chance to leave that school of yours behind."

"I probably would if it didn't mean losing you as my coach again."

"I'm not quite ready to cut you loose yet." Pete pulled up to a stoplight and glanced over at her. "You know, this thing with Todd is going to keep eating at you until you face it. Running away won't really solve the problem."

"I know. I was talking with Jonah about that. I have to find out a way to stand up to Todd, or I'm going to feel like he won."

Pete was quiet for a moment. Then he said, "I have an errand to run for my wife. Do you want to come along?"

"Sure. Where are we going?"

"There's a rental house she wanted me to look at," Pete told her. "It's in the same school district as the one you're in now. That could be a benefit."

"Why would it matter if your house is in my school district?" Bianca asked.

"Well, you probably won't feel safe in your apartment now, and if I know my son, he'll do everything he can to convince your sister to stay here in Virginia Beach."

Bianca's brow furrowed, still not sure what that had to do with her.

Pete parked beside the curb, and Bianca shifted to look at the house in front of them with the For Rent sign in the yard. The two-story house was larger than Pete's house in Miami, and it appeared to have been recently painted.

"Apparently, the owners wanted to sell it but weren't able to find a buyer for the price they needed." Pete opened his car door, and Bianca followed suit.

The Realtor got out of his car, which was parked in the driveway. "Mr. Wellman?" He reached out and shook Pete's hand. "I'm Bruce Molinski. It's good to finally meet you in person."

"You too."

Bruce started toward the door. "Like I told your wife on the phone, this house has five bedrooms, two on the main level and three upstairs."

"She mentioned that there's a private entrance for the downstairs bedrooms."

"That's right. Those two rooms are located in the back of the house, and there's a side entrance that leads to that section of the house."

He unlocked the door and waited for Bianca and Pete to walk inside. "I'll let you and your daughter take a look around. Just let me know if you have any questions."

Bianca nearly opened her mouth to clarify, but when Pete didn't say anything, she figured he didn't see a reason to correct the false assumption.

She walked inside, glancing at the living area to the right before following Pete past the stairwell to their left and into the kitchen. The cabinets were outdated, but the space was open and seemed pretty organized. The large family room stretched along the back wall of the house, and a set of french doors opened up to the backyard.

Pete led the way through the kitchen and into a hallway leading to a laundry room. Past the laundry room were three doorways. Bianca looked in the first to find a modest bedroom. Across from it was a bathroom that had the feel of recent remodeling.

"What do you think?" Pete asked from just outside the doorway on the end.

"It's pretty big for just two people," Bianca told him.

"Actually, it would be for five people."

"Huh?"

Pete motioned inside the bedroom at the end of the hall. Bianca peeked through the door. The room was enormous. "Is this the master bedroom?"

"I think the master is upstairs." Pete started back toward the staircase.

Bianca trotted after him. "You said five people would be living here? Who?"

"You know your sister and Jay are going to get married eventually."

"Yeeaahh," Bianca said, drawing the word out. "It's kind of obvious they're heading that way."

Pete led her up the stairs and paused to look at the master bedroom. He motioned toward the two bedrooms down the hall. "So which room do you want?"

"Wait a minute." Bianca held up a hand as she finally started catching up with what Pete was talking about. "Are you planning on Carina and me moving in here with you?"

He nodded casually like everything was already settled. "We'll turn one of these upstairs rooms into a guest room for when my other kids come to visit. After they get married, Jay and Carina can have the big room downstairs, and Carina can use that little one for her office or as a guest room for Gianna when she's home from school."

Bianca let herself visualize the scene, finding it surprisingly easy to imagine. It would be almost like her life before her mom died—a real house, someone besides just her sister to talk to. The thought of having a real family again brought tears to her eyes, and she quickly blinked against them. "Are you sure you'd want us to live with you? What will your wife think?"

"I already talked to her." Pete gave her a knowing look, and his voice was gruff when he added, "She said you're already family anyway. Besides, if she's helping cook for you, maybe you'll stop trying to sneak hamburgers and pizza."

"I was good yesterday," Bianca said, and her stress started to ease away. She looked up at Pete, her eyes sparking with mischief. "How do we talk Jay and Carina into it?"

Pete just arched an eyebrow. "Oh, I don't think it will be too difficult."

CHAPTER 14

"I DON'T UNDERSTAND WHY THIS is so difficult." Her Southern drawl might have slowed her words, but the man beside her shifted his weight uncomfortably, clearly aware of her displeasure.

"We had a little trouble tracking her after she visited her father. We were able to follow her as far as Nashville . . ."

"Which means you lost her in Nashville," she concluded.

"Yes, but we did manage to catch a break. The man you caught in Raymond's office indicated that Marciano Perelli has men looking for her."

"How does this help us?"

"We learned Marciano went to Virginia Beach yesterday. Two of his men are still there."

Understanding dawned. "He found her."

"We believe so."

Dark emotions swelled inside her, the need for revenge cresting above all else. "You know what to do."

"Yes, ma'am."

* * *

Jay had spent countless hours plotting and planning how he would ask Carina to marry him. For weeks he had wondered how long to wait, how he could be sure she was ready to take that next step with him. This afternoon hadn't been anything like he had thought it would be.

Somehow, the complexities of Carina's situation and the simplicity of their feelings for each other had made this special time uniquely theirs. He hadn't bought a ring yet, hadn't had the time since returning from his last mission. Besides, he had always wanted her to help pick it out. As soon as she had said yes, he had convinced her to go shopping.

Now, after two hours of searching four different jewelry stores, a round diamond sparkled from Carina's left hand. They had just started home when they received the news from Seth that Riley and Tristan had had their baby boy. Jay had expected their stop at the hospital to only take a minute, but instead he had found himself in the waiting room with the rest of the squad for nearly an hour before they were allowed to see the new mother and her little one.

Seeing Riley holding her newborn had left Jay with an odd sense of longing and anticipation. The feeling settled deep inside him as they drove back to his apartment and discussed their future.

"I suppose you're going to want to wait to get married until I can take you to the temple," Jay said, even though he was secretly hoping that wouldn't be the case. He understood the whole reason for temple marriage now, but he found himself anxious to start their life together.

"I guess I assumed we would wait for that," Carina said, her voice a little hesitant.

Jay took her hesitation as a good sign. He drew a breath and mustered his courage. "How would you feel about maybe getting married sooner than later?" Before she could answer, he pressed on. "Then we could go through the temple on our first anniversary."

She was quiet for a moment. "Are you sure we aren't rushing this? It's not just us we have to think about. I still have Bianca at home for at least two more years."

"I know we won't start our life together like most people, since it won't be just the two of us, but I would really love being able to come home to you, whether it's at the end of every day or at the end of a long mission." He pulled into a parking space near his apartment. After he turned off the car, he shifted in his seat to face her. "I know I want to get married now, but I've had a lot of time to think about it over the past couple weeks while I was gone. The question is, what do you want?" Jay reached for her hand and gave it a squeeze before continuing. "If you want to wait until I can take you to the temple, I'll be okay with that."

Her eyes were dark and serious. "Right now, all I want is to be with you."

"We could always pray about it," Jay suggested.

"I'd like that." Carina glanced around the quiet parking lot. "Do you think we could do that now?"

"Here?" Jay asked.

"This may be the most privacy we get until I figure out what to do about my apartment."

Jay glanced at his dad's car parked beside them. "You're probably right."

Together, they folded their arms, and Carina offered a sweet, heartfelt prayer. Jay was surprised by the warmth burning through him the moment she posed the question of when they should marry. When the prayer ended, she looked up at him, and her eyes were moist.

Jay wasn't sure what her tears meant, and he was afraid to ask. He reached for her hand and waited.

Carina took a moment before speaking, but Jay wasn't sure if she was fighting her emotions or waiting for some kind of answer. Finally, she asked, "Do you think you will be home for the holidays this year?"

"I'm supposed to be. Right now, our next scheduled deployment isn't supposed to happen until March."

"How would you feel about a December wedding?"

"Really?" A well of emotions bubbled up inside him, anticipation dominating them all.

She spoke almost hesitantly again when she said, "I always assumed we would want to wait until you could go through the temple, but I don't think we're supposed to wait."

"I think you're right. Otherwise, we wouldn't be getting the same answer." Jay shook his head in amazement. "I still can't get used to this."

"What?"

"The whole idea that God can give us answers for stuff like this."

"I don't know if I'm used to it either, and I've been a member of the Church a lot longer than you." Excitement filled her voice when she added, "Should we go tell your dad and Bianca the news?"

Jay gave her an apologetic look. "Um, Dad kind of already knows."

Confusion lit her eyes. "What?"

"He knew I was planning on asking you to marry me. He just didn't know it was going to be today."

Slowly, Carina's lips curved up into a smile. "So he doesn't mind the idea of me being his daughter-in-law?"

"Are you kidding? My dad loves you. So does my mom."

Carina's smile widened. "The feeling's mutual."

* * *

"It's about time," Pete grumbled when he heard Jay's apartment door open. He and Bianca had returned from the house they would soon call home over an hour before to find Jay's apartment empty. During that time,

Bianca had been driving him crazy worrying that they wouldn't be able to convince Carina to move in with him and his wife.

Pete wasn't about to admit that he had similar reservations. But he had moved forward with the plan to have Sandra travel up to Virginia on the train as soon as the movers finished loading all of their belongings. If he had his way, they would all be settling into the new place by next weekend.

"Where have you been?" Bianca asked impatiently when she saw Carina.

Carina glanced back at Jay with a funny expression. Then she grinned at her and said, "Shopping."

"Shopping?" Bianca asked a little indignantly. "You're all freaked about our uncle showing up, you have me pack up most of my stuff to come stay here in a one-bedroom apartment with three other people, and then you go shopping?"

"Yeah."

"I can't believe . . ." Bianca trailed off, her focus finally shifting to the hand Carina held up and the diamond ring that sparkled from a very significant finger. She stared for a second and then she shrieked, "You're engaged?"

"Told you they'd end up together." Pete smirked at Bianca before stepping forward to slap Jay on the back. "Congratulations."

Bianca also extended her congratulations, and Jay and Carina shared their plans to marry sometime during Gianna's Christmas break. Pete hadn't expected them to marry quite so soon, but he kind of liked the idea of a holiday wedding. That would give his wife the chance to convince their other two children to come visit for both the wedding and Christmas. He imagined the big house he had just rented would be busting at the seams in no time and was surprised at how much he liked that particular image.

They all settled into the living room, and Pete asked Jay, "How much longer do you have on your lease here?"

"I'm already on a month-to-month. I just have to give thirty days' notice," Jay told him. "I thought I would rent a two-bedroom place that Carina and Bianca can live in until we get married."

"Actually, I have another idea." Pete told them about the house he had just rented. "Besides having enough room for all of us, it will keep both of you from putting a lease in your names for a while. If you're still worried about Carina's family finding her, we can clean out her apartment and ship her stuff to somewhere out of state to make it look like she moved away from here."

"That's certainly not something I had thought of," Jay said, considering. He turned to Carina. "What do you think?"

"I don't know." She paused, the possibilities clearly working through her mind. "Pete, are you sure you and Sandra would be okay living with combined households like that?"

"Sandra loved the idea. She misses having people in the house."

"Then I guess that could work . . ." Carina said.

Jay nodded agreeably and added, "Most of the stuff you have you just picked up at yard sales. We could send all of that to some charity somewhere else and sneak anything you really want to keep out of your place."

"There's another thing," Pete said, his voice serious. "I think Bianca should change her name."

"What?" Bianca narrowed her eyes. "Why?"

"Your family knows what name you're using, and they might be able to track you down through your school records. I thought maybe you'd consider using my last name. Carina will be a Wellman soon enough, and with you living at our house, everyone will just assume you belong to Sandra and me."

"That's actually a really good idea," Jay said, his voice hopeful. "We could file the paperwork in a different city so it wouldn't be easy to find."

Bianca stared at them, the shock of Pete's suggestion apparently melting into acceptance. "So we would all be Wellmans?"

"You're going to be part of the family soon enough anyway," Pete said.

A flash of wonder appeared on Bianca's face, and Pete noticed her blinking against tears.

After a long moment, she finally said, "I guess I would be okay with that."

Satisfied, Pete fished his new house key out of his pocket. "Why don't the two of you go take a look at the house. The furniture won't get here until Thursday, but we can start moving stuff in at any time."

Jay took the key and wrote down the address Pete gave him.

Pete felt a ripple of satisfaction when Carina smiled at his son and said, "It looks like it's going to be a busy week."

CHAPTER 15

"I didn't expect to see our new coach at church yesterday," Jonah said as he parked his car in the student parking lot.

"Yeah." Bianca grinned at him. "He grumbled about coming, but Jay convinced him that a little religion wouldn't hurt him. Pete still isn't so sure about it all, but he lasted through sacrament meeting at least."

They got out of the car and started walking toward the school. Bianca noticed the way Jonah rolled his shoulders as though trying to stretch out the muscles there. "Did Pete tell you to ice your shoulders yet?"

Jonah nodded. "I thought he was kidding, but now I'm starting to think he was serious."

"After a week or two, it'll get better." Bianca rolled her own shoulders. "At least, I keep telling myself that."

"Do you really think I'll be able to beat Todd after I've been working with Pete for a while?"

"Yeah, I do," Bianca said with conviction. "Of course, I wouldn't announce that to Todd yet. I think you should surprise him. Just make sure I'm there for it. I can't wait to see the expression on his face."

"He's really been giving you a hard time, hasn't he?"

Bianca felt her cheeks flush with embarrassment. "I was talking to Pete about it. I've got to stand up to him. Maybe if I do, he'll leave me alone."

Jonah pulled the door open for her, and they walked into school together. When he fell into step beside her, he said, "Is there anything I can do?"

"No, thanks. I appreciate the offer though." Bianca turned toward her locker. "I'll see you later."

"Come find me at lunch. We can eat together."

Bianca's stomach jumped at the idea of feeling normal again. She had spent the last month hiding out in the library during lunch. "I'd like that."

"I'll see you later."

Bianca made her way down the hall to her locker, now accustomed to the dirty looks and evil stares. She'd rather deal with those any day than have to face Todd.

That thought had barely crossed her mind when a hand gripped her shoulder and spun her around. She found herself facing the angry version of her current nightmare.

"What did you tell Pete Wellman?" Todd demanded.

"I don't know what you're talking about," Bianca responded, trying not to notice the curious glances being cast their way.

"I saw you walking out of the rec center with him." Todd stepped closer, and Bianca took an automatic step back. "Did you tell him not to coach me?"

"I didn't say anything to him about who he should coach."

"Then why would he pick Jonah over me? I am way faster than Jonah, and my tryout went great."

Bianca took another step back only to find herself up against her locker. Pete's words echoed in her mind. No one could push her around without her permission. It was time to make sure Todd understood he was in her space and it was time for him to leave.

She forced herself to stand a little straighter and looked him in the eye. "You know, the one thing about Pete is that he cares as much about the character of his swimmers as he does about their abilities. Clearly, he saw what you're really like."

"What's that supposed to mean? And how would you know what Pete Wellman looks for in a swimmer?"

Bianca's chin lifted a little higher. In a matter of days, she would share the same last name as Pete, and she wondered briefly what Todd would think of that development. She reminded herself that she didn't have to explain her friendship with Pete and that it was time to put Todd in his place. In her mind, his place was anywhere she wasn't. "You've been stalking me for weeks. Pete would never want to coach anyone who tries to tear others down. You can't blame me because Pete saw through this act of yours and realized for himself that you're nothing more than a bully."

Bianca winced when Todd slammed a hand on the lockers beside her head. "I'd watch what you say about me if I were you." He leaned down so their faces were close together and lowered his voice. "Believe me, I can make your life a living hell if you aren't careful."

She bristled, but that didn't stop him from slipping his free hand around the back of her neck and brushing a kiss across her cheek. "Have a good day, sweetheart."

Bianca could feel her face flush, and her gaze dropped to the floor when Todd stepped back and sauntered down the hall. She looked down, annoyed to see her hands shaking. She couldn't keep living like this, she told herself yet again. Maybe Pete was right. Maybe it was time to talk to the principal to see if someone could figure out a way to get Todd to leave her alone.

* * *

Sitting in the driver's seat of the borrowed van, Jay looked through the binoculars at their target, searching for anything out of place. The Saint Squad normally preferred to operate at night, especially for their clandestine missions, but this one called for a daylight approach.

Seth's voice came over his communications headset. "We've checked for motion detectors and listening devices. It's all clear."

Brent's voice sounded next. "What about anyone on surveillance?"

"A single car parked across the street," Seth told him. "Full visibility of the front entrance."

Jay looked around the back alley behind the building to make sure he was still alone. He spoke through the miniature microphone attached to his headset. "The back is clear."

"Let's do this," Brent said.

Jay got out of the car and headed for the back wall just below the balcony of his target. He glanced around and then quickly climbed onto the edge of the concrete wall that surrounded a main-floor apartment's patio. He gripped the railing above him, found a good foothold, and began the short climb onto the balcony above him.

By the time he reached for the sliding-glass door, he could already see Quinn and Tristan inside Carina's apartment. Tristan flipped the lock on the patio for him so he wouldn't have to pick it and then slid the door open.

Brent hefted the coffee table and carried it out the door to load it in the moving truck parked outside.

"Seems to me that we almost got arrested the last time we did this." Quinn sent Jay a dark look.

Tristan nodded in agreement. "Yeah, and we were only rescuing clothes and photographs that time, not moving a couch."

"If you don't want to help, you can always go back to the office and work on those readiness plans," Jay suggested mildly.

"Yeah, like any of us would actually choose to do paperwork when there's another option." Quinn shook his head.

Jay smothered a grin. "Yeah. That's what I thought."

"Come on, Tristan. Grab the other end of this." Quinn leaned down to lift his end of Carina's couch. He stopped, set the couch back in place, and motioned to Jay. Using hand signals, he motioned for Tristan to help him turn the couch on its side. Quinn then ran a hand along the bottom edge of the couch.

Jay moved closer to see what had caught Quinn's attention. Right where the wooden leg gave way to fabric, he saw the small piece of material that nearly blended into the color of the couch. On closer inspection, he recognized the nearly undetectable tracking device: proof that someone had indeed been in Carina's apartment since they had been here last.

Jay backed up, leaving the tracking device in place. He then motioned for Tristan and Quinn to move the couch out to the moving van.

"I'm going to go pack up the girls' stuff." Jay picked up two of the packing boxes Tristan and Quinn had brought inside, and he headed for Carina's bedroom. After their previous experience of leaving their apartment in Miami and not being able to return, Carina and Bianca had both known to pack up the majority of their clothes. Jay started with the single bookshelf in the corner of the bedroom. He pulled the books and sketch pads off the shelves and stacked them in the boxes, checking each item for any additional tracking devices. Finding none, he hefted the boxes and took them into the living room.

Brent walked in through the front door. "I can help you pack. Where do you want me to start?"

"Bianca's room." Jay picked up a box of trash bags and then grabbed two more boxes. He led the way down the hall and handed some trash bags to Brent. "We're taking everything we can except the furniture. Just make sure we don't have any extra surprises coming with us."

"Got it."

For the next ten minutes, Brent and Jay stuffed bags and packed boxes. By the time Quinn and Tristan came into the bedroom to start moving furniture, the bedrooms and bathroom were packed.

"How come you guys get the light stuff?" Quinn complained.

"Sorry, but we can't take a chance that Carina's family might recognize me," Jay responded with an unapologetic shrug.

"And I'm in charge." Brent grinned, pulling rank on the two enlisted members of the squad.

Quinn shook his head and picked up a mattress.

For the next twenty minutes, the men worked together to pack up the few belongings Carina had purchased since moving to Virginia.

"You and Quinn take the last of this stuff out and then take off," Brent said, motioning to a couple of chairs and a box of books. "Hopefully our friend outside will take the bait. Jay and I will take care of the rest."

"We'll let you know when we get back from Baltimore." Tristan hefted the box and shifted it into Quinn's arms when Quinn walked inside empty-handed.

Quinn juggled the box to get a better grip and asked Brent, "You did arrange for a return flight for us, right?"

Brent pulled a folded piece of paper from his pocket and handed it to Quinn. "It's a cargo flight coming out of Andrews."

"Oh, joy." Quinn shot Brent an annoyed look.

Jay watched Tristan pick up the last two chairs and realized what a huge favor both of these men were doing for him, especially since Tristan's baby was only days home from the hospital. Packing and moving were bad enough, but now they had to drive most of Carina's belongings to Baltimore in the hopes that her family would believe she had relocated. Flying back home in the back of a cargo plane was a long way from first-class accommodations.

"So, I'll owe you one," Jay told him lightheartedly.

"Oh, you'll owe us all right." Sarcasm dripped from Quinn's voice.

"Personally, I'm looking forward to getting a little sleep tonight," Tristan said.

"Is that baby of yours keeping you up?" Jay asked.

"Let's just say my son has very healthy lungs." Tristan chuckled. "This little exercise was the perfect excuse for my mother-in-law to get to come play with the baby."

"Glad to help." Jay grinned.

"Good luck," Tristan offered before heading outside.

Brent led the way back into the living room, where everything Carina and Bianca wanted to keep was stacked by the balcony door. He grabbed the ropes he had rigged to lower the bags and boxes down to the van. "Let's hope this works."

"What are the chances that someone is going to call the cops on us?" Jay asked, leaning down to help with the rigging.

"Don't know." Brent shrugged. "Seth is monitoring the police channels."

"I hope the plan works if we can't get out clean."

"Only one way to find out," Brent said, looking down at his watch. "Jay, you go downstairs to load; I'll feed everything down to you."

"Okay." Jay went out onto the balcony and climbed down to the ground level, grateful that Carina's apartment was only on the second floor. His feet had barely hit the ground when Brent lowered the first box.

Seth's voice came over his headset as he loaded the box, and Brent started throwing the bags of clothing down to him. "Our boy out here took the bait. He's just pulled out of the parking lot behind the moving truck."

"Keep listening for police activity," Brent responded.

"Roger that."

Jay loaded the boxes Brent continued to lower to him, but the process didn't proceed quite quickly enough. Jay was just loading the last box when Seth's voice came over his headset. "We've got a 9-1-1 call about a suspected robbery."

"Great," Jay muttered.

"Jay, take off," Brent told him. "Seth, you run interference by the alley, and I'll close up here."

"Got it," Seth agreed.

Jay tossed the last box in, climbed into the driver's seat, and started down the alley. He reached the edge, hoping and praying there wasn't a patrol car in the neighborhood. A siren sounded, his prayer not being answered the way he had hoped.

"I may need some interference," Jay announced.

"I'll block the path to the alley," Seth told him. "The cops are coming from the south."

Jay turned north, catching a glimpse of Seth's car blocking the alley entrance on the south side and the flash of lights heading toward them.

Following the prearranged plan, Jay took a quick turn into a neighborhood and then took several more quick turns until he came to a small park.

"Status?" Jay asked.

"They're about a minute behind you, and they have backup on an intercept course at Princess Anne."

Jay pulled into the parking lot beside the park, choosing a space just beyond an identical minivan already parked in the lot. He hopped out and pulled off the fake magnetic license plates he and Seth had put on earlier and quickly slapped them on the other van.

Jay then pulled farther into the parking lot, taking position behind a small grove of trees.

"The plates have been switched. Where are they now?"

"They should reach the park in about thirty seconds."

Sirens sounded. "I hear them."

"I'm heading your way," Brent told him. "Get ready."

"Tell me when," Jay said.

Jay could see the flashing lights through the trees and counted down the seconds until the car would stop to investigate the other vehicle.

The moment the police car parked beside the other van, Brent said, "Now!"

Jay pulled out of his spot and headed for the back entrance. Brent drove toward him, waiting until just after Jay got onto the road before pulling in slowly to make sure the police couldn't make an easy pursuit.

Jay cut through another neighborhood before finally entering the main road. A moment later, Brent announced, "You're all clear. Meet Seth at his house. He'll help you transfer everything into my SUV so you can move it to your dad's house. Seth will return the van to base."

Jay let out a sigh of relief and hoped the other part of their plan was working too.

CHAPTER 16

BIANCA WALKED TOWARD THE CAFETERIA, debating whether she should really meet Jonah for lunch. For all she knew, if he was seen with her, his social status would plummet just by being associated with her.

She hesitated, preparing to head to the library instead. Then Jonah appeared in front of her.

"Come on. Dan is saving us seats over here."

"Who?" Bianca asked, unfamiliar with the name.

Jonah didn't answer until they were standing beside a table near the center of the room. "Bianca, this is Dan and Mariah. They're in the other ward."

"Wait. You're Mormon?" Mariah looked at Jonah and then back to Bianca.

Bianca nodded, taking the seat Jonah nudged her toward.

"Wow. I didn't know that."

Jonah just shook his head and responded, "I already told you she isn't going out with Todd."

"What happened with Todd this morning?" Mariah asked now. Jonah sent her a glowering look, and she returned it unapologetically. "I'm just asking because everyone is talking about it."

"Great," Bianca said under her breath.

"What did happen?" Dan asked bluntly. "Maybe we can help."

"He's ticked off because he thinks I convinced Pete not to coach him."

Understanding dawned in Jonah's eyes. "He must be steaming that Pete chose me instead of him."

"Yeah. He can't accept that you're a better swimmer than him." She didn't miss the surprise in Jonah's eyes. "You *are* better than him," she continued. "Todd just doesn't know it yet."

Jonah shifted in his seat as though embarrassed by the compliment. "Dan's right. There has to be something we can do to help."

"I don't know how." She glanced across the room to where Todd was sitting beside the girl Allison had pointed out as his girlfriend, Margot. Not surprisingly, Margot noticed her look toward them and sent her a responding glare. "Margot believes I'm chasing after Todd instead of it being the other way around."

"Maybe you should talk to her," Mariah suggested. "You could explain what's really going on. I mean, I'd want to know if my boyfriend was chasing after another girl."

"Why would she believe me? From what I hear, they've been together for like two years."

"I guess we need to find a way to prove it to her. And to everyone else."

"That'll be the day." Bianca rolled her eyes. She wasn't quite sure what to think of the knowing looks Dan and Jonah exchanged. "What?"

Jonah was smiling. "I think I may know a way to help you out after all."

"How?"

"I'll tell you later," Jonah said, giving her a meaningful look after glancing around the crowded cafeteria. "When we don't have so many people around."

"You realize you've got my curiosity piqued now."

Jonah put a hand on hers. "Some things are worth waiting for."

* * *

Jay sat down across from Jonah and Bianca and listened to Jonah's somewhat elaborate plan. It wasn't the plan that surprised him so much as the reason why it was necessary. He had anticipated putting his efforts into researching Bianca and Carina's family and any threats they might pose, but now he found himself dealing with a much different challenge, one that was taking priority.

"Bianca, why didn't you tell us you were having trouble at school?" Jay asked.

Bianca looked down and shrugged. "I thought I could handle it."

"Hey, look at me," Jay insisted, waiting for her to lift her eyes to meet his before continuing. "It doesn't matter what's going on with you, if it's good or bad, your sister and I want to know. We want to be part of your life."

"Todd just makes me feel stupid. I know I shouldn't let him get to me, but the more I think about what I'm going to do the next time he corners me, the worse it seems to get."

"Well, we're going to put a stop to that now," Jay said, pleased to see Jonah nodding in agreement. He considered for a minute. "I'll help you with this plan of yours, but tomorrow afternoon, we're going in to talk to your principal."

Dread curled in Bianca's stomach. "That's what Pete said we should do."

"He's right. The school needs to be aware of what this guy has been doing, and we need to make sure you're protected if things escalate."

"I don't think they can get much worse."

"Maybe not for you." Jay gave her a determined look. "But they're about to get a lot worse for Todd."

* * *

Carina couldn't believe what she was hearing. It was bad enough that Bianca hadn't felt she could confide in her about her problems at school, but now she was sitting here listening to Bianca's principal insinuate that he didn't believe what Bianca was telling him. She wondered if the principal would take them more seriously if he were facing an irate parent instead of a concerned older sister who was only six years removed from high school herself.

"I'll certainly look into the situation, but this is the first I've ever heard of any problem with Todd." He looked skeptically at Bianca. "Are you sure this isn't just a lovers' quarrel?"

"Haven't you heard anything Bianca has said?" Jay asked from his seat beside Carina. "She just told you the problem has stemmed from this boy acting like they're dating when that has never been the case."

Principal Smythe looked at Jay doubtfully. "This young man Bianca is accusing is one of our most respected students."

"I told you so," Bianca said under her breath. "All anyone on the faculty sees is that he's on the student council and he gets good grades."

"What about changing Bianca's schedule so she doesn't have to be in class with Todd anymore?" Carina suggested. "From what I understand, they have several classes together. Quite frankly, he's affecting her ability to succeed here."

"I'm sorry, Miss Channing, but we are not in the habit of changing students' schedules just because they can't get along with an old girlfriend or boyfriend," Mr. Smythe said. "As I already told you, I will look into the situation. If your sister's claims have merit, we can look into making some changes to her schedule."

"I think we're done here," Jay said evenly, and Carina could tell he was holding back his temper. He stood up, and Carina and Bianca followed suit. "I suggest you have a chat with the young man involved and explain to him that this behavior needs to stop immediately."

Principal Smythe stood also, his posture now defensive. "As I said, I will look into the situation."

"I'll look forward to hearing what you find," Carina said stiffly. She didn't say anything more until they had exited the office. "He's not going to do anything, is he?"

"It would probably be better if he didn't do anything," Bianca said tensely. "If he really calls Todd in and talks to him, it will only prove to Todd that he's right. The rules really don't apply to him."

"I think we need to help Jonah with his plan," Carina said firmly.

Jay looked down at Bianca. "Did you make a copy of your schedule for me?"

Bianca handed him two pieces of paper. "Here's my schedule and a map of the school."

"Okay." Jay looked over the information. "I'll get everything set up. You just do what you normally do."

"I hope this works," Bianca said, her voice low. Even though they had waited until after school ended to meet with the principal, several students were still lingering in the halls.

"Trust me," Jay said with a determined look in his eyes. "I'll make it work."

"What do we do first?" Carina asked.

"First, we're going to walk Bianca to her locker so I can get a look around. Then I'm going to talk to my dad about letting Jonah and Bianca leave practice a little early tomorrow. I think there may be a few things I'll need them to take care of for me."

The three of them walked through the nearly empty hallways until they reached Bianca's locker. Jay turned around as though analyzing the space.

"Is this where you normally get cornered?"

"Here and when I go into my history class."

"Let's see if we can talk to your history teacher," Jay suggested.

"Do we really have to keep rehashing this?" Bianca asked. "I already tried talking to her once, but she didn't seem like she really wanted to know what was going on."

"Let's just see if she's noticed anything," Carina suggested, hoping they could find some adult to give her sister positive support.

"Her classroom's this way." Bianca showed them to a door at the end of a short hallway.

Carina reached for the door handle, only to find it locked. "She must have already left for the day."

Jay leaned forward and looked through the glass window in the door. He glanced back at Bianca. "Where do you sit?"

"In the back corner. You can't see it from here."

"And where does Todd sit?"

"Right behind me."

Jay looked up at the ceiling and then said, "Stand right there behind me."

"What are you going to do?"

"I'm going to set up a hidden camera so we can film what's going on in that corner."

"The door is locked," Bianca reminded him.

Jay just arched a brow. "Stand there and act like you and Carina are talking in case someone comes along. It will only take me a minute."

Bianca positioned herself beside her sister while Jay stepped behind them and pulled a little metal tool from his pocket. A few seconds later, she heard the door open. Less than a minute after that, he reemerged from the room and flipped the lock.

"Let's go."

"You're done already?" Bianca asked in amazement.

"Let's just say you and Jonah came to the right person for help," Jay told her smugly.

"Can we put a camera by my locker too?"

"I'll have you and Jonah put a couple up tomorrow morning. If we do it now, the custodial staff might find them." Jay motioned down the hall. "Now let's go home. I think it's time for a crash course in self-defense."

CHAPTER 17

NERVES BATTLED IN BIANCA'S STOMACH. She was used to her stress level going up a notch when she arrived at school each day, but today was different. For once, she actually wanted Todd to bother her. She had to be insane.

"Are you ready?" Jonah asked after he parked and turned off his car.

"I don't think so."

"Everything's going to get better after today," Jonah promised. "If you get lucky, Todd will back off after Principal Smythe talks to him. Worst case, he'll act like he normally does, and we'll record it."

"Unless we can't get it on video." Bianca took a deep breath in an effort to settle her stomach.

"Mariah, Dan, and I are going to help. We'll get you what you need."

Bianca tried to let herself believe his words. "Let's go."

Together, they went inside and walked straight to her locker. Since Pete had let them leave their morning practice early, the halls were still empty, except for a couple of staff members making their way to their classrooms and duty stations.

Bianca reached into her pocket and fingered the miniature camera Jay had given her. Jonah gave her an encouraging nod and pressed one of the minicameras against the top of the lockers across the hall. Bianca followed suit, hoping the borrowed cameras would give her the results she hoped for.

"Now what?" she asked.

"Now we go study for our AP history test and let whatever happens happen."

Bianca started down the hall with him. "How is it that we have almost all of the same teachers, but we don't have any classes together?"

"I don't know." Jonah shrugged. "You know, you could see if you could get your schedule changed. Then you wouldn't have to deal with Todd all of the time."

"We actually tried that yesterday. Mr. Smythe said that if we could prove I'm telling the truth, he'd think about it."

"Then I guess we'd better prove it." Jonah tossed an arm casually around her shoulders and steered her toward the cafeteria.

Bianca tilted her head up toward him and felt some of her nerves settle. "In case I haven't already told you, I appreciate your help."

"Anytime."

* * *

Jay watched the camera feed on his computer at work, wishing the picture came with sound. Since he would have been required to go through the police to get permission to set up full surveillance with audio, a tactic that would likely have resulted in notifying the principal of his actions, Jay had instead given Bianca a hidden microphone so he could hear what was being said around her.

If Bianca did have an incident with Todd today, Jay would have to match up the video with the audio, but it was the best he could do under the circumstances. He was probably already pushing the legal limits by helping Bianca and Jonah set up the cameras, but he wasn't about to sit around and let some kid get away with bullying Carina's little sister. After all, she was about to become his little sister too.

His lips curved slightly at the thought. At this time last year, he had been content with his bachelor lifestyle. Now he was looking forward to marriage and children. Gaining a younger sister was a bonus, although he sincerely hoped his role as big brother didn't include helping her with her homework.

The audio feed coming through the earphone in his left ear proved that the English curriculum hadn't changed much over the years, and he certainly didn't want to relive that particular class from high school. He thought of everything Bianca had already been through in her life and supposed dissecting the works of Shakespeare was the least of her worries.

His mind drifted, and he found himself wondering how his marriage to Carina would impact Bianca. Jay had never before been in the situation of dating someone with any kind of parental responsibilities. He was a little torn on the living arrangements his dad had proposed. He wasn't thrilled with the idea of living under his parents' roof again, especially as a newlywed, yet the safety the arrangement would offer more than compensated for the lack of privacy. Besides, as his father pointed out, he and Carina would likely have more privacy living with his parents than if they had ended up in a two-bedroom apartment somewhere else with Bianca.

He also knew that having his parents around would help ease the day-to-day time pressures on Carina. Bianca would be able to go to and from practice with his father, alleviating Carina from that responsibility, and Jay knew his mom was looking forward to having people around to cook for again besides just his father. He also loved knowing that his dad would be around to keep an eye on things the next time he deployed.

Seth walked into their shared office and looked at him, surprised. "I thought you were taking today off."

"I am."

"Then why are you here?"

"Because I needed to use the computer here to help me solve a little problem."

"Looking into Carina's family again?"

"I haven't had time yet," Jay admitted.

Seth dropped his keys in his desk drawer and looked over at Jay's computer. "What is that?"

"Video feed from Bianca's school."

Seth looked at him suspiciously. "I'm probably going to regret asking this, but why do you care what's going on at Bianca's school?"

"She has a bully problem."

"Have you talked to the school?"

"Yeah." Anger bubbled up inside him at the thought of their encounter with the principal the day before. "The kid bothering her is one of their star students. The principal didn't want to hear about it."

Seth huffed out an annoyed breath. "What can I do to help?"

"This isn't exactly a matter of life and death."

"It probably feels like it to Bianca." Seth moved across the room to stand behind Jay. "Where are these images feeding from?"

Jay pointed at each of the three images currently displayed on his screen and explained the layout of the school and where the cameras had been placed.

"Do you have audio?"

Jay nodded, tapping the earbud in his ear.

"Anything worth hearing?"

"Not right now. According to her schedule, she won't be out of class for another five minutes."

"Unplug the audio. I want to hear it too."

Jay did as he was asked.

"What's the audio source?"

"I've got a mic on Bianca. I didn't want to deal with the legalities of putting audio on the cameras."

"Good thinking." Seth stood patiently behind him while the teacher gave the next day's homework assignment and the bell rang. A moment later, the halls filled with students.

"That's her there," Jay said, pointing at the video feed coming from the camera across from Bianca's locker. "She said this guy usually corners her there or in her history class."

Jay tapped a finger on his desk, watching the boys in the hallway. Bianca had told him the troublemaker was about six foot two and had blond hair, so that narrowed down the suspects a little.

They could see Bianca exchange her English book for her math book and slam the locker shut. Jay was a little disappointed that Todd didn't appear on the screen. "Maybe the principal already talked to him and the guy actually got the message."

"It's possible," Seth agreed just as a tall, broad-shouldered boy stepped in front of Bianca in the hallway, causing her to take a step back. "Then again, maybe not."

Jay leaned closer to the screen and turned up the audio, his temper sizzling the moment he saw the expression on Bianca's face.

* * *

Bianca braced against the anger vibrating from Todd. Anger, not his typical arrogance.

"That was pretty pathetic," he said with a sneer in his voice. "Going to the principal about me. You should have known he wouldn't believe you."

It was time for things to change. Finally, she would have proof that Todd wasn't who he appeared to be. A tremor worked through her body, but she forced herself to look him in the eye. "I just want you to leave me alone. Is that so much to ask?"

"You know you like the attention." He reached out and cupped the back of her neck with his hand.

"No," she batted his hand away and gave him a very deliberate stare, "I don't."

His next comment was crude and unoriginal. Bianca tried to ignore his words and let her temper surface. "Just back off." She took a step to her left only to have Todd mirror the movement.

"That's not going to happen," he told her, his voice low, his expression smug.

"Why don't you go hang out with your girlfriend? Obviously, she must like you."

"Maybe I'm looking for some excitement in my life."

"This isn't excitement. It's harassment," Bianca countered. Determined, she took another step to the left and started to push past him. This time Todd didn't just mirror her movement but put both of his hands on her shoulders and pushed her back against the locker.

Though she could feel her body trembling, Bianca's voice was low and even. "Get your hands off me, and don't ever touch me again."

"I'll put my hands wherever I want."

Bianca was spared from responding when one of the teachers came walking down the hall. "Let's go, people. Get to class."

Todd kept Bianca pinned against the locker for another moment, long enough to lean down, kiss her cheek, and whisper, "I'll see you after school. This isn't over."

The instant he released her, Bianca sagged against the locker. Her heart was pounding wildly in her chest, a sickening feeling churning in her stomach. So used to these confrontations, she had nearly forgotten today's was different. She looked across the hall at the camera hidden on top of the lockers. "Jay, if you're listening, I'd really appreciate anything you can do to keep me from having to deal with Todd again. He's usually worse in history."

Her breath shuddered out, and slowly, she started down the hall.

CHAPTER 18

CARINA SAT ON THE FLOOR of her new bedroom and opened the packing box nearest her. Methodically, she stacked the contents on the bookshelf she had purchased the day before.

Her emotions pitched in her stomach as she let the events of the past few days roll through her. Excitement and anticipation about her upcoming marriage to Jay, frustration that Bianca was dealing with so much at school, and disappointment that her sister hadn't confided in her.

She supposed Bianca's struggles were one of the factors that played into persuading her to combine households with Jay's parents. It grated a bit that Bianca had opened up to Pete instead of her. Carina knew that with working for Riley, starting her business, and spending time with Jay, she hadn't been as available for her sister as she would have liked to be. Still, she couldn't deny that she was grateful Bianca had finally told someone what was really going on.

She pushed the now-empty box aside and reached for another. If she hadn't been so worried about how Bianca's day was going, she would have taken the time to imagine how life was going to change in a couple of months when she and Jay would marry.

The house Pete had rented was laid out as though it had been designed for them. Her bedroom, office, and bathroom were all tucked away from the rest of the house and even had a door that separated the short hallway connecting the three rooms with the laundry room and kitchen beyond.

Of course, she wouldn't have the joy of setting up her entire house the way she wanted, but the prospect of having help with Bianca and cooking meals more than balanced out her desire for control in that area. With the help Pete and Sandra were offering, she would be able to focus her energy on her new business and still have quality time with Bianca.

Carina's cell phone rang, and she fumbled to pull it out of her pocket. "Hello?"

Jay didn't greet her, and she could hear the tension in his voice. "Carina, you need to meet me at the school."

"Is Bianca okay?"

"Yeah, but we need to have another meeting with her principal. It's time to get her schedule changed."

Carina quickly stood and grabbed her purse. "I'm on my way."

"I'll meet you in the visitor parking lot."

"Okay." Carina hurried out to her car and prayed that Jay had found a way to end Bianca's troubles for good.

* * *

"Are you heading to the school?" Seth asked.

"Yeah. Carina is meeting me over there."

Seth stood and started for the door.

"What are you doing?" Jay asked.

"I'm coming with you," Seth announced and followed Jay into the hall.

Jay turned back to look at Seth. "Excuse me?"

"This is a family emergency. Bianca's family."

Tristan appeared in the doorway of the office across the hall. "What's going on?"

"Bianca's having a problem at school," Seth said. "I think it's time the guy bullying her gets some firsthand knowledge of what her support system looks like."

Quinn's voice was hopeful when it echoed into the hall. "Road trip?"

"Looks that way," Tristan called over his shoulder. He started down the hall. "I'll go tell Brent where we're going."

Jay looked at him, bewildered. "I can handle this."

"Jay, it's not a matter of handling it. It's a matter of showing Bianca we've still got her back," Seth told him firmly. "We're coming with you."

Jay wasn't sure how it happened, but ten minutes later, he pulled up in the high-school parking lot with Seth sitting beside him. Parked two spaces down was Brent with the rest of the squad in tow.

"I can't believe you guys insisted on coming with me," Jay muttered under his breath.

"Hey, nobody messes with our little sister."

"She's not even *my* little sister yet."

"Close enough."

Jay climbed out of the car and looked up to see Carina standing nervously by the front door. He noticed the way her eyes widened when she saw the rest of his squad falling in behind him. Jay closed the distance between them, glanced over his shoulder, and muttered, "Don't ask."

Carina took a deep breath, and Jay laid a comforting hand on her arm. "It's going to be okay. We have everything we need now to show the administration they put their faith in the wrong kid."

"I hope you're right."

* * *

The receptionist looked up when they walked in, her eyes widening as she studied the new arrivals. Jay supposed they were a formidable-looking group.

"May I help you?" she asked, shifting her attention to Carina.

"Yes." Carina stepped forward and laid a hand on the counter.

Before Carina could continue, Jay moved beside her and announced, "We need to speak with the principal immediately."

"I'm sorry, sir, but he's in a meeting."

"We'll wait," Jay said, clearly unwilling to budge.

"I also need to speak with my sister, Bianca Channing."

"May I ask what this is regarding?"

"I'm afraid it's a private matter," Carina told her with a shake of her head.

"We aren't in the habit of pulling students out of class without a reason, especially without the parent's permission."

Carina straightened. "I'm her guardian."

The receptionist looked at Carina and then shifted her attention once more to the men flanked behind her. "I'll see if the principal is available to see you."

A moment later, the principal emerged, his eyes narrowing when he saw Carina and Jay. Then his shoulders straightened, and he seemed to posture with authority when he saw the rest of the Saint Squad. "You asked to see me?"

Jay nodded. "We have that proof you asked for."

"Perhaps it would be best if we discuss this in the conference room." The principal ushered them into a room a short distance from the receptionist's desk.

Carina offered introductions, and everyone took a seat except for Jay. Jay moved to the television in the corner of the room. He retrieved a flash drive from his pocket and plugged it into the television monitor. After making a couple of quick adjustments, he turned on the screen.

"Mr. Smythe, you indicated that you didn't think it was possible that Todd was really harassing Bianca. I think you might change your mind after you see this." Without waiting for a response, Jay turned on the television and started the video feed, complete with the audio enhancements from the hidden microphone Bianca had worn.

The principal stared in stunned silence until the clip ended. His face flushed. "How did you get this?"

"When we realized you didn't believe Bianca, we took precautions to protect her."

"What? That's illegal to set up surveillance without my permission."

"Actually, it isn't. And if you had taken the appropriate actions when we brought this problem to your attention, it wouldn't have been necessary. However, as I told you yesterday, I'm not going to sit back and let Bianca get bullied." Jay turned off the television and unplugged the flash drive. "Now, I suggest you have another talk with the young man in question and make sure the problem is resolved this time. If this happens again, we will be taking the problem to the school board."

Mr. Smythe's jaw clenched, and he stared in silence for a long moment. Then he stood and crossed to the telephone in the corner. "Miss Quincy, please call Todd Layton to the office. I need to see him immediately. Would you also please call Bianca Channing to the office?"

As soon as Mr. Smythe hung up the phone, Jay said, "Sir, with the past history between Todd and Bianca, I would appreciate it if you would allow me to escort Bianca here to the office. I don't want to take the chance that she will run into him in the hall."

Jay could tell the principal wanted to object, but instead he said, "I believe you know your way around the school. The receptionist can tell you what class she is in right now."

Jay nodded in response and then handed the flash drive to the principal. "This is a copy for you. I thought you might need this while discussing the situation with Todd and his parents."

Mr. Smythe took the offering. "Thank you."

* * *

Bianca had hoped to get pulled out of class before she had to face Todd in history next period. What she hadn't expected when she walked into the hall was to find Jay waiting for her. She let the door close firmly behind her before asking, "Did you already talk to the principal?"

"Oh yeah." Jay smiled darkly. "Mr. Smythe already called Todd to the office, and I didn't want to take the chance that you would run into him without backup."

Bianca gave him an appreciative look. "Good thinking."

She walked with Jay down the hall, her eyes widening when they walked into the office and she saw the rest of his squad standing there with her sister. "What are all of you doing here?"

Before anyone could respond, the door opened, and Todd walked inside. His gaze landed on Bianca, and she felt Jay's hand come down on her shoulder. She deliberately straightened and forced herself to keep her eyes on Todd.

Carina spoke in a calm, clear voice. "Bianca, I wanted to make sure you knew the situation has been resolved and you won't be having any more problems."

"But if you do, we'll all be here for you," Jay finished for her, his eyes landing on Todd. "No one picks on my little sister and gets away with it."

Bianca didn't miss the way Todd swallowed hard as he approached the receptionist's desk. Feelings of relief spread through her, but when she spoke, her voice was a little shaky. "That's good to know."

Jay gave her shoulder a squeeze. "You have a great day."

"Thanks, Jay," she said, trying to force some confidence into her words. "I'll certainly try."

CHAPTER 19

CARINA WAITED ANXIOUSLY FOR BIANCA to arrive home. Pete had picked her up from school to take her to practice, and Carina could barely stand waiting for the news of how the rest of her day had gone. She was also excited for Bianca to see their new home now that her bedroom was complete.

After their impromptu meeting with the principal, Jay had returned with Carina to Pete's new house to help her put together the bedroom set Pete had bought for Bianca. Carina still felt a little awkward about Pete spending money on her sister, but he had insisted. According to him, a box spring and mattress weren't real furniture by themselves and teenagers needed a chance to decorate their own rooms to feel at home.

Carina had also taken the time to move Bianca's things from Jay's apartment and put her clothes in her closet. The rest of her belongings were still in boxes, but Carina imagined Bianca would want the chance to put the finishing touches on her room herself.

The principal had called only an hour ago to inform her that in light of the new evidence, Bianca's counselor would be meeting with Bianca first thing in the morning to make any changes to her schedule that would help her situation. He wouldn't tell Carina the exact punishment the boy harassing her would receive, but he had assured her that the matter was being dealt with.

The front door opened, and Carina rushed down the stairs to hear Bianca talking to Pete.

"Why are we stopping here? You said the movers aren't getting here until tomorrow."

"My stuff isn't getting here until tomorrow. But your stuff is already here," Pete said.

Carina reached the bottom of the stairs, and Bianca turned to face her. Awareness flickered across her face. "I already have my new furniture?"

"Seth and Brent picked it up from the store after they left the school, and then Jay put it together. Come take a look."

Bianca raced up the stairs to the room she had chosen as her own. Her eyes lit up, and she turned to look at Carina, a grin on her face.

"I can't tell you how great it is to see you smile again," Carina said.

"It was so nice today going into history and not having to see Todd."

"At least your problems with him are finally over," Carina said. "Your counselor is already working on changing your schedule. We meet with her first thing in the morning."

Bianca's smile faded. "It's not over completely."

"What do you mean?"

"There's one more thing I have to do," Bianca said wearily.

"What's that?"

"I need to make sure the other victim in this whole fiasco knows what's really going on."

"Who are you talking about?"

"Margot, Todd's girlfriend. She deserves to know the truth," Bianca said. "Do you think Jay can give me a copy of the recording he made?"

"Yeah, I'm sure he will, but are you sure you want to do this?"

"It's the right thing to do."

* * *

"What do you mean you can't find her?" Marciano looked up at Nick Baldino, one of the up-and-coming young men in his organization, a man who had earned a great deal of trust over the past several months. "You said they moved to Baltimore."

"We traced the moving truck there, but the girls never showed up." His voice turned apologetic when he added, "It appears their belongings were delivered to a thrift store there."

Marciano glared at Nick. "So this was a wild goose chase?"

"We think so." Nick appeared to brace himself before asking, "What do you want us to do now?"

"Find them. There has to be a way to figure out where they went."

"We're trying. She still has GPS blockers on her car and her cell phone. The only way we were able to find her the last time was by following her home after she visited her father."

"You can be sure she won't make that mistake again."

Nick acknowledged the truth of Marciano's words and asked, "Has anyone found anything else out about Raymond's family or who might be looking for Carina?"

"You don't need to worry about any of that. Just concentrate on finding her yourself."

* * *

Bianca turned the corner and checked the numbers on the houses as she passed. Carina had offered to drive her to Margot's, but when Bianca found out Margot lived only a few blocks away from their new home, she opted to walk instead.

She slowed as she approached the faded-yellow house with the big oak tree in the yard. She reached into the back pocket of her jeans, pulled out the flash drive Jay had given her, and swallowed hard. She didn't know if Margot would even talk to her, but she knew she had to at least try to set the record straight.

Mustering her courage, she crossed the lawn and climbed the two steps onto the front porch. Her heartbeat quickened, but she forced herself to raise her hand and knock. Words tumbled through her head, words she might say, how she would explain who she was if one of Margot's parents answered the door.

Footsteps sounded inside, and Bianca braced. Then the door swung open, and she found herself face-to-face with Todd's girlfriend.

Bianca tightened her grip on the flash drive in her hand. "We haven't met. I'm Bianca Channing."

Margot crossed her arms and stared. "I know who you are."

"No, you only think you know who I am." Bianca took a steadying breath and forced herself to continue. "I know you think I've been sneaking around with Todd. I want you to know that isn't true. It's never been true."

She huffed out a breath. "Why should I believe you?"

"Because I don't have any reason to lie." Bianca held up the flash drive in her hand. "And because I brought you this."

"What is it?"

"It's a video clip. Please watch it. If you do, you'll know what's really been going on."

Margot stared at Bianca for several seconds. Then she reached out and took the offered flash drive.

"I promise you, I haven't done anything to hurt you." Bianca took a step back. "I guess I'll see you at school."

A little wrinkle formed on Margot's brow as though she were deep in thought. Then, without a word, she stepped back and closed the door between them.

* * *

Carina examined each of the bridesmaid dresses for the eighth time. She had been up much of the night preparing for Kendra's visit until she had finally collapsed out of sheer exhaustion. The experience of visiting Kendra in Nashville had been surreal, but she hadn't ever believed she would have a superstar coming to visit her at her own home. Technically, it was the Wellmans' home, but still, the unbelievability factor was off the charts.

Carina had known better than to tell Bianca about Kendra's expected visit. Bianca was already dreading going to school today, and Carina knew a visit from Kendra Blake would have been a pretty good excuse to stay home. Not that Carina could blame that kind of thinking. After all, how often did a sixteen-year-old have one of her favorite singers show up at her house? Still, Carina didn't want to appear unprofessional, and Kendra having a fan swooning at her feet probably wouldn't be a good way to start a meeting.

The doorbell rang, and she heard Sandra's greeting followed by Kendra's voice. Carina moved through the kitchen and living room to where Kendra was now standing. She was dressed in a basic white button-up and jeans, but unlike last time, today she looked every bit the woman on the covers of her albums.

"Kendra, it's so good to see you."

"It's good to see you too." Kendra stepped forward and gave Carina a friendly hug as though they were old friends.

Swallowing her surprise, Carina said, "I see you've met Sandra."

"I did." She nodded. "Were you able to finish the rest of the dresses?"

"Yeah. I won't hem them until after the initial fittings, but they're basically done." Carina motioned toward the back of the house. "Come on back and take a look."

Kendra followed and grinned as soon as she walked into the room Carina now used as an office. Carina took a dress off the portable rack to show Kendra, the rose-colored fabric hanging sleekly from the hanger.

"I can make adjustments if you need me . . ." Carina's voice trailed off as she looked up at Kendra expectantly.

"They look even better than they did in the pictures you sent." Kendra took the dress and ran a hand down the silk as she inspected the nearly finished product. She studied it for a moment and then pointed to the bodice. "What do you think about doing some adornments through here?"

"That's definitely an option," Carina said, relieved to discuss adjustments rather than a complete redesign. Together, they looked over different embellishments and discussed ideas until, finally, Kendra smiled in satisfaction.

"Carina, I can't tell you how much I appreciate all of your hard work. You have been a godsend."

"Are you kidding?" Carina looked at her in amazement. "Designing your wedding dress is an amazing opportunity."

"I'm glad you think so." Kendra's attention shifted to a framed photo of Carina with her two younger sisters. "I thought your sister would be here this morning. I was looking forward to meeting her."

"She has swim practice before school." Carina tensed slightly as she thought of what today would be like for Bianca. Undoubtedly, rumors would be flying about Todd getting suspended.

"Does she come home before school?"

Carina shook her head. "Unfortunately, she doesn't. She's going to be so bummed that she missed you. She's a huge fan."

"Really?"

"Oh yeah. I had to keep your visit a secret to make sure she would go to school today. She was already looking for an excuse to stay home."

"She doesn't like school?" Kendra asked.

"She always did before we moved, but making new friends hasn't been easy here," Carina said. Then she shook her head. "I'm sorry. I shouldn't be boring you with my family's problems."

"Maybe I can help."

"I'm sorry?" Carina looked at her, completely at sea.

"I'm planning on spending the day with Amy to talk wedding plans, but I'm sure she wouldn't care if I took a few minutes to swing by and see Bianca."

Carina's jaw dropped open. "You aren't serious."

"I'm totally serious. It would be fun."

"You'll probably get mobbed."

"Nah." Kendra shook her head. "Unless I'm out where people expect to see me, they're usually too timid to talk to me." She took a step toward the door. "Come on. You can come with me so I can meet her, and if you aren't busy, I'd love it if you could join Amy and me today."

The surreal took a wild turn into fantasy land. "I would love it."

"Great. Let's go."

CHAPTER 20

BIANCA GRIPPED THE STRAP OF her backpack, wishing she and Jonah were heading anyplace besides school.

"You know, it's possible that no one even knows what happened with Todd yet," Jonah said as though sensing her trepidation.

"Todd can hardly blow his nose without everyone talking about it." She shook her head. "I don't know which is worse, worrying about running into Todd when I knew what was going to happen or walking into the school and having no idea what to expect."

"The truth will come out eventually, and when it does, all of those nasty rumors will go away."

Bianca thought of her conversation with Margot the night before, still not sure if Margot believed anything she'd said. Some of her biggest fears were that Margot wouldn't look at the video clip or that she would somehow misunderstand what she was seeing. She shifted in her seat and looked over at Jonah when he put the car in park and turned off the engine. He had been such a good friend to her, and he didn't deserve to get the spillover from her bad luck.

"You know, I'll understand if you don't want to be seen with me today."

Jonah gave her an incredulous look. "Are you kidding? I'm lucky you're willing to hang out with me." He swallowed and then added, "In fact, I was hoping maybe you'd go out to dinner with me tonight."

Bianca's eyes widened. "You mean, like a date?"

She could see the insecurity flash in his eyes, but he nodded. "Yeah, I'm talking about a date."

Bianca's eyes brightened. "I'd like that."

Jonah's face lit up, and he grinned at her. "Great." He motioned toward the school. "Are you ready?"

"No," Bianca said bluntly. She took a moment to muster her courage and willed herself to open the car door.

"Come on." Jonah pushed out of the car and fell into step with her. "Don't worry about what anyone else does or says. You already have friends who believe in you."

"Thanks." She followed him inside, and instantly, she felt the wave of silence followed by hostile glares.

Jonah nudged her forward and leaned down to speak in a whisper. "Don't worry. It will all blow over."

"I'm not so sure," Bianca muttered as they made their way to the cafeteria, Bianca trying to keep her eyes straight ahead so she wouldn't have to face the evil looks. She saw Margot on the far side of the room but couldn't tell if her visit yesterday had yielded the desired results. Feeling the continued stares, Bianca turned to look up at Jonah. "I don't know if I can do this."

"You are doing this. I'm right here to help." Jonah reached down and took her hand, giving it a squeeze before leading her to a table where Dan and Mariah were sitting.

Bianca clung to his hand, drawing comfort in the gesture. When they got to Dan and Mariah, Bianca forced herself to ask, "Okay, tell me. What are the rumors going around?"

Mariah looked at Dan before giving Bianca a sympathetic look. "Todd is saying you made up a story to get even with him when he refused to break up with Margot to go out with you."

The ball of lead that had taken up residence in Bianca's stomach churned. "This nightmare is never going to end."

To Bianca's surprise, none of her friends responded. Instead, Mariah and Dan were both staring past her.

"Is that . . . ?" Mariah trailed off, nodding toward the door.

Bianca turned around, her jaw dropping when she saw her sister standing at the cafeteria entrance with none other than Kendra Blake. *The* Kendra Blake. Had Jonah not been standing right behind her, Bianca likely would have fallen over when both Carina and Kendra waved at her.

Excitement and bewilderment filled Mariah's voice. "That *is* Kendra Blake!"

Speechless, Bianca stood where she was as a flurry of whispers erupted in the cafeteria. Kendra and Carina crossed to where Bianca and Jonah were standing. Bianca knew Carina was designing Kendra's wedding dress, but she had been sworn to secrecy about all of the wedding plans and had promised not to mention Kendra to anyone.

Admittedly, Bianca had been jealous that Carina had met Kendra, especially since she didn't expect to ever get the chance to meet the singer herself. Carina had brought her home a signed photo of Kendra after her trip to Nashville, and Bianca had figured that was the end of it. Now, here she was, standing in the same room with Kendra Blake with several hundred of her fellow students homed in on them.

Carina reached Bianca first and gave her a quick hug. "Just play along," Carina whispered before stepping aside. Then, to Bianca's astonishment, Kendra reached out and hugged her as well. "Bianca, it's so good to see you."

Somehow, Bianca managed to find her voice. "It's great to see you too. I definitely didn't expect this."

Kendra gave her a warm smile as though they had known each other for years. "Are these the friends you were telling me about?"

"Yes." Her stomach still fluttering with excitement, Bianca turned to make introductions. "This is Jonah, and this is Mariah and Dan."

"It's great to meet all of you. I really appreciate you being such good friends to Bianca," Kendra said with complete sincerity. She chatted with them for a moment, and Bianca found that her sister hadn't been kidding when she said what a genuinely nice person Kendra was.

A crowd started forming around them, students staring openly as they tried to edge closer to Kendra. As though she knew the requests for autographs were inevitable, Kendra spoke to Bianca once more. "Your sister and I are going to be with Amy all day today, but we're having a little get-together tonight; I'd love it if you could join us."

Bianca nearly answered automatically. She couldn't believe she would get to hang out with Kendra Blake. Then she felt Jonah shift slightly beside her and remembered she already had plans. Torn, she managed to find her voice. "I would love that, but Jonah and I already made plans."

"Jonah, you're welcome to come too. That is, if you want."

Bianca looked up at him hopefully, smiling when he quickly replied, "That would be great."

The crowd seemed to close in even more, and Bianca caught a glimpse of Margot. Instantly, she felt a pang of sympathy for all that Todd had undoubtedly put her through. "Kendra, do you have a minute to meet one more of my friends?"

"Absolutely."

Bianca took a moment to look around and then started weaving her way through the crowd. The whispers flurried again and then silenced completely when Bianca and Kendra stopped in front of Margot. "Kendra, this is my friend Margot. We haven't had a lot of time to spend together yet, but we've shared a lot of memories."

"It's nice to meet you, Margot," Kendra said, extending a hand.

Margot goggled at her and seemed to struggle to find her voice. Then she held up the notebook she held in her hand. "Could I . . . ? Would you give me your autograph?"

"Of course." Kendra signed her name, gave the notebook back to Margot with a smile, and then turned to Bianca. "Your sister and I have to get going, but we'll see you tonight."

"I can't wait," Bianca said with an excited grin.

Kendra gave her a quick hug good-bye and then led the way back toward the door, with Carina falling in beside her.

The moment they disappeared, the excitement level among the students spiked. Bianca could feel their eyes on her again, but now they were filled with curiosity rather than loathing. She waited for Margot to say something, but she remained silent, with a look of stunned disbelief. The bell rang, and Bianca took a step back.

"I guess I'll see you later," she said.

Then, with a trail of whispers following her, Bianca headed for her locker. When she remembered that Todd wasn't at school to bother her, she grinned. Her mother had always told her that anything worth having was worth fighting for. Maybe this was one of those times her mother was talking about.

She reached her locker and, for the first time in weeks, opened it without fear of getting cornered. When a student in her English class walked by and greeted her by name, she felt those first stirrings of hope that maybe she could salvage the new life she hoped to make for herself here.

* * *

Jay stood beside Brent on the back porch of Amy and Brent's house and stared through the window at the buzz of activity going on inside. Amy's brother Charlie was inside, his arm wrapped around Kendra's waist. The rest of the squad and their wives mingled in the kitchen and living room, along with Bianca and Jonah.

Carina stepped up beside Bianca and whispered something in her ear. Jay found himself smiling when their laughter rang out. Only two more months and Carina would be his wife. He could hardly believe it.

"It's kind of weird, huh?" Brent said.

"What?"

"Having Kendra Blake hanging out with a bunch of Navy SEALs," Brent commented. "Of course, I guess it's not any stranger than the idea that she's marrying an FBI agent who happens to be my brother-in-law."

"Yeah. Amy definitely has an interesting family."

When Jay continued to stare through the window, Brent asked, "Is something bothering you?"

"I was actually thinking about how weird it is that I'm getting married."

"That's not weird." Brent chuckled. "That's terrifying."

"Yeah." Jay breathed the word out and leaned back against the deck railing. "I just wish we knew what the deal was with her family."

"I assume you haven't seen any sign of her uncle since we cleared out her apartment."

Jay shook his head. "So far, it looks like they followed the moving truck. I'm sure they know by now that Carina isn't really in Baltimore, but at least they seem to think she isn't here either."

The door leading onto the deck opened, and Charlie emerged as Brent asked, "Did you figure out if there's any truth to Marciano's claim that someone from Alexander's family might be looking for her?"

Charlie crossed the deck to where they were standing and asked, "Are you guys talking about the Perelli family?"

Jay nodded. When Carina and Bianca were threatened last spring, Charlie had been instrumental in ensuring the girls' safety. "Yeah. Now that Bianca's problems at school seem to be solved, I'm hoping to start running background checks on their family."

"Why?" Charlie asked. "Has something happened?"

"Marciano Perelli showed up last week here in Virginia Beach."

"What?" Charlie looked from Jay to Brent and then back at Jay again. "I hadn't heard anything about that."

"Marciano said he found evidence that Raymond Alexander's family is after the key Giovanni sent Carina."

"And, of course, he wanted Carina to hand it over," Charlie concluded shrewdly.

Jay shoved his hands in his pockets. "We think it isn't the key they're after so much as the clue to where the door is that it unlocks."

"Any luck figuring that out?"

"We've got some ideas, but for now, I just want to make sure there isn't anyone out there who is going to show up looking for Carina again."

"Tell you what," Charlie said. "Give me what you've got and I'll run the background checks for you. That way, if anyone has set any alarms on any of the names, they'll trace the searches back to the FBI rather than to you guys."

Brent looked at him hopefully. "Are you sure you don't mind?"

"It's not a problem. Kendra and I are heading up to D.C. tomorrow. I can run the searches out of FBI headquarters, and then I'll e-mail them to you. You'll have the information by tomorrow night, and no one will know you are even involved."

"Charlie, that would be great."

"It's the least I can do. Kendra can't stop raving about Carina. We didn't think there was any way we were going to be able to keep our wedding plans quiet, but so far the press hasn't even found out Kendra and I are engaged."

"Carina definitely knows how to keep a secret," Jay agreed. He turned his attention back toward the house, where he saw Carina talking to Kendra. Feeling an unexpected kinship with Charlie, he waved a hand toward their fiancées and added, "How in the world did we get so lucky?"

Charlie just grinned. "I ask myself that every day."

CHAPTER 21

MARCIANO PASSED THROUGH THE DINING room of the elegant Italian restaurant with a sense of purpose. He didn't take the time to appreciate the fact that every table was full and that several couples were waiting by the entrance to be seated. The dripping chandeliers and floor-length tablecloths went unnoticed as did the muted music and the quietly efficient wait staff.

The mouthwatering scents from the kitchen conjured images of fried calamari and chicken marsala. His stomach grumbled, reminding him that he hadn't yet eaten dinner. He reached the far side of the room and turned down a long hallway. He passed the restrooms and continued on until he reached the door at the end of the hall and pushed it open to reveal his private dining room.

A long table was set with a dozen settings, but the man inside wasn't sitting. He was pacing.

"What was so important that it couldn't wait?" Marciano asked Stanley, one of his longtime informants from the FBI.

"Someone from FBI headquarters ran a background check on you today."

"Who?"

"It was a secretary, so I'm not sure who requested it, but that's not all." Stanley rushed on. "Whoever it was also ran backgrounds on the rest of your family, several known associates, and the Alexander family."

"You think they're starting up another investigation?"

"I don't know. If they are, I should have heard something, but there wasn't anything mentioned in any of our briefings this week. I also don't know why something like this would originate out of FBI headquarters. With Alexander gone, no one would have any reason to suspect another security breach."

"What have you found out about the Alexanders?"

"The flow of drugs from Mexico has more than doubled in the past year, and Alexander's death hasn't changed that. Someone within the Alexander family is working with the Vasquez cartel, and their power within the city is growing."

"Does it still look like they're searching for my nieces?"

Stanley nodded. "As recently as yesterday there was an extensive search on all of their names. Utilities, leases, vehicle registrations, property taxes."

"Was there anything to find?"

"Not that I can tell. Now that they're on the move again, it's hard to know when they'll slip up and put something in one of their names."

"Has anyone tried searching school records?"

"Those types of records are self-contained. We'd need a way to narrow the search in order to be effective."

"Start looking in Philadelphia."

"Why there?"

"They were in Miami, then North Carolina, followed by Virginia Beach. Their stuff was shipped to Baltimore. It looks like they're moving north, and that's the next major city."

"It's worth a try."

"And get someone to watch all of those social media sites. It's only a matter of time before someone leaves an electronic signature out there for everyone to see."

Stanley took a step back. "I'll take care of it."

* * *

Bianca couldn't believe the change. People she had never spoken to were saying hi to her, and the whispers behind her back now held excitement rather than the pointed daggers of hostility she always expected to come her way. It was amazing how one person's random act of kindness could have such a positive impact.

Even better than the reaction she was now getting at school was the knowledge that the feigned friendship Kendra had shown her yesterday at school now felt real. Last night had been like a dream. Sure, she and Jonah were the only teenagers there, but everyone had been so cool.

Seth had helped keep Tristan and Quinn from harassing Jonah too much, although a freestyle race between Tristan and Jonah now appeared inevitable. Kendra had hung out with them, answering questions and telling them about what life was like when she was on tour and how much she loved just hanging out with her guitar and writing music.

Kendra had even talked a little bit about her wedding plans and acted like it would be okay for Carina and her to come to the big event. Bianca couldn't even imagine what that would be like, to be at a wedding the press didn't even know about but would be dying to see. It would be a "no paparazzi allowed" kind of event.

She was deep in thought when she and Jonah sat down with Dan in the cafeteria. Before Bianca could even utter a greeting to Dan, Mariah rushed toward the table, her face glowing with excitement.

"Did you see it last night?" Mariah slid into the seat across from Jonah and Bianca and put both palms firmly on the table. "We were on TV!"

"What?" Bianca could feel the color draining out of her face. After her uncle Marciano's appearance, she had gotten the familiar lecture of staying out of the spotlight. "When? Why?"

"Someone called into the local station and told them about Kendra stopping by our school yesterday."

"There wasn't anything about me, was there?" Bianca asked cautiously.

"I don't think so." Mariah's brow furrowed in concentration, completely clueless as to the reason for Bianca's question. "They just showed the outside of the school and talked about how Kendra was in town visiting friends and that her publicist said she thought it would be fun to thank some of her fans in person. Then they showed a clip from her last video, you know, the one where she's walking through the trees in the snow."

"That's a great video," Dan commented.

Jonah leaned over and whispered in Bianca's ear. "Are you okay?"

Bianca took a deep breath. "I think so."

Jonah seemed to understand the source of Bianca's concern. He shifted his attention back to Mariah. "Are you sure the reporter didn't say anything about why Kendra chose our school to visit?"

"Yeah. They made it sound totally random." Mariah looked a little annoyed. "I was kind of bummed they didn't do more on the story. It would have been cool if they would have said she came to see Bianca."

"Actually, I'm glad they didn't say anything about me," Bianca admitted. "Why?"

Bianca thought for a moment, preparing to bend the truth a little. "Kendra is pretty private, and the last thing I want is to have people trying to get to know me just because I know her."

"I have a feeling that's exactly what's about to happen," Dan mumbled.

"What?"

"Excuse me, Bianca. Do you have a minute?"

Bianca turned to see Margot standing behind her. "Sure."

"I was hoping we could talk," Margot added. "Privately."

Bianca gathered her books and stood. "I'll see you guys later."

Margot led the way out of the cafeteria and into a relatively empty hallway. "I watched the video," she said without preamble.

"I'm sorry about everything. I didn't know how else to show you what was really happening," Bianca said, her voice soft.

"I have to admit, I never would have believed you if you hadn't given that to me."

"I still don't understand why he acted that way with me. He completely ignored me until he heard me tell someone I didn't really like him. After that, he just wouldn't leave me alone."

"I don't know." Margot shrugged. "Before you got here, there was another girl who was supposedly hitting on him. I don't know if it was true or if he was making it up like he did this time." Her shoulders lifted again. "I wonder how long it will take for it to blow over this time."

"You aren't seriously planning on staying with him are you?"

Her voice was soft, resignation humming through it. "We've been together for a long time."

"Why would you want to stay with a guy like that? He isn't worth it."

"Are you kidding?" Margot asked, a flash of insecurity evident on her face. "He's the most popular kid in school."

"I don't think so. I think you are."

"No one would even know who I was if it wasn't for Todd."

Bianca thought for a moment and then slowly shook her head. "For the past two months, everyone in this school has hated me. The only reason they had to hate me is because they like you."

Margot fell silent as she absorbed Bianca's words. Finally, she said, "You're a lot different than I thought you would be."

Bianca felt some of the stress ease out of her shoulders. "I can't tell you how relieved I am to hear you say that."

CHAPTER 22

PETE STOOD ON THE POOL deck and surveyed his new kingdom. Admittedly, the facilities weren't up to the same standards he'd left behind in Miami or that he'd always dreamed about building himself, but the talent in the pool more than made up for the minor inconveniences.

The tryout with Bethany went even better than he had hoped. He had already seen her swim at the world championships the year before and knew she had talent, but he was thrilled to find out she also had an excellent work ethic. Her ego was solid enough that she believed she could be the best but not so overinflated that she wasn't willing to hear what he had to say.

He could already see improvement in his other new swimmers' strokes, and he found himself looking forward to taking them on the journey from good to exceptional.

He glanced down at his clipboard, considering the upcoming meets in the area. One had caught his attention, mostly because it was local but also because Bianca and Jonah's old team would be there.

He knew it was probably petty of him to want to put Bianca's old coach in his place, but he figured it would benefit Jonah too. The sooner the kid learned to live outside of Todd's shadow, the better. Pete was sure Jonah was ready to take that step. He just had to make sure Jonah knew it.

He moved closer to the pool's edge, where Jonah and Bianca were stroking into the wall. Jonah stopped and stood, looking up at Pete skeptically.

Pete held his finger and thumb an inch apart. "You're still crossing over by this much."

Bianca looked up at him as well. "Let me guess. I'm still pulling short on my freestyle."

"Actually, it looked pretty good." His voice warmed with humor. "I just wish you weren't so darn slow."

Bianca chuckled, obviously recognizing the sarcasm in his voice. "Thanks, Pete."

"Do it again." Pete glanced up at the pace clock and counted off the seconds. "Go."

Pete moved to the next lane to give Dillan and Nathan instruction. As soon as he had everyone moving smoothly through the water again, he let himself enjoy the rhythm of the water and the swimmers cutting through it.

He smiled to himself. It was time to let the locals get a glimpse of the talent that was now in town.

* * *

Jay studied the files Charlie had sent him earlier that morning. He hoped and prayed he would find some clue as to whether one of Raymond Alexander's family members was really after the key Carina's father had sent her or if maybe Marciano Perelli had made the story up.

Charlie had been thorough in his research, providing Jay with not only background checks on the names he had given him but also the recent financial activity on the people he was most concerned about: Marciano Perelli; Raymond Alexander's mother, Helen; his widow, Linda; and their son, Levi.

Jay looked through the widow's finances first, not seeing anything unusual, other than a couple of large deposits that were undoubtedly the proceeds from life insurance policies. The son appeared to be living off of a hefty trust fund his father had established for him, the deposits the result of regular proceeds from investment income.

Helen Alexander's financial portfolio was much more complex than the rest of the Alexander family's. Hidden assets, offshore accounts, unidentified payments that were likely sourced by laundered money. If anyone was likely to be behind some attempt to find Carina, the ambiguity of Helen's assets would put her at the top of Jay's list.

The Perelli family's assets hadn't changed much since the last time he had searched through them. An apparent cash flow problem still existed. The best he could tell, the Perelli assets had been distributed to various family members when Carina's grandfather had passed away nearly a year ago. Carina had said Marciano told her her grandfather had left many of the family's assets to Giovanni and him. Perhaps her father's imprisonment was causing part of Marciano's current financial struggles.

An alarm sounded on Jay's computer, a calendar reminder that he was supposed to be heading to the helipad for today's training. He secured his computer and headed for the door. With the paperwork already in process to change Bianca's name, as well as Carina's willingness to live with his parents, hopefully they would have plenty of time to figure out exactly what Carina's family was up to.

* * *

Bianca stared out at the pool, watching the early-morning sun glisten on the water. She could hear Pete talking to Eric behind her, but her thoughts weren't on the conversation. Rather, she found herself wondering how life would be at school now that Todd's suspension was over.

For the past week, life had been almost perfect. After seeing the video clip of her last altercation with Todd, the principal had consented to change her schedule. The changes had worked well in her favor, giving her two classes with Jonah and another one with Mariah. Kendra's appearance at school on the first day of her new schedule had helped smooth out any awkwardness that might have otherwise occurred.

The principal had even gone to the extreme of changing her locker. Now, instead of having her locker in one of the hallways, she enjoyed a locker in the cafeteria in a section normally reserved for seniors. With the changes, she hoped she wouldn't even have to see Todd, but she knew she would eventually have to face him again.

Pete and Eric stopped talking, and Pete stepped beside her. "What's going on with you? You look worried."

"Todd comes back to school today."

"He won't be bothering you again," Pete told her with certainty. "And you need to stop thinking about that guy. If you stop letting him matter, then any power he had over you will be gone."

Bianca drew a breath and slowly let it out. "You're right."

"I'm always right," Pete said with such arrogance that Bianca laughed.

"Of course you are. How could I forget?"

"Beats me." He motioned behind him, where Dillan was talking to Jonah. "You'd better get going. You don't want to be late for school. It's time you show everyone you aren't afraid of anyone."

"Thanks, Pete."

Pete just nodded. Bianca was nearly to the pool entrance when he called after her, "And no more french fries at lunch. You're in training."

"How did you know . . . ?" Bianca trailed off and then narrowed her eyes at Jonah, who was right beside her. "You told Pete I was eating french fries?"

"He asked," Jonah said sheepishly. "Have you ever been interrogated by him before? He's scary."

"Yeah." Bianca just shook her head and chuckled. "He's scary all right."

* * *

Carina stirred some peaches into her oatmeal and looked up to see Sandra walking into the kitchen. Even after a week of living with the Wellmans, she still wasn't quite used to sharing space with someone she wasn't related to. "Good morning," she said.

"Good morning." Sandra pulled the refrigerator open and retrieved the orange juice. "What are you working on today?"

"Wedding plans."

"Yours or Kendra's?"

"Mine." Carina sighed. "There's only one weekend that Gianna will be home during Christmas that isn't a holiday, and we're having a hard time figuring out where we can hold our ceremony. Normally, we would just use the church, but with all of the holiday parties scheduled, that isn't an option."

"What about one of the hotels?"

"The one we liked that was reasonably priced is already booked that weekend. Everything else is either too expensive or not what we really want."

"What do you want?" Sandra asked.

"Simple elegance," Carina said. She felt a pang as she longed to have her own mother here to talk over wedding plans. She let the feeling sweep over her and then forced herself to push it aside. Nothing could change the past, but she could take advantage of the hand she had been dealt. "Can I show you something?"

"Absolutely."

Carina went into her room and retrieved the scrapbook she was using to help plan her wedding. In it were the designs for her wedding dress and magazine clippings showing everything from flowers to food to venues. She carried it to the kitchen table and flipped to a photo of an elegant colonial home with a wide lawn.

"I would love something like this, but everything I've found in the area is already booked."

Sandra stared at the photo for a moment. "How set are you on having the wedding here in Virginia Beach?"

"I don't know. I just figured it would be the easiest place to have it since all of Jay's friends are here. Why?"

"How would you feel about having your wedding at someone's home?" Sandra asked. "Jay knows someone up near D.C. who has a great house, one that looks very much like this one."

"I guess that could work," Carina said before asking, "Whose house is it? And do you think they'd let us use it?"

"Senator Whitmore's."

Carina stared in disbelief. "Senator Whitmore. As in Kendra Blake's future father-in-law? *That* Senator Whitmore?"

"He's also Amy's father," Sandra reminded her.

"Yeah, but how random is that to ask if we could get married at his house, especially during the holidays?" Carina shook her head. "There has to be something we can do here."

"I'm sure there are a lot of places you could get married here, but it sounds like you would have to settle. No one should have to settle when they're getting married, at least not on the things that matter most," Sandra insisted. "We can talk to Jay about it tonight and see what he thinks."

"I guess it can't hurt to talk to him about it," Carina said, even though she was sure nothing would come from the conversation. She flipped a page in her book and looked around the organized kitchen. "I know you've been busy getting all moved in, but do you think you might be willing to help me plan my wedding?"

Sandra beamed at her. "I thought you'd never ask."

CHAPTER 23

"ARE YOU SURE YOUR PARENTS are okay with this?" Jay asked Amy, a rapelling rope in one hand and a climbing harness in the other.

"Absolutely. All I had to do was ask. They are excited about meeting Carina after all they've heard about her from Kendra and me."

"Yeah, but this isn't just stopping by your parents' house for dinner. We're talking about hosting a wedding there."

"I know." Amy shifted the clipboard in her hand and scribbled a note. "My mom actually suggested that you two make a weekend trip up to visit so you can decide how you want to set everything up. Personally, I think you should do the ceremony in the living room next to the Christmas tree."

"I don't know when we're going to have time. We'll be gone this weekend for training, and then the next weekend, I'm planning on taking Carina up to New York."

"Are you going to fly or drive?"

"Drive. I don't want to go anywhere unarmed right now. Not until I find out who's looking for Carina."

"Does Carina still carry a gun too?"

"Oh yeah." Jay nodded. "From what she's told me, she started carrying one right after her mom died. Except when she has to fly, she keeps it with her all the time."

"I don't blame her with what she's been through," Amy said. Then she added, "Why don't you stop by my folks' place on your way back from New York? Brent and I will be up there visiting anyway. I'd love to show Carina around and maybe talk over some ideas."

Jay considered for a moment, going over the timeline in his mind. He had already planned on taking next Friday off so he and Carina could drive up together and then have all of Saturday and Sunday in New York before heading back to Virginia Beach that Monday. Making a stop in Northern Virginia would be right on their way. "That actually might work."

Amy gave a satisfied nod. "Good. I'll let my mom know, and she can talk details with Carina."

"Amy, I really appreciate this."

"Happy to help." Amy pointed to the obstacle course. "You'd better get started. I have all of you guys down for advanced driver's training this afternoon."

Jay headed for his morning training session and found that Seth was already there. "Amy said she has us down for advanced driver's training this afternoon."

"I could have sworn we just passed that off a few months ago," Seth complained.

"Apparently not."

"How are the driving lessons going with Bianca?" Seth asked as they approached the rapelling wall.

"Great, actually. I taught her the basics, and now my parents are taking over. Dad's been getting her to drive to practice every day, but she prefers going out with my mom on her errands."

"How come?"

"I have a feeling french fries and milkshakes are involved."

"Ah. Contraband."

"Exactly." Jay put his harness on and heard footsteps in the gravel behind him as the rest of the squad approached.

Brent stepped beside him. "I just got off of the phone with Amy's brother, Charlie."

"Is everything okay?" Jay asked.

"Charlie just talked to one of the agents in Chicago who has been working on the Perelli case," Brent told him, his voice serious. "Apparently someone discovered a reward notice that had Carina's name on it."

"What?" The rapelling rope Jay was holding slipped out of his hand, but he didn't lean over to retrieve it. Instead, he played over the facts that Marciano Perelli had relayed to Carina. "Carina said her uncle Marciano told her about the reward for the key her father sent her."

"They aren't just looking for the key. They're looking for any of the Perelli girls or for the location of Giovanni's safe house."

Jay could feel his face pale as he considered the ramifications of this latest news. "Are they sure? Marciano didn't tell Carina there was a reward for her and her sisters."

"Charlie said the information was very reliable."

"Then everyone in organized crime is going to be looking for them."

"No one knows they're here," Brent reminded him. Then he asked, "Did you know anything about a safe house?"

Jay shook his head. "My best guess is that the safe house must be what the key goes to, but we're still trying to figure out where it is."

"The real question is, why is someone so interested in it?"

"If we're lucky, Carina and I will figure that out over Veterans Day weekend."

"The sooner the better." Brent leaned down, picked up the rope Jay had dropped, and handed it back to him. "Let me know if there's anything we can do to help."

"Thanks, Brent. I appreciate it." Jay took a moment to check his gear while letting this latest news sink in. If Carina's family really was looking for her again, it might just be a matter of time before someone decided to show up to see if *he* knew where she was. What if by keeping Carina close to him, Jay was putting her in danger?

"I know what you're thinking," Seth said, stepping beside him.

Jay turned toward him, still deep in thought.

"Don't let the fear of Carina's family get in the way of your happiness."

"But what happens if someone connects me to her again? We're pretty sure her uncle Raymond found her in North Carolina by following me somehow."

"Jay, it would be just as risky for her to try to move," Seth insisted. "You're doing everything you can to keep her and her sisters safe. And at least here she has the rest of us to help watch her back."

"I know. I just want all of this to end."

"It will," Seth assured him. "I think after we wrap up for the day, maybe we should put in an extra hour to see if we can dig up any more information on the Perellis."

"Seth, we've already done everything we can think of."

"Yeah, but maybe the latest info from the FBI will help us narrow down exactly who is looking for Carina. If we know who, we might be able to figure out why."

"You're right. It's at least worth a try," Jay agreed. Somehow, he had to unravel this mystery surrounding the key. Only then would Carina and her sisters finally feel free from the family they had spent years hiding from.

* * *

"Did you see this?" Marciano held up a printout of a personal ad from the newspaper and handed it to his son. Although the words were cleverly disguised, there was no doubt that this was the latest in a string of reward notices that had been released by Alexander's family.

Marciano watched while his son read it. Silvio looked up and shook his head in disgust. "They've stooped to offering a reward for my cousins now too?"

"They obviously haven't had any luck figuring out where Giovanni stashed everything. This must be a last-ditch attempt to take over before it's too late."

"You don't think they'll be able to find them, do you? It's only a couple more weeks until they lose their ability to take control."

Marciano's shoulders lifted. "I hate not knowing where they are."

"I guess your visit must have scared them off."

Disgust crossed Marciano's face. "Carina has lost all perspective of how this family works."

"She's been away for a long time."

"That's no excuse. She's still a Perelli," Marciano said tersely. "See if our friend at the FBI has any more information about who might be accessing the case file on Alexander or our family. Maybe we can figure out who is behind this ad by uncovering who is on the inside helping them."

"Do you really think the Alexander family still has access to the FBI's information?"

"Absolutely. Alexander was an agent for twenty years. It would make sense that someone in his family would be able to get one of his friends to help them gain information."

"I'll see what I can dig up."

* * *

Seth's idea to dig up some more information on Carina's family was unsuccessful, so Jay decided to go straight to the source. He picked up the phone and made a secure call to Charlie Whitmore in hopes that the FBI knew more than the limited information that had already been passed on.

"Charlie, it's Jay Wellman," Jay said as soon as he heard Charlie's voice on the other end of the phone.

"Hey, Jay. How are the wedding plans going?"

"I try to stay out of those details as much as possible." Jay didn't want to think about all of Carina's lists and the magazines and sample books that now littered his parents' house.

"I know what you mean." Charlie chuckled. "Kendra tried to get me to help pick out the color of tablecloths last night. Like I care what color the tablecloths are."

"I'd rather deal with tablecloths than flower arrangements."

"Yeah. I had to deal with that last week." Charlie laughed. "So what's up?"

"Brent told me someone put a reward out for Carina and her sisters."

"That's right. It was posted in the form of a classified ad in the Chicago newspaper. The mob has long used this form of communication, disguising an employment opportunity or a personal message to send out information to a wide range of people."

"Do you know who might be behind this?" Jay asked. "Could it be her uncle Marciano?"

"It's hard to say," Charlie admitted. "We know Raymond Alexander was involved in some drug activity within the Vasquez cartel. The flow of drugs hasn't slowed since his death, but we aren't sure who took over that part of his business."

"Do you think that has anything to do with Carina?"

"Let me see what the analysis in the file says." Charlie fell silent for a moment before he continued. "This is all confidential, of course, so you can't pass this along to anyone who doesn't share our top-secret clearance, but according to this, we have open investigations into Raymond Alexander's son, Levi and his wife, Linda."

"From the stories in the press, I got the impression his wife didn't know what her husband was into."

"We don't think that's the case. I don't know how she could be unaware that her husband was bringing in millions of dollars of income each year. Trust me. FBI agents don't make nearly that kind of money," Charlie said wryly. "Personally, my guess is that it's the son who is currently working the drugs. From what we can tell, after Raymond Alexander died, Marciano Perelli succeeded in pushing the Alexanders out of the family business, but there is still income flowing through their bank accounts. A lot of it."

"That's consistent with what Marciano told Carina when he came to see her."

"One of the analysts here also searched through the asset records for the Perellis and their known holdings."

"And?"

"From what we can tell, around the time that Sergio Perelli stepped down, he transferred his assets to his three sons. About two hundred million in liquid assets went to Raymond Alexander, and reportedly, he was given operational control of the family's business. Another two hundred million dollars' worth of assets related to the gambling side of the operation was handed over to Marciano Perelli, but most of it was put in trust to be used to support the family business."

"What about Carina's father?"

"Giovanni was apparently left with the majority of the family's legitimate assets. Almost a hundred million in cash and assets was given to him outright, but another hundred million was placed in trust. From what we can tell, the assets in the trust were the businesses, and we suspect they were used to hide the family's real income from the IRS."

"Why would he divide the business that way?"

"Our insiders say Sergio Perelli was worried about his sons working together. Tradition demanded that Raymond Alexander take over control since he was the oldest son, but since his access to the family had been so limited, Sergio split up the operating assets and used trusts as a way to force them to work together."

"Who controls these trusts?"

"We don't know. The only reason we even know they exist is that one of our informants told us. Apparently, they are well hidden behind a legal maze of companies and subsidiaries."

"The real question is, does any of this have to do with why someone is so anxious to find Carina or what that key goes to?"

"Possibly. The reward on this latest ad is significant. If the Alexanders and Perellis are warring over assets, it's possible they think Carina has somehow gained access to her father's piece of the pie."

"I don't understand why her father wouldn't just tell her why he sent her that key or what it's for."

"I don't know," Charlie admitted. "We looked into the concern Carina expressed that Giovanni felt like he was being watched."

"And?"

"Nothing popped up, but that doesn't mean he wasn't right. The mob has a funny way of paying people off and finding the information they want when they want it."

"I just pray that I can keep Carina and her sisters hidden."

"If anyone can handle the challenge, it's you and your squad."

CHAPTER 24

BIANCA WATCHED AS A GROUP of swimmers walked past her, their matching swim bags over their shoulders, deck passes from numerous big meets clipped to the outside. She didn't have any of those deck passes, and she watched them wistfully for a moment, wondering what it would be like to flit from meet to meet without any cares other than who would be the fastest at the end of the day.

Today would be her first meet since leaving Miami, but she wasn't about to display her few pieces of swimming memorabilia to this crowd. She was already paranoid enough that someone from her family might take notice of her.

Changing her last name from Channing to Wellman had been surprisingly simple, but it had been harder than she expected to let go of that last link to her mother. Part of her hoped the name change would only be temporary, that eventually she would be able to change it back to Channing. Another part of her kind of liked the idea of sharing the same last name as the people she lived with. And when Pete had handed her his heat sheet so she could write down her events, she'd looked through it twice before remembering what name she was looking for.

She had to admit that it was weird wearing the last name before Carina did. Carina wouldn't officially become a Wellman until December when she and Jay got married.

Bianca reached her arms over her head to stretch and saw Jonah heading her way. His cap was still in place from warming up, his goggles pushed back on his forehead.

Bianca recognized Jonah's nerves in the rigid way he stood. She put a hand on his shoulder and asked, "Are you ready?"

"I don't know about this," Jonah admitted. He glanced behind him, where their old team was crowded at the corner of the pool, Todd standing in the middle of the group. "What if Todd beats me?"

"Don't think about him. Think about you," Bianca insisted. She refused to look over at Todd, willing herself not to notice him. His return to school had been surprisingly uneventful, except for the rumor mill that had started after news spread that Margot had broken up with him.

"I *am* thinking about me, and I don't know if I can really beat him."

Before Bianca could continue her pep talk, Pete stepped up beside them, his focus on Jonah. "I heard you raced Tristan the other day."

"Yeah," Jonah admitted, his tone indicating that he wasn't sure if he was about to get a lecture or receive praise.

"Did you beat him?"

Jonah held up his hands eighteen inches apart. "By about that much."

"And those Navy SEALs think they're fast." Pete shook his head. "You'd better get up there. And don't forget to build your speed into your turns."

Jonah swallowed hard and nodded.

"You've got this," Bianca assured him, taking up position along the side of the pool beside Pete. As soon as Jonah was out of earshot, she asked, "He is going to beat Todd, isn't he?"

"We'll see soon enough." Pete glanced up at the board that displayed the times from the first heat of the one hundred freestyle. "What did Jonah say his best time was for this event?"

"A high forty-eight."

"Let's see where he's at now." Pete fingered his stopwatch in preparation for Jonah's heat. The whistle blew, and the swimmers stepped onto the blocks. Jonah was in lane seven, with Todd two lanes over in the center of the pool. "Here we go."

The swimmers started nearly simultaneously when the buzzer went off. Bianca could almost hear Pete's constant instructions rattling through her mind as she watched Jonah use his powerful dolphin kick to propel himself through the water. Todd surfaced first, but when Jonah emerged several yards later, he was already in the lead.

Bianca cheered with the crowd, willing Jonah to swim faster. Todd had closed the distance between them by the first turn, but the moment they hit the wall, Jonah again pulled out ahead. The race intensified as the swimmers surged toward the finish, Jonah in the lead, with Todd closing in behind him. The crowd roared with excitement when Jonah slammed his hand into the timing pad, beating Todd by three tenths of a second.

"Not bad," Pete mumbled, checking the time on his stopwatch and then comparing it to the time illuminated on the board.

Bianca looked up, grinning when she saw Jonah's time. 47.93. Nearly a full second faster than his personal best. She saw Jonah's expression when he read the board, his eyes narrowing as though he didn't quite believe the time illuminated there was real. Then excitement replaced his shock.

She was so focused on Jonah's delight that she nearly missed the looks that passed between Pete and her old coach. Russell was clearly stunned that Todd had been beaten, and the fact that it had been one of his former swimmers had to be like salt to the wound. Bianca put a hand on Pete's arm. "You know, I'd tell you that you're a great coach, but it would just go to your head."

"Yeah, you're probably right," Pete agreed. "Now go get warmed up. I want you to show that idiot over there what you're really capable of."

"You got it."

* * *

Carina sat in the stands, her meet program gripped tightly in her hand. She wished Jay could have been here for Bianca's meet, but unfortunately, he had some training mission this weekend. At least, she was pretty sure it was a training mission. He had known when he was leaving and said he would be back before church on Sunday. The short time away meant he was likely staying within the U.S.

On the pool deck below, Carina saw Bianca listening to some last-minute instructions from Pete; then she saw Jonah standing right behind them. Carina noticed the way Jonah put an encouraging hand on Bianca's arm before she headed for the starting end of the pool.

"I think my son is smitten with your sister," Rhonda Zimmerman said from the seat beside her.

"I was wondering about that," Carina said, noticing the way Bianca glanced back at Jonah. "It looks like the feeling is mutual."

"I really appreciate Bianca's help in getting Jonah a tryout with this new coach."

"He made the team on his own merits. Bianca just helped open the door."

"Still, she was an answer to a prayer. I can't believe what a change there's been in Jonah's confidence. We didn't realize how bad the situation had become with his old team until after he started swimming with Pete."

"Bianca said it was getting pretty bad," Carina admitted. "I'm just glad things are finally settling down."

"You and me both."

* * *

Bianca passed the door at the end of the pool and looked through the glass panel. The man standing just outside the door looked vaguely familiar, but she continued forward, her mind already on her race to come. She made it only another two steps before Todd stepped in her path, fury evident on his face.

"This is all your fault. If you hadn't told Pete not to coach me, I never would have lost to Jonah."

Bianca took a step back. "Just leave me alone."

Venom filled his voice. "You don't have all of your friends to protect you here."

Bianca took a step back and considered whether she had time to circle around the pool to avoid Todd or if she should try to flag down one of the safety marshals to help her. When she glanced around, the man standing outside the glass door caught her attention again. The thought had barely formed in her mind that he looked like her uncle when the lights flickered and then went out.

The crowd let out a collective groan, and awareness dawned. Lights didn't just go out like this. Someone must have turned them out.

Suddenly, Bianca didn't care about Todd's threats or the people preparing to compete against her. She didn't care about the swimmers in the pool or the spectators in the stands. Her only thoughts were about the man outside, the man who was coming to get her.

Fear, pure and paralyzing, pulsed through her. She gasped for breath, not able to fight the frightening images of her past. She could almost feel the cold barrel of Raymond Alexander's gun pressed against her skin. She remembered too well the sound of the gunshot she had thought was meant for her.

Panic speared through her, as did an overwhelming urge to flee.

Disoriented in the darkness, she took a step away from where Todd was standing. Her shin connected with the starting block, and she gritted her teeth against the pain. Someone jostled into her in the dark, and she stifled a scream as she bumped into another unfamiliar figure.

A split second later, the light streaming through the glass shifted and changed when the door opened. The familiar shadow was no longer safely outside. Now he was inside, and he was heading for her.

Terrified, Bianca pushed her way farther into the darkness. She managed to find the back wall of the natatorium, her thoughts focused solely on a way to escape.

Even as the announcer asked everyone to stay where they were while the maintenance people looked into the problem, Bianca used the wall to guide her and fought her way through the darkness, urgently searching for safety. She quickly considered her options. She could hide in the locker room. Or try to make it to the security office in the next building. The security office, complete with armed guards, won the quick internal debate.

She stubbed her toe on the steps leading to the bleachers and the doors that would take her into the main hallway. Ignoring the pain, she groped for the stair railing and made her way up the handful of steps. She bumped into someone, barely able to keep a scream from escaping her.

She could see more light now, this time streaming through the emergency exit at the end of the main hall. Stumbling past several more people, she pushed her way toward the light. Her heart was still pounding when she reached for the door. Her hand pressed against the cold metal of the handle just as a hand came down on her shoulder.

"Where do you think you're going?"

A muffled yelp escaped her when the hand jerked her back and spun her around. Then she looked up into the familiar face and couldn't make a sound at all.

CHAPTER 25

"WHERE DID SHE GO?" JONAH asked the moment the lights flashed back on.

Pete didn't answer, his eyes already searching the crowd. The lights had been off for only a minute or two, but in that short period of time, Bianca had disappeared. "Go warm up for your next race. I'll be back in a minute."

Leaving Jonah and his other swimmers behind, Pete worked his way through the throngs of coaches and swimmers at the pool's edge. He had watched the exterior doors during the power outage, and even though one of them had opened, he had only seen someone enter, not exit. That meant Bianca was still here or she had disappeared through the doors leading to the hall.

Pete prayed that wherever she was she had gone there of her own accord.

Bianca's race was called once more as the officials prepared to resume the meet. The swimmers stepped up, but the starting block in Bianca's lane remained vacant.

"Where could she have gone?" Jonah asked, rushing to catch up to Pete rather than heading for the warm-up pool as he'd been instructed.

Recognizing the concern in Jonah's voice, he let the kid tag along. "She had to have gone out this way."

Pete jogged up the bleacher steps and pushed his way out the door. He caught a glimpse of Bianca's red hair, and his protective instincts surfaced when he saw that she was backed up against a wall, a tall figure looming over her.

He heard the male voice speaking in low tones. "Do you have any idea how much trouble you've caused?"

Pete didn't take time to absorb the words or the voice that spoke them. He reached out, gripped the arm of the figure looming over Bianca, and shoved him back against the wall. Relief speared through him when he saw Todd's startled face.

"I thought my son made it clear that you need to keep your distance from Bianca," Pete said, his voice even.

"I . . . I don't know what you're talking about."

"Let me spell the situation out for you. You are going to stay away from Bianca from now until forever," Pete told him, his hand still gripping the boy's arm to hold him in place. "If you don't, Bianca can't be held responsible for what her Navy SEAL brother-in-law and his loyal buddies might do to you."

Pete had the satisfaction of seeing Todd swallow hard, his Adam's apple bobbing up and down in a wordless stupor.

"Are we clear?" Pete asked sternly.

Todd looked sideways to where Bianca was standing with Jonah right beside her. Silently, he nodded.

"Good." Pete released him, not surprised when the boy took two tentative steps back and then scampered back to the safety of the pool area.

As soon as Todd was gone, Pete turned his attention to Bianca. "Are you okay?"

Bianca let out a shuddering breath, her face pale.

"What happened?" Jonah asked Bianca urgently. "The lights came on, and you were gone."

A tremor worked its way through her body, and Pete could see that her breathing still wasn't quite steady. "I thought I saw someone outside the door near my block. I thought maybe my uncle was here, that he was the reason the lights went out."

"Hey, it's okay. You're safe. No one from your family knows where you are." Pete pulled her into his arms, fully aware that she was still fighting against her fears and the emotions they invoked. "You missed your first race, but you still have a few more today. Are you up for them?"

"I don't know," Bianca managed to say.

"I really think it's time you show that old coach of yours what an idiot he is," Pete said, cockiness in his tone.

"I don't know . . ."

Pete took a step back and studied Bianca. "Was it really just coincidence that the power went out right before your 400 IM, or did you pay someone off to flip the switch so you wouldn't have to swim it?"

Jonah looked at him, obviously confused by Pete's dry tone, but Bianca's eyes cleared, and she seemed to push past the panic he had seen in her expression when he'd first stepped into the hallway.

"Getting out of the IM today isn't going to help you much," Pete continued. "You know I'll just make you swim it at the next meet."

She seemed to consider. "I really do like the backstroke better."

"Come on." Pete motioned to the door. "Jonah, you need to get warmed up for your next race, and, Bianca, we need to talk strategy. It's time you take home a gold for that backstroke."

Bianca hesitated, her tone serious once more. "Do you know why the lights went out?"

Pete shook his head. "Tell you what, while Jonah warms up, we'll go check in with security to find out exactly what's going on."

Bianca relaxed marginally. "Thanks, Pete."

* * *

The security guards said the power outage had affected the whole area, not just the natatorium. Bianca continued to run that fact over and over in her mind. No one was after her, at least not today. Carina had found her and Pete at the security office, worried when Bianca had missed her race.

Even though Jonah didn't have another race for more than an hour, he stood behind the blocks in a show of support. Bianca tried to think of the people who were here to cheer her on instead of letting past memories swallow her whole.

The heat before hers finished, and she glanced up at the scoreboard to read the times. She could beat them. That thought surfaced, along with Pete's insistence that she could win this race. Her best time would put her in the finals, but she had two of her old teammates swimming in this heat with her, both of whom her old coach had insisted were faster than she.

The whistle blew, and she stepped into the water. She let herself sink beneath the surface before gripping the edge of the pool and placing her feet on the wall in anticipation of the start.

When the buzzer sounded, she reacted instantly, plunging her body backward into the water, her powerful dolphin kick propelling her forward. In that moment, she forgot her fears and lost herself in the comfort of the familiar.

Adrenaline pulsed through her, the good kind of adrenaline rather than the kind born of fear. Pete's instructions rattled through the back of her mind, but in the forefront was her absolute joy of the sport.

She could sense the girl beside her falling behind, but Pete had trained her too well for her to waste any effort in looking at her competitors. She powered through her first turn, feeling stronger with each stroke. When she slammed her hand into the timing pad for her finish, she found herself at the wall alone for a full two seconds.

Her eyes skimmed over the crowd to where Pete was standing. She had the satisfaction of seeing his grin before turning to congratulate the girl beside her. That was when she caught a glimpse of her former coach with a scowl on his face. Feeling both liberated and vindicated, Bianca let herself enjoy the moment, determined that before the day was over, she would bring home gold.

CHAPTER 26

Jay FELT LIKE HE WAS right back where he'd started six months ago. The incident at the swim meet on Saturday only served to show that Bianca had not recovered from her previous emotional trauma and that she didn't feel safe. He was sure the situation with the jerk from her school had aggravated the situation, but the bottom line was that Bianca's fears were justified even if no one had been looking for her at the swim meet.

Somewhere out there, people were actively searching for her.

Gianna was apparently still safely hidden from the Perelli family. Like he had done with Carina, Jay had insisted that Gianna's apartment at BYU be subleased so no one could search for her using any kind of rental or property records. All of her information in the school directory was also listed as private so her name couldn't be found through any of the university's search engines.

The fact that Marciano had found Carina once already was Jay's bigger concern.

He was grateful Bianca's last name had already been changed, but now he worried that maybe he should have pushed to have her change her first name as well since it was rather unique. At the time they had gone through the paperwork for the change, he had considered the new last name to be an extra precaution. He had thought that once the Perellis thought Carina and Bianca had disappeared, the family would stop looking for them. Now he knew better.

Not only was someone still searching for them, but the personal ad Charlie had referred to offered a tempting reward. It also noted a deadline. That deadline was only two weeks away, on Carina's twenty-fifth birthday. Jay tried to consider the possible implications of that information, not sure if the deadline meant Carina would be safe after her birthday or if the reward would hike up even more if she wasn't found before then.

Seth's voice broke into his thoughts. "Um, Jay, you'd better take a look at this."

"What?" Jay rolled back in his chair and leaned over so he could see Seth's computer. He looked from the screen to Seth in confusion when he saw that it was the video clip of Todd bullying Bianca. "Why are you watching that?"

"Jay, I'm not replaying our video feed. This is on the Internet."

Jay's face paled. "What?"

"Did anyone besides the school have a copy of this?" Seth asked.

"I'm not sure," Jay admitted. "I gave Bianca a copy. She wanted to show Todd's girlfriend what was really going on, but that was a couple of weeks ago."

"That doesn't make sense. Why would it pop up now?"

Jay edged closer. "Is Bianca's name listed with the video at all?"

Seth shook his head. "Not that I can see, but look at how many hits this has had already."

Jay looked down to see that the clip had over a hundred thousand hits; the caption below it read *Scorned*. "What in the world?"

"It looks like someone uploaded it and tagged it with a caption that happens to be the same as a new movie coming out this weekend. I think that's what's driving the number of hits."

"There's got to be a way to take it down."

"The easiest thing to do would be to call Charlie. He should be able to use his FBI credentials to yank it since it could conceivably endanger Bianca and Carina."

"I'll call right now." Jay made the call, and Charlie agreed to contact the website to have the video pulled.

As soon as Jay hung up the phone, Seth asked, "Were you planning on taking Bianca with you to New York?"

"I was going to have her stay home with my parents, but after what happened at her meet on Saturday and now this video hitting the Internet, I'm leaning toward taking her with us. Besides, we were going to stop at the Whitmores' on our way home. It would be nice for Bianca to come with us to see where we're planning on getting married."

"Maybe you should take off a day early and reverse those plans," Seth suggested.

"What do you mean?"

"Amy told me this morning that the dive we had planned for Thursday just got canceled because of the storm that's supposed to hit tonight. I'm sure Brent would let you take off a little earlier than planned," Seth told him. "You could drive up to the Whitmores' on Thursday afternoon, spend the night there, and then keep on going up to New York."

Jay shook his head. "I can't just call up a U.S. senator and ask if I can stay at his house. It's weird enough that he's invited us to visit and that I'm probably getting married there."

"Senator Whitmore has an open-door policy when it comes to this squad. All of us have stayed there at one time or another."

"I don't know." Jay hesitated. He had to admit that it would be nice to break up what would otherwise be a seven- or eight-hour drive. And the holiday traffic would undoubtedly add to that if they waited until Friday to leave.

"Come on." Seth pushed back from his desk. "Let's go talk to Brent. We'll let him know about this video and see what he thinks about changing your plans."

With a last look at Seth's computer screen, Jay nodded. Whether he stayed at the Whitmores' house or not, getting Bianca out of town and out of school for a couple of days might be the best way to reassess how to keep her safe.

* * *

Bianca didn't know what had changed, but the moment she stepped into the school cafeteria, she could feel the whispers and stares. She looked over at Jonah. "Do you know what's going on?"

"I have no idea."

Mariah rushed across the room to where they were standing. "Did you see the video on YouTube?"

"What video?"

"The one you showed Mr. Smythe."

"What are you talking about?" Jonah asked.

"The video of Todd harassing Bianca is on YouTube. It's spreading all over the Internet."

Bianca could feel the color drain from her face. She struggled to find her words. "How could that have happened?"

Jonah laid a comforting hand on her back. "Do you think Margot might have put it up?"

"I don't know why she would do that now. I gave it to her two weeks ago." Bianca looked across the room and saw Margot rushing toward her, a look of alarm on her face.

"Bianca, I'm so sorry," Margot told her without preamble. "I swear, I didn't know she was going to do that."

"Who?" Jonah asked before Bianca managed to find her voice.

"My friend Gabby was at the swim meet last weekend, and Todd told her all sorts of stuff that wasn't true."

"Stuff about me?" Bianca asked.

Margot nodded. "She came to my house and told me Todd wanted me back and that you were lying about everything."

"And you showed her the video," Bianca finished for her.

Again, Margot nodded. "After she watched it, she insisted on watching it again. That must have been when she uploaded it onto YouTube."

Bianca looked around the room, still feeling the stares of many. Then she saw Todd storming toward them. "Great. Here comes trouble now."

"How could you do that?" Todd demanded. "I swear you're trying to ruin my life!"

Bianca took an automatic step back. "I didn't do it."

"Yeah right," Todd sneered.

Remembering that she had been the victim in this whole situation, Bianca straightened her shoulders. "If you didn't want anyone to see you acting like such a jerk, maybe you should have thought of that when I asked you to leave me alone."

"She didn't do anything," Margot said before Todd could respond. "And she's right. You're the one who started this thing by making her life a total nightmare."

"You stay out of this," Todd growled at her. He gestured toward Bianca. "She made me out to look like some kind of monster, and then she put this video online for the whole world to see."

"Gabby's the one who did it," Margot blurted out. She seemed to instantly regret her words, but she took a steadying breath and continued. "I guess she wasn't thrilled when she found out you had been lying to her too."

Todd's hand clenched into a fist, and his face reddened. To Bianca's surprise, Jonah stepped forward and squared off against Todd, but his voice was calm when he spoke. "Todd, no one wants any trouble here. If you want, we can go talk to Mr. Smythe to see if he can have Gabby come into the office so we can have her take down the video."

"What good would that do? Thousands of people have already seen it."

"Well, we can at least keep it from being seen by thousands more." Jonah motioned toward the office.

Todd glared at Bianca and Margot, and for a moment, Bianca thought he was going to spit out another threat against one or both of them. But instead, he just gritted his teeth and headed toward the office with Jonah.

CHAPTER 27

CARINA LOOKED AT JAY SKEPTICALLY. "You want to leave tomorrow and stay the night at the Whitmores' house?"

"I pretty much had the same reaction when Seth suggested it, but Brent thought it was a great idea. The principal at Bianca's school made sure the video clip was pulled off of YouTube, and the FBI is working to track down anyplace else it might still be accessible."

"What's the likelihood that any of my family saw it?"

"I have no idea. The hits were pretty widespread, but the good news is that Bianca's name wasn't associated with the video at all."

Carina threw her hands in the air. "I can't believe that every time it looks like we're safe again, something happens to turn everything upside down."

"It will all get worked out," Jay told her, but Carina noticed the hesitation in his voice.

"Is there something else you aren't telling me?"

"Charlie Whitmore called. There's a new reward posted for finding you."

Carina's stomach clutched. She tried to sound calm when she asked, "More money?"

"Not just that. There was a deadline on this one. It's for a week from Thursday."

It took a moment for Carina to put the dates in place. "That's my birthday."

Jay nodded.

"You think that might be significant?"

"I'm not one to believe in coincidences." Jay stepped closer and took her hand in his. "I do know I'll feel a lot better if we can put some distance between us and Virginia Beach, at least until we're sure no one from your family saw that video."

"How can we be sure of that?"

"The FBI is going to set up surveillance at Bianca's school to watch for anyone from your family looking for her."

"And we'll be out of town in case they show up," Carina finished for him.

"Exactly."

"How soon did you want to leave?"

"I have a training exercise early tomorrow morning, but I should be done by two. I thought we could leave after that."

"What about Bianca? Should I keep her home from school?"

"I think so," Jay said. "I hate to get her worked up over this, especially after what happened at her meet, but I really don't want to take a chance that someone might find her there."

The front door opened and then slammed shut. A second later, Bianca stormed into the living room. "You aren't going to believe what happened."

"Some girl at your school uploaded the video of you and Todd, and now it's all over the Internet?" Jay suggested helpfully.

Bianca blinked and stared for a brief moment. "Okay, so maybe you will believe what happened."

"I already talked to the principal," Jay told her. "He said the video has been pulled down. The FBI is trying to track down anyplace else it might have popped up."

Bianca dropped onto the chair across from them. "We aren't going to have to move again, are we?"

Jay shook his head, but there was a touch of uncertainty in his voice when he said, "Your name isn't associated with the video anywhere, so chances are that everything will be fine."

"You are going to need to miss school for the next couple of days though," Carina told her.

"What?" Bianca turned her attention to Carina. Then she looked back at Jay. "Why?"

Jay proceeded to explain their plans to leave for Northern Virginia the next afternoon for an early holiday.

"If we aren't leaving until tomorrow afternoon, can't I at least go to school until we're ready to go?"

Jay shook his head. "The FBI is setting up surveillance to make sure you're safe. It would be best if you aren't around in case someone does show up looking for you."

Fear lit her eyes. "I thought you said you weren't too worried."

"*If* someone from your family noticed you on that video, the only way they could find you would be to back-trace the Internet connection to who uploaded it. If that happens, they could logically figure out what school you go to."

"How could they figure that out? It was uploaded from Margot's house, not the school."

"Yes, but if someone figures out Margot's address, they would know what school she's zoned for. Not to mention that she lives really close to you."

Dejected, Bianca struggled to keep her voice steady. "So we might have to move again."

"There's a good chance that whatever is going on with your family will end on your sister's birthday," Jay told her. "Let's give the FBI the chance to do their job, and then we'll figure out what to do from there."

"Okay." Bianca stood up. "I guess I'd better go e-mail my teachers so I can get my homework assignments."

"Why don't you let me take care of that," Jay suggested. "I don't want you to contact anyone at the school for now."

"Great," Bianca muttered. "What about practice?"

"That should be fine, and I'm sure my dad will be more than happy to give you workouts for while we're gone."

Pete stepped into the room. "You've got that right." He motioned toward the stairs. "Go get started on your homework. We need to leave a little early for practice."

Bianca rolled her eyes, but she didn't argue. "Okay."

As soon as Bianca left the room, Pete sat down in the chair she had just vacated. "You know, Jay, I'm not sure if you should be the one to talk to the school. Now that Bianca shares our last name, if someone is keeping an eye out for her, we might want to keep our distance."

"What do you suggest?" Carina asked. "Assuming the best, that no one does show up looking for her, she needs to keep up with her schoolwork."

"Jonah has almost all of the same classes as Bianca. Why don't you let me talk to him. Maybe Jonah can get the assignments for us."

"Most of Bianca's teachers also put their homework assignments up on the school's website," Carina said.

"If Jonah's willing, we can have him get the assignments for her and pass them along. Since he's already a student there, no one would suspect that anything is out of the ordinary."

"That's a good idea," Jay agreed. "Can you talk to him tonight at practice?"

"Yeah, I'll take care of it," Pete assured him. "You just make sure you keep that girl in the water for me while you're gone. She's really starting to drop time, and I don't want any setbacks. Besides, it will be a good distraction for her."

"You got it."

* * *

"Bianca!" Sandra's voice carried from the kitchen when the doorbell rang. "Can you get the door?"

Bianca's stomach jumped in anticipation. She slapped her history book closed and barely resisted running down the stairs, expecting that Jonah would be on the other side of the front door.

When Jonah had found out about the situation, he agreed to get Bianca her assignments while she was in New York. He had also offered to lend her the one book she would need but hadn't brought home.

Casually, she pulled the door open and smiled when she saw him standing on her doorstep looking a little nervous. "Hey, Jonah. Come on in."

He stepped inside and looked around at the empty living room. "Where is everyone?"

"Jay and Carina went to the store to get some stuff for our trip, Sandra's in the kitchen making banana bread, and Pete is in his office plotting how to torment me over the next few days while I'm gone."

"He's sending workouts with you?" Jonah asked.

"Oh yeah." Bianca grimaced. "Just think. With me out of the pool this weekend, he'll have more time to pick on you."

Jonah rolled his shoulders at the thought. "At least when Pete picks on us, he knows what he's talking about."

"Don't say that too loud," Bianca said in a mock whisper. "His ego is already big enough."

Jonah chuckled. He held up a book. "I brought you my chem book. I'll see if I can borrow one from class tomorrow."

"Actually, I wrote down my locker combination for you so you can just take mine." Bianca pulled a slip of paper out of the back pocket of her jeans and handed it to him.

"Oh, okay. Thanks." He took the paper, stuffed it in his front pocket, and then opened up the front cover of the chemistry book, where a piece of notebook paper was tucked. "I also wanted to give you this."

"What is it?" Bianca took the book from him and looked down at the name and numbers scribbled on the paper.

"My aunt and uncle's address and phone number. My cousin Sara swam with us at practice for a couple of days at the end of the summer right after you joined the team."

"Why are you giving this to me?"

"Remember, I told you they live in Manhattan? My dad wanted me to give it to you in case you need anything while you're in New York."

"Thanks, Jonah." Bianca looked up at him. "I wish you were coming with us."

"Me too." He shifted his weight. "I'd better get going."

Bianca tried to hide her disappointment. She wasn't sure what she'd expected with Jonah coming over, but it certainly wasn't him rushing off only a minute or two after he got there. "I guess I'll call you tomorrow night to get my homework assignments."

"Okay." Jonah shoved his hands in the pockets of his jacket and took a step toward the door. Then he turned back to face her. He seemed to gather his courage before he blurted out the words, "Do you think maybe we can go out sometime when you get back?"

She stared for a moment. Then her lips curved. "I'd like that."

Now Jonah returned her smile. "I'll talk to you later."

"Thanks, Jonah." Bianca watched him pull the door open.

He stepped outside onto the front porch and turned back to her. He reached for her hand and gave it a squeeze. "Be safe."

"I will. Thanks."

CHAPTER 28

THE NERVES WARRING IN CARINA'S stomach had started the moment she'd woken up. Now that they were nearing Senator Whitmore's home, the sensation was nearly unbearable. From the driver's seat beside her, Jay kept his focus on the road and on the car in front of them. Amy and Brent had decided to take off that afternoon as well so they could drive up with them.

Even though Carina knew Amy was a senator's daughter, Carina had always just thought of Amy as a friend. Of course, now, with Kendra Blake's wedding approaching, Amy and her mother were also clients. That fact alone was enough to keep her mind racing in anticipation.

The garment bag containing the finished mother-of-the-groom's dress was hanging in the backseat of Amy and Brent's SUV, along with the bridesmaid dresses. Amy's was already complete, unless any last-minute alterations were needed. All of the others were awaiting the final touches once the fittings were complete.

Carina fiddled with her engagement ring, her thoughts consumed with what Katherine Whitmore would think of the dress Carina had designed for her to wear at her son's wedding. The fact that Amy had been thrilled with her dress gave Carina a little boost of confidence.

At six feet tall, Amy was rarely able to find clothing that fit well, and she had been pleased that the design Kendra had chosen for the bridesmaids was actually one they could wear again after the wedding was over. Carina prayed that Katherine would be equally pleased.

From the seat behind Jay, Bianca seemed oblivious to everything around her, her focus on her math homework and the constant flow of text messages coming from Jonah. At least, Carina assumed they were coming from Jonah.

"I still can't believe Brent and Amy were willing to take an extra day off to come with us today."

"It wasn't really a day off. Brent worked it out with the team's commander for us to shift our canceled training to next week so everyone will have a longer weekend than planned."

Carina stared out the window at the enormous houses as they drove by. Memories of her childhood pushed to the forefront of her mind. Her neighborhood in Chicago had been very much like this one. Huge houses, manicured lawns, three- and four-car garages undoubtedly filled with luxury cars.

When Jay turned into a driveway behind Brent and Amy, Carina studied the elegant colonial home. The front lawn was expansive, lined with mature oak trees.

Jay glanced back at Bianca, who was still staring down at her cell phone. "We're here."

Bianca looked up and raised her eyebrows in consideration. "Yeah, I can see how this place would work for your wedding."

The dry humor in her tone helped loosen some of the knots in Carina's stomach. They all got out of the car, and Jay started unloading their luggage.

Feeling extremely awkward to be carrying luggage up to the home of people she had never met, Carina hung back as Amy and Brent led the way up the front walk.

Amy gave two quick raps on the door and then pushed it open and motioned everyone inside. "Mom! I'm home!"

Footsteps sounded from somewhere deep in the house as Carina reluctantly followed Amy inside, where she noticed a large picture of the Washington D.C. Temple hanging on the wall in the entryway.

Amy showed them into the enormous living room to the left. A moment later, her mother entered from a doorway on the other side of the room. "Hi, sweetie. It's so good to have you home."

The elegant brunette extended her arms and greeted her daughter warmly before turning to embrace Brent. To Carina's surprise, she then turned and gave Jay a warm greeting and a hug as though he was a frequent visitor.

"Sister Whitmore, this is my fiancée, Carina, and her sister Bianca."

"I'm so glad to meet you both. Carina, I feel like I already know you from talking to you on the phone, but it's nice to put a face to the name."

"Yes, it is," Carina agreed, her earlier anxiety fading.

"Let me show you to your rooms so you can get settled in, and then we can take you on a tour of the house and talk wedding plans."

"That sounds great," Carina said.

Katherine turned to Jay. "Jay, I was going to have you stay in the downstairs guest room. You know the way."

Jay nodded.

"Wonderful." Katherine started toward the staircase.

"Mom, I'm going to finish unloading the car," Amy said.

"Okay." Katherine showed Carina and Bianca up the stairs, stopping at the first open doorway on the left. "We have plenty of space if you would like your own rooms. Or if you would prefer, you can share this one in here."

Katherine motioned into a guest room with two twin beds. "Charlie's room is right across the hall, so one of you is welcome to stay in there too."

"This is fine," Carina assured her. "We really appreciate you letting us invade your house like this."

"It's not a problem. You're welcome anytime," Katherine said.

Carina was amazed to hear the sincerity of her words. She set her suitcase down just inside the door, and Bianca stepped past her to set hers down as well.

"Come on. Let me show you the lay of the land here," Katherine offered. She showed them the other upstairs bedrooms, including where Amy and Brent would be staying. She then took them back downstairs, circling through the large formal dining room, the expansive kitchen, her husband's study, and the guest room where Jay would be staying.

They ended back in the living room, and Katherine motioned to where the wide windows overlooked the front lawn. "I thought somewhere in this room would be best for your ceremony. We'll be rearranging the room anyway to decorate for Christmas. We can decide how it will work best and then go from there."

Before she could continue, Bianca said, "If it's okay, I'm going to go upstairs and get some more of my homework done."

"Of course," Katherine said. "Please make yourself at home while you're here."

Carina watched Bianca leave and then turned back to Amy's mother, a look of wonder in her eyes. "I can't believe you're willing to do all of this for Jay and me."

"Brent and Amy have told us a little about what you're going through. My oldest son and his wife went through something very similar to this many years ago," Katherine told her. "Let's just say we're glad we're in a position to help."

Amy walked into the room holding the garment bag containing Katherine's dress. "Mom, I think you need to take a break and look at this."

Katherine's face lit up. "Is that my dress?"

Hesitation and nerves sounded in Carina's voice. "If it isn't exactly what you want, just let me know, and we can make any changes you want."

Amy unzipped the garment bag to reveal the rose-colored dress with the varied-length hemline.

Katherine reached out and took the dress from Amy. "Oh, this is beautiful."

"Is it okay?"

"It's perfect." She took a step toward the stairs. "I've got to go try it on. I'll be right back."

Amy waited until her mother had left the room before leaning closer to Carina and whispering, "I think she likes it."

"I hope she likes it as much once she tries it on."

"We'll find out soon enough."

Carina managed to keep from pacing while they waited, but Amy must have sensed how nervous she was.

"Don't worry," Amy assured her. "She already loves it. If it doesn't fit quite right, you'll fix it."

Carina hoped it would really be that easy. A moment later, Katherine walked into the room wearing her new dress. Instinctively, Carina studied the fit of the waist and the length of the hem. The delight on Katherine's face gave her the courage to step forward. "I think we might need to take it in just a bit at the waistline. What do you think?"

"Maybe just a little," Katherine agreed. Delight danced in her eyes when she added, "I think I may have just scored a coup to get to be among the first to wear one of Carina Channing's designs. Or will it be Carina Wellman?"

"Actually, I'll use my company name, Eleganza, to avoid any security issues from my family."

"I'm sure this craziness will end soon," Katherine assured her.

"My mom's right. These things have a way of working themselves out, especially when the Saint Squad gets involved."

Katherine ran a hand down the fabric of her dress. "One thing you can be very certain of is that as soon as Charlie and Kendra leak the photos from their wedding, you are going to be very popular."

"I thought Charlie and Kendra weren't going to allow anyone at the wedding to have cameras."

Katherine gave her an amused smile. "They have a friend who will do the official photographs for them, but when the timing works well for them, they'll leak a few they've approved."

"And, of course, the name of your company will leak with the pictures," Amy added.

"You know, people in the fashion industry dream of a break like this. I can't believe all of you have been so kind in helping make this happen," Carina said.

"We're glad to help," Katherine said delightedly. "The fact that you're immensely talented just makes it easy on us."

* * *

Jay sat beside Brent at the Whitmores' kitchen table, both of them tapping away on their laptops. The latest information from the FBI was unexpected and opened a whole new realm of possibilities. The Bureau had discovered that Raymond Alexander's mother, Helen, had been living in a nursing home for the past year as she struggled with cancer.

The new tidbit of information, discovered by looking through the nursing home's visitor logs, was that Raymond Alexander had a sister. Rosa Alexander had been born eighteen months after Raymond, and like her older brother's, her birth certificate did not name her father.

Noting the timing, that she was born almost two years before Carina's grandparents married, the FBI believed Sergio Perelli was also the father of Rosa. The fact that the payments Sergio made to his ex-wife had increased right after Rosa's birth supported that analysis.

"I was hoping we could narrow down our list of suspects," Jay muttered as he continued to look through the FBI's report. "Instead, we keep expanding it."

"At least we're sure Helen Alexander couldn't be involved. According to the nurses at the nursing home, the treatments she is on have really affected her mental capacities," Brent said.

Jay lifted a hand and rubbed at the stiffness in his neck. "I guess our next step is to see if we can help figure out where Rosa is now."

Bianca wandered in and plopped down in the seat beside Jay. "What are you two working on?"

"We're still trying to figure out who's looking for you," Jay told her.

"Anything I can do to help?" Bianca asked.

"Not really." Jay shook his head. "A lot of this information is classified, and I'm afraid you aren't cleared to access it."

"Seriously?" Bianca's eyebrows lifted. "There has to be something I can do. I'm *so* bored."

"Give me a few more minutes with this, and then I'll take you down to the rec center so we can put in a practice," Jay said.

"Have you seen the workout your dad sent with me? I said I was bored, not suicidal."

Jay chuckled and gave her a sympathetic look. He had to admit, even with all of his constant training with the SEALs, he wasn't particularly looking forward to swimming his dad's workout with Bianca tonight.

"Actually," Brent interrupted in a considering tone, "maybe there is something you can do to help."

Bianca's expression instantly brightened. "What?"

"Go ask Amy's mom if you can borrow one of their laptops. You can get online and figure out the addresses for the buildings on that card your father sent Carina."

"How can I do that?"

"You can start by using Google Earth. There are a couple of other programs that can help us narrow them down," Brent told her. "Don't worry. I'll show you how."

"Okay. I'll be right back."

As soon as she left the room, Jay said, "You do realize that when we get to New York, we can just drive down the streets around Central Park and get the same information, right?"

"Yeah." Brent gave him a knowing look. "But this will give her something to do."

"Good point."

CHAPTER 29

"THIS IS HOPELESS." CARINA SAT in the passenger seat of Jay's car as they crawled through the snarled traffic in Manhattan. They had driven around the area for several hours the night before, searching for clues but ultimately ending up back in their overpriced hotel rooms with nothing to show for their efforts. "Even though the picture my dad sent only has half of Central Park's skyline in it, there are way too many possibilities."

"It won't hurt to keep looking," Jay told her. "It's not like we expected this to be easy."

"I know you're right." Carina sighed and looked over at Jay. "You know, even if we don't figure out what this key goes to, I really appreciate all of your help."

Jay reached over and gave her hand a quick squeeze. "Hey, I have as much at stake here as you do. I just want you and your sisters to be safe and for us to be able to live happily ever after."

Carina smiled. "I'd like that too."

"Sometimes you guys sound like a Hallmark movie," Bianca quipped from the backseat.

"Hardly," Jay said with a roll of his eyes.

"You aren't the ones sitting back here watching the show. It's getting a little sappy," Bianca said. "And boring. After we eat lunch, can you guys drop me back off at the hotel?"

"Bianca, I don't want you anywhere right now by yourself," Carina answered, her eyes still focused on the road.

"Oh, come on, Carina. It's not like anyone knows we're here."

"You're sister's right." Jay glanced back at Bianca with a look of sympathy. "You're stuck with us, kid."

"Maybe I can go hang out at Jonah's aunt and uncle's house. His cousin Sara is my age. Supposedly, they live around here."

"You don't even know them."

"Sure I do. Don't you remember? We met them when they came to visit over Labor Day weekend," Bianca told her. "Jonah gave me their address and phone number. It wouldn't hurt to call to see if they're around." She gave her sister a hopeful look and added a drawn out, "Pleeease?"

Carina tried to recall the bishop's sister, whom she had met briefly at church two months earlier. She hated the idea of imposing on her, but the thought of dealing with Bianca all day when she had already reached this state of boredom was even worse. "Let me see the phone number."

Bianca dug a piece of paper out of her purse and handed it to Carina. Carina looked down at the string of numbers, at first confused to see a string of only six numbers. Then she noticed the small *th* written at the end of seventy-eight. It took her a moment to realize the first four numbers represented the house number, and 78th was the street. Her mind whirled as another thought crashed into her mind. "Oh my gosh."

"What?"

Carina looked up to see that they were on Central Park West. "Can you cut over and see if there is something at 995 Fifth Avenue?"

"Where did you get that from?" Bianca asked, even as Carina could see the confusion in Jay's eyes slowly turn to awareness.

"The numbers on the card Dad sent me were 9-9-5, then a space followed by another 5. What if that was an address? 995 Fifth Avenue."

"And he sent you the photograph so you would know what city to look in." Jay shook his head in disbelief. "That's brilliant. Everyone is busy looking for the key, figuring there is some clue with it when, really, it was the note that held the important information."

Carina watched impatiently as Jay maneuvered through the city traffic and finally made his way over to Fifth Avenue. Right across the street from the Metropolitan Museum of Art was a sixteen-floor condo building with a long green awning stretching from the front door out across the sidewalk. She read the numbers on front of the awning. *995.*

"This could be it." Carina pointed excitedly.

"Let me find someplace to park, and we'll check it out." Jay found a spot in a parking garage at the museum, and they all walked toward the condos.

A uniformed doorman greeted them when they approached. "May I help you?"

Carina nodded, but it took a moment to find the right words. She had denied having the key for so long that she had to remind herself it was okay in this situation to offer an explanation. "My father sent me a key, and I believe it may be to one of the units in this building."

The doorman sized them up for a moment, shifting his attention from Carina to Bianca to Jay and then back to Carina again. "Your name?"

Carina took a steadying breath. "Carina Channing."

The doorman reached back and pulled open the door for them. "You'll need to speak to the concierge."

"Thank you." Carina led the way inside, noticing the way the building had a historic feel, with its gorgeous coffered ceiling and elegant furnishings. She looked around the lobby area, then led the way to the concierge's desk.

She greeted the distinguished older gentleman who stood behind the desk and repeated what she had told the doorman.

"Do you have your key?"

Again Carina hesitated, but she reluctantly reached into her purse and retrieved the key. The concierge took the key from her, turned it over in his hand as he studied it, and then handed it back. "Yes, this is the key to your storage room."

Carina's heartbeat quickened. Could they really have found the door that this key opened? "Can you show me where that is?"

"Yes, miss." He motioned her across the room and then showed her to the private storage rooms for the building. He pointed at a door and said, "This is yours."

"Thank you."

"Is there anything else?" he asked.

"I think we're good for now," Carina told him. "We appreciate your help."

"If you have any further questions, please let me know."

"Thank you." Carina waited for him to leave them alone before sliding the key into the lock. Her breath caught when it turned smoothly. She tried to imagine what could be inside that was so important that people would be willing to kill for it.

What she found inside definitely wasn't what she had expected.

"This is it?" Bianca asked from beside her, staring at the nearly empty room. A single filing cabinet occupied the far corner, and a small round table sat close beside it. Other than that, the room was completely empty.

Always cautious, Jay took the time to check the doorway and then the rest of the room for any kind of surveillance devices or booby traps. When he indicated that it was all safe, Carina crossed to the filing cabinet and pulled open the top drawer.

Several files lay inside, neatly organized and labeled. Each one appeared to refer to a different company, but Carina wasn't familiar with any of them.

"What is all of this?" Jay asked.

"I don't know." Carina pulled the first file out, opening it to see legal documents referring to the sale of a pizzeria in Chicago. "This business was in Chicago, but I honestly don't remember it."

She flipped through the files, finding a wide variety of movie theaters, bowling alleys, and restaurant chains. Each one included documentation of the company's sale, each of them dated during the six months before her mother's death.

She didn't have time to process the significance of that before Bianca said, "What's in the next drawer?"

Carina replaced the file she had been holding, closed the top drawer, and opened the second. "It looks like the legal documentation for the stuff in the first drawer."

She opened the next drawer to find even more legal documents. She fingered through them and was all the way to the back when the last file caught her eye. Rather than a company name on the label, it read *Protection*.

"This might be something." She opened it up, her eyes widening at the contents. At the top of the page was the name Raymond Alexander. Beneath it were two columns. One column was entitled FBI. The other header was Vasquez cartel. A dozen names were split between the two columns. "Jay, look at this."

Jay took the paper Carina handed him. "The Vasquez cartel is the one the FBI said Raymond Alexander was working with. This must be a list of his contacts within the cartel."

"Then the names under the FBI column could be people who were on his payroll." Carina read through the names and found a familiar one. "Look at this. Frank Tesan is on here."

Beside her, Bianca tensed. Her voice was unsteady when she spoke, undoubtedly fighting back the frightening memory of the one and only time she'd seen him. "He's the one who came after me in Miami."

"It's okay, Bianca," Jay assured her. "We know he can't hurt you now."

Bianca nodded and drew a cleansing breath. "Yeah, and we definitely know he was working for Raymond Alexander."

Carina looked down at the next paper in the file, her eyes widening again. "Oh, wow."

"What?"

"This looks like a list of payouts. Dates, amounts, names."

"These must be the people your family has working for them."

Carina read through the names and slowly shook her head. "I don't recognize any of these names. They must be people Raymond was paying off."

"You've been away from your family for a long time," Jay reminded her. "It's possible the people on their payroll have changed over the years."

"Yeah, but not all of them." She shook her head. "There are several government officials I'm sure would still be working for my family, but none of them are named here."

"Let me see that for a minute." Jay took the file from her, put it on the table, and used his cell phone to take pictures of the documents. After he finished, he returned everything to the file and handed it back to Carina. "Go ahead and put it back where you found it."

"What are you going to do with the pictures?"

"I'll send them to Charlie to see what he can do to track them all down. It's possible that whoever is looking for you is on this list."

"Are you sure you want to keep the list here?"

"I want to make sure it stays secure," Jay said. "Besides, I have the pictures with the information."

"Okay." She replaced the file. Then she opened the bottom drawer to find it empty, except for a carved wooden box. She leaned down and lifted it out, placing it on the table beside them.

"What is it?" Jay asked before Bianca had the chance to.

Carina lifted the lid to reveal an oddly shaped key and a handwritten note.

"*Another* key?" Bianca asked.

Carina nodded. She lifted the note and began reading the words written in Italian, translating it automatically.

Carina, Gianna, and Bianca,

What's mine is yours now. I have to pay for my mistakes, but know that everything I leave you is from the good in my life. 16th Floor. It's paid for, and it's yours. Live well and know that I have always loved you.

Papa

"What's on the sixteenth floor?" Bianca asked.

"There's only one way to find out." Carina lifted the key out of the box and motioned to the door. "Let's go."

CHAPTER 30

JAY ITCHED TO GET SECURE Internet access so he could research the files in the storage room, but he settled for using the encryption mode on his phone to send a picture message to Brent with the request that he forward it to Charlie through secure channels. He didn't want to take the chance that someone on the list of corrupt FBI agents might discover that Charlie was digging into Raymond Alexander.

Jay found himself wondering what else Carina's father had hidden away. He had to admit, his curiosity was piqued, especially since there wasn't anything in the storage room files about anything in this building. The concierge had instructed them on how to gain access to the sixteenth floor using the elevator key Carina's father had left for her. Now the three of them rode the otherwise empty elevator in silence.

The elevator doors chimed open. Ever cautious, Jay stepped onto the hardwood floor of a wide hallway. He looked around, expecting to see a traditional hall with regularly spaced doors to the various condos. It took him a moment to realize they were already standing in a residence.

He heard Carina and Bianca follow him into the gallery-style hallway, all of them looking around in stunned silence. Jay barely glanced at the paintings hanging on the wall or the single-person benches situated beneath the artwork as he walked forward to look through the wide doorways. Windows stretched along the far side of an enormous living room, framing a breathtaking view of New York's Central Park.

Two white couches flanked the ends of the room, each accompanied by a cluster of chairs and a complement of accent tables and silk floral arrangements. The tables were free of dust, and a hint of lemon oil scented the air. The hardwood floors also appeared to have recently been cleaned.

"Is this your dad's apartment?"

"I don't know." Carina moved farther into the room and turned in a circle. "Nothing here looks familiar."

"Look at this view!" Bianca crossed to the windows directly in front of them and looked out over the splendor of autumn visible in Central Park below.

"Let's take a look around," Jay suggested. He glanced toward the dining room and then headed in the opposite direction to where a smaller living area was situated.

He took Carina's hand and looked at the cozier living room, with its L-shaped couch and square coffee table. With all of the little decorating touches on the built-in shelves and the occasion tables, he had to guess the place had been professionally decorated. Beyond the smaller living area, they discovered a library accessible from the hall or through the bathroom situated between it and the living room. Across from the library was a decent-sized bedroom with twin beds and a private bath.

"Do you think Dad bought this place for you when you were going to do your graduate work here?" Bianca asked.

"I don't think so." Carina shook her head. "The place Mama was buying was expensive, but nothing like this. My guess is this place would go for close to ten million dollars."

"Ten *million*?" Bianca asked incredulously.

Carina nodded. "Our family has always invested pretty heavily in real estate, but even this is over the top unless someone is living here."

"Do you think someone is living here?"

"I don't think so. Otherwise, the concierge would have said something."

"I knew Dad's family was rich, but I never really put a dollar amount to how much he had," Bianca admitted.

"Let's check out the kitchen," Jay suggested. "With a place this size, there must be another bedroom somewhere."

They crossed through the hallway in front of the elevators and found the kitchen . . . and a very long hall with half a dozen doors opening off of it.

"Um, I think this place may be a bit larger than we first thought," Bianca said, her eyes bright. She opened the door on the right to reveal the laundry room and then proceeded to check out the string of four bedrooms on the right, each of them with private bathrooms. Another hallway led to a media room that had a Murphy bed in the corner in case it needed to double as yet another bedroom.

"This is the largest bedroom. I wonder why they have the master set up as a media center," Carina mused.

"I don't know." Jay left Carina to look around the media room and wandered farther down the hall. When he reached the final doorway, he thought it was a long hallway that led back to the library. When he realized it was a master suite, complete with two bathrooms and two dressing rooms, all he could do was stare. It took him a moment to find his voice, and he called out, "Um, Carina. I think you'd better take a look at this."

Carina appeared at the main entrance to the master suite. "What?"

"Come here." Jay motioned for her to join him by the bedroom door. He couldn't help but smile when he saw the expression on her face when she looked past him.

"Oh," Carina breathed the word, moving with him to look out the window where they could see the New York skyline. "Wow."

"I have a feeling this place is worth a bit more than ten million," Jay told her. "It takes up the whole floor. From what I saw of real estate prices when we were researching this part of town, I think it would probably go for more like thirty million."

"But what did my father intend for us to *do* with a place like this?"

"Maybe he planned on you living here eventually," Jay suggested.

"That's possible," Bianca agreed. "He must have known that you went to school at NYU and Gianna used to talk about coming here for school too."

Jay's phone rang, and he pulled it out of his pocket to find his father on the other end of the line. "Hey, Dad. What's up?"

"The principal from Bianca's school called a few minutes ago. He said a reporter showed up at the school looking for Bianca. I guess they wanted to talk to her about that bullying video that went viral," Pete told him. "The principal wanted to know if it was okay to give the reporter our number."

"I assume you told him no."

"Obviously," Pete said with a touch of indignation in his voice. "But that's not all. I thought our friends at the FBI would want to know about it since they're staking out the school."

"Yeah. And?"

"And when they called the television studio this guy was supposedly from, they'd never heard of him."

"They're sure?"

"Oh yeah," Pete said with certainty. "They're pulling the surveillance videos from the school now to run facial recognition. They promised to let me know if they get a hit."

"You'll let me know when they call back?"

"I will. You be careful up there. I don't like how this is going right now."

Jay saw Bianca walk into the room, her eyes wide. He tried to ignore the sense of dread in his stomach but couldn't quite manage it. If someone had tracked Bianca to her school, there was no way of knowing where they might try looking next. "I know what you mean. I'll talk to you later."

As soon as he hung up, Bianca asked, "Do you have to ship out?"

"No. Nothing like that." Jay shook his head.

Carina put a hand on his arm. "Is something wrong?"

"I was just thinking." Jay took a look around the room before looking back down at Carina. "How would you feel about extending our trip for another week? We could go back to Virginia the day after your birthday."

"I don't know. The hotels here are so expensive."

"Carina, take a look around. We don't need a hotel."

"You want to stay here?" Carina asked, the reality apparently not quite sinking in that this enormous condo currently belonged to her. "Can you even get the time off? You were planning on taking a couple of weeks for our wedding and honeymoon."

"I'm sure I can work something out."

"But what about our wedding plans? I still have a lot to do. And Bianca would be missing school and practice."

Jay reached out and tucked a strand of hair behind her ear. "These are all details we can work out. I just think it might be a good idea for you to lay low until after your birthday. Maybe by next week we can figure out what the significance of that day is." Then he added, "If we stay here for the next few days, Charlie will hopefully have time to track down the people on that list."

Carina looked around the room again, and Jay could tell she was working through her concerns, a sense of excitement beginning to overshadow the logistical details.

"Well . . . ?" Jay asked.

Carina slowly nodded. "I guess I could stand celebrating my birthday in New York."

"Great." Jay waved a hand to encompass the room. "Why don't you and Bianca take a closer look around, and I can go get our stuff and check out of our hotel."

"We can come with you," Carina offered.

Jay shook his head. "I'd rather keep both of you out of sight as much as possible."

"Why do we need to stay out of sight?" Bianca asked. "No one knows we're in New York."

"Just humor me," Jay said, not wanting to share the details of his father's phone call with Bianca. He led the way out of the master suite and back down the hallway to the elevators. "I can also see if I can find somewhere to have a couple of extra elevator keys made so we don't have to all share the same one."

"That would be great," Carina said, "but do you have any idea where you can get that done around here? It's not like there's a hardware store on the corner."

"I'll ask the concierge downstairs. I was going to stop and ask him who else might have access to this place before we settle in."

"What do you mean? It doesn't look like anyone is living here."

"I know. But after three years, you'd think there would be dust on everything, and there isn't. Someone is at least coming in and cleaning on a regular basis. I don't want anyone showing up unexpectedly."

"I hadn't even thought about that."

"My guess is there's some kind of cleaning service contracted to come in," Jay told her. "I also need to ask the concierge where the closest pool is," Jay said.

"You're going to make me practice this week?" Bianca asked, insult in her tone.

"Absolutely," Jay said without missing a beat. "For now, why don't you go decide which bedroom you want."

Bianca looked at him, considering. Then she said, "I can do that."

CHAPTER 31

PETE WALKED INTO THE REC center, his thoughts still on the principal's phone call. He could barely fathom, after all of their efforts to help Bianca fix her school troubles, that danger had apparently found her and Carina again.

When he had first suggested that they all live together, his motives had been altruistic. Carina and Bianca needed a safe place to stay, and he had the means to help them. Now that he was faced with the prospect of them being in danger if they stayed, he could admit, at least to himself, that he liked having them around. He had missed the sounds of family in the evenings and the conversation and bantering that occurred at dinnertime.

Somewhere over the past many months, Carina and Bianca had become family in every sense of the word. He imagined that with a little time, Gianna would quickly fall into that category as well.

Pete's eyes landed on his swimmers who had gathered across the pool deck to stretch. Already, it seemed odd to not have Bianca here. He hoped the situation with the video wouldn't chase her away from his team for a second time. When he counted only five swimmers on deck, he did a quick attendance in his head and noted that Jonah was also missing.

His eyes shifted to the lanes where his team would practice in a few minutes, instantly annoyed when he saw a swimming instructor with a group of six-year-olds working in one of his lanes. A lifeguard approached him before he had the chance to complain. "Excuse me, Pete, but I wanted to see if there's any way you can go down to one lane for your practice today. I'm afraid we overbooked."

"This is the third time this has happened this month."

"I know. I'm really sorry about that. I'm afraid our lessons coordinator thought you only rented one lane since you only have seven swimmers."

Irritation hummed in Pete's voice. "Is this going to keep happening?"

"For now, it looks like the conflicts only happen on Saturdays. Once we get through this set of lessons, we'll make sure we adjust to give you the space you need."

"How long until this set of lessons is over?"

"Only another five weeks."

"Great," Pete muttered. He left the lifeguard behind, striding over to where his swimmers were waiting for him.

He was just about to ask where Jonah was when his cell phone rang. "Hi, Pete. This is David Zimmerman, Jonah's dad."

"Is everything okay with Jonah?"

"Yeah. He's actually on his way right now. His car battery died, and we had to run out and buy a new one."

"Thanks for letting me know."

"There's one other thing. I'm sorry for the late notice, but I wanted to let you know we have a family thing out of town. We'll leave tomorrow after church, and we won't be back until late on Monday. I'm afraid that means he won't be able to make practice on Monday."

"I see."

"Jonah didn't want to miss, so I told him I would see if there was any way you could give him some workouts to do."

"Yeah, I can do that," Pete said gruffly. "Remind him to stretch before he starts them though."

"I can do that," David said. "Thanks for understanding."

"Yeah, sure," Pete said unconvincingly before saying good-bye.

He turned back to his remaining swimmers, opened his mouth to give them the warmup, and winced when a little girl's squeal pierced the air. With a shake of his head, he motioned his swimmers to get in the water and muttered, "I've got to find a new pool."

* * *

He weaved his way through the outskirts of town, constantly checking his rearview mirror to make sure he wasn't being followed. This meeting was too important for him to miss, and under no circumstances could anyone else know of it. After circling the area several times, he finally made his way to the designated meeting place.

He pulled into the parking lot of the hotel, driving to the rear corner of the building, where his contact was waiting. He pulled up to the curb and waited for him to climb in. Then he drove to the far corner of the lot and parked before he asked, "Did you find Bianca?"

Nigel shook his head. "She wasn't in school today."

Impatience vibrated through his voice. "Where was she?"

"The secretaries weren't very helpful, but since the FBI was staking out the place, I have to think that she and Carina have gone into hiding."

Frustration simmered into anger. "I told you how important it is that we find them. We're running out of time."

"I know. That's why I talked to some of the other kids at school."

"And?"

Nigel handed him a folded piece of paper. "Trace the calls on this cell number, and I think you'll find her."

"Whose number is this?"

"It appears Bianca has a boyfriend."

* * *

Jay crossed the lobby to the concierge desk. "Excuse me. I wonder if I could ask you a few questions."

"What may I help you with, sir?"

"The unit on the sixteenth floor. Do you know who provides the cleaning service?"

"That is handled through our office. It is scheduled for once a month," he told him. "It is billed with the monthly maintenance fees."

"Can you tell me where the bills are being sent? Or who is paying them?"

"I'm sorry, sir, but I'm not at liberty to say."

"Can you at least tell me if the payments are up to date?"

The man hesitated for a moment and then nodded.

"Thank you," Jay said. He held up the elevator key and asked, "Can you tell me where I can get more keys made? And where I would find the nearest grocery store?"

"There is a touch-screen intercom in your unit that will allow you to schedule food deliveries. As for the key, we have a local locksmith we contract with to handle that for us. How many additional keys do you need, and how soon would you like to pick them up?"

"I need to pick up our things at our hotel. I should be back in about an hour so I'll need my key back by then." Jay offered his key.

"We can use the master key we keep for the cleaning service to have the new keys made." The concierge motioned to the front entrance. "The doorman can call a cab if you wish."

Jay shook his head. "I have a car parked across the street."

"In that case, the doorman can instruct you where to park so you can use our valet parking service."

"Thank you." Jay took one step before turning back. "One more thing. Where is the closest swimming pool?"

"La Palestra, the private fitness center in this building, has a pool."

Jay's eyebrows lifted. "Really?"

"Yes, sir. It is solely for building residents," the concierge told him. "I will have the information for La Palestra available for you when you return to pick up your keys."

"I appreciate all of your help." Jay made his way outside, stopping long enough to talk to the doorman so he would know where to drop off the car when he returned. Then he pulled out his phone and called Brent.

"Hey, Jay. I'm afraid I haven't heard back from Charlie about that list of names you sent me."

"I figured he probably wouldn't be able to get too much done over the weekend. There's actually something else I was hoping either you or Charlie could help me with."

"What's that?"

"I'm trying to track down who is paying for the maintenance on a condo here."

"Sure. Whose condo?"

"It looks like Carina's father purchased it. The concierge confirmed that the fees are current, but he wouldn't tell me who's paying them."

"Charlie should be able to track that down, but I'm sure he'll need a warrant."

"Which means we'll probably have to wait until Tuesday."

"Exactly."

"Just let me know when you hear something."

"I will. Also, I have a phone number here for you so you can call Charlie directly if you need to. He picked up a burn phone so it can't be traced to you."

"Great. I don't have anything to write with. Can you e-mail it to me?"

"No problem. Stay safe."

"That's my plan. Thanks again for your help."

CHAPTER 32

JAY WAS BARELY OUT THE door before Bianca started checking out the bedrooms again, ultimately choosing the large corner room across from the master suite. When Jonah called and she disappeared into her room to talk to him, Carina wandered through the house, again wondering about her father's motives.

The legal documents they had found in the storage room indicated that he had sold all of those companies while their mother was still alive. Had he used the proceeds from those sales to purchase this condo? Could her mother have known about this place? And if so, why had the note with the elevator key only been to his three daughters?

She couldn't for the life of her figure out why her father would have chosen to buy something here in New York, a city where her family had no business holdings. In fact, her understanding was that the Perellis deliberately steered clear of New York City to avoid any conflicts with the New York mafia.

Carina entered the enormous kitchen and pulled open a cabinet door at random. Plates and bowls were neatly stacked inside, ready to be used. Methodically, she opened each cabinet and drawer. Pots, pans, cooking utensils, silverware, glassware—everything that one would need to cook was neatly arranged, but all of it looked brand-new.

The refrigerator was completely empty, the tags from the manufacturer still inside. When she walked into the pantry, the empty cupboards confirmed what she had already suspected. No one had ever lived there. Not a single item of food was in the apartment.

She supposed she would have to talk to Jay about picking up some groceries after he got back from the hotel. Surely he would be okay with her going out to do some basic shopping so they wouldn't have to order out.

Making her way back down the hall, she headed for the master bedroom in search of any personal items her father might have left behind. Clean sheets and towels were folded in the linen closet, but there weren't any toiletries of any kind. She checked inside the medicine cabinets and inside the bathroom cabinets to find them all empty.

The bedroom also appeared to be just as the interior decorator left it. After an unsuccessful search of the dressers, she found a closed door near one of the bathrooms. Assuming it was another linen closet, she pulled the door open to find a room about the size of a normal bedroom.

Two armchairs faced a fireplace with a small round table situated between them. A beautiful Chippendale partners desk was angled in front of one of the windows, an executive chair tucked behind it.

The contrast of modern and antique was enough to pique Carina's curiosity. She crossed to the desk and lowered herself into the chair. When she opened the center drawer, she was surprised to find an executive pen set and a few loose paperclips.

The drawers on the right side of the desk were empty, but when she pulled open the top drawer on the left, her breath caught in her throat. Inside was a framed photograph of her parents shortly before her mother had taken them away from Chicago. Gently, Carina drew it out and set it on the corner of the desk, her throat closing with emotion as she remembered the horrific way her mother had been murdered.

Trying to push those memories aside, Carina opened yet another drawer and discovered a thick file with a handwritten note clipped to the outside that said *Girls' trust*.

She picked up the file and discovered a photo album hidden beneath it. She remembered the album vividly from her childhood and the way her mother had always kept it on a high shelf so little fingers wouldn't ruin the photographs.

More interested at the moment in memories than documents, Carina pushed the file aside and set the album on the desk, flipping it open to the first page. Photos of her childhood, of her parents, grandparents, and cousins, filled the pages. Taking her time, she let herself remember in a way she hadn't done in years.

She reached what she expected to be the end of the album and was stunned to see photographs of her and her sisters after they had left Chicago: school photos, her high school and college graduations; a photograph of Bianca when she received her first gold medal after moving to Colorado; another of Gianna in her volleyball uniform.

Lost in memories, Carina started when Jay called out from down the hall. "Carina?"

She tried to shake off the past and bring herself back into the present. "I'm in here."

It took a minute for Jay to make his way into the master suite and find her in the study. "What are you doing?"

"Looking at old pictures." She waved a hand at the album. "I remember my mom putting photos in this album when I was a kid." She looked up at him, her eyes moist. "There are pictures in here of my sisters and me after we left Chicago. My mom must have been sending them to my dad over the years."

"From everything we've found over the past few months, that makes sense. It seems like your parents still loved each other and that your father sent all of you away to protect you."

"I wish he would just tell me what he's protecting us from," Carina said with a sigh. "I keep wondering if all of these precautions are really necessary. Maybe that reward on my sisters and me is just a mistake. It could have been arranged a long time ago, before Raymond died."

Jay lowered himself onto the arm of the chair closest to her. "I wish that were true, but we both know it isn't."

"You know, I look around this condo, at the incredible views and beautiful furnishings, and then I remember where my family's money comes from." Carina shook her head. "I don't know what my father was thinking, buying this place. What does he want from me?"

"I think he probably started out buying it to protect himself from his half brother. We know Raymond had control of the family business. Your father must have felt threatened by him enough to hide away evidence that could incriminate him."

"But Raymond is dead. Why would anyone care about finding us now?"

"I don't know." Jay looked over his shoulder as though listening for Bianca. "I didn't want to say anything in front of your sister, but someone showed up at her school today looking for her. The guy said he was a reporter and that he wanted to do a story on the video clip that got posted on the Internet."

"The last thing we need is for Bianca to talk to a reporter."

"I agree. The problem is, this guy wasn't really a reporter."

"Are you sure?"

Jay nodded. "When the FBI called the television studio to check him out, they had never heard of him."

Carina pressed her lips together and fought a fresh wave of emotion. If it wasn't safe for them in Virginia Beach, how would she and Jay ever be able to build a future together? "You think it was whoever is looking for us."

"Yeah. I called Charlie when I went out. He's sending me over the surveillance photos of the guy so we can see if you might recognize him."

"And in the meantime?"

"For now, we make ourselves at home here and try to keep things as normal as possible for Bianca until we figure out what's really going on," Jay told her. "I stopped by a little corner deli on my way over here and picked up some sandwiches. The concierge downstairs said there's an intercom system up here that we can use to order groceries."

"That's convenient."

"Yeah." Jay stood up and noticed the file on the desk. "What's that?"

"I'm not sure. I think it may be some of the documents from the trust the FBI was telling you about."

"Do you mind if I take a look?"

"Help yourself." Carina handed it to him. "I think I'm going to go eat. After skipping lunch, I am starving."

"Me too." Jay stood up. "After we eat, I thought Bianca and I could go practice, and maybe you can take care of the grocery list."

"I'm definitely getting the better side of that deal. You're going to have a tough time getting Bianca off the phone."

"No, I won't." Jay shook his head and grinned. "Jonah has to go to practice in twenty minutes."

"It sounds like you have those two figured out."

"Oh yeah."

CHAPTER 33

BIANCA SAT DOWN AT THE round table in the kitchen and rubbed a towel over her wet hair. She wasn't sure how she felt about the news that there was a high-end fitness center downstairs in their building. The setup was amazing, including a workout pool. Unfortunately, the easy access to a pool also meant she could pretty much live within the walls of 995 Fifth Avenue and not ever have a reason to leave. She had rather hoped to have the chance to explore New York City while they were here.

Carina stirred something on the stove and looked up at her. "How was the workout?"

"Pete is trying to kill me."

"You said the same thing right after you started working out with him in Miami," Carina reminded her. "After a couple of months, you stopped remembering to complain. And you know you love the results."

"Yeah, I guess." Bianca had to admit that she had enjoyed stepping onto the medal stand at the last meet to collect her gold medal in backstroke, while the girl who received the bronze was one of her former teammates. Russell hadn't looked too thrilled about the results of that particular race or the one in which Jonah had beaten Todd.

"Did you get all of your homework done?"

"Most of it. Jonah is at practice right now, but after he gets home, he said he would call so we can work on our history."

"You're working on a project together?"

Bianca shook her head. "No, but we have a report due on Tuesday. Since I won't be back before then, Jonah said I could e-mail it to him so he could turn it in for me."

"That's nice of him."

"Yeah." Bianca glanced at her watch, calculating how long it would be before Jonah could call.

"You like him," Carina stated in a no-nonsense tone.

"What? I didn't say that."

"That wasn't a question," Carina said humorously. "Has he asked you out yet?"

Bianca could feel the blush rising to her cheeks. "Actually, he said he wanted to take me out when we get back. We just didn't know we would be here for so long."

"If all goes well, we can head home next Friday." Carina turned the burner down and looked into the next room. "Where's Jay?"

"I think he was in the library," Bianca told her. "You know, there's something that doesn't make sense to me. Why would our family be so anxious to search for us? If Dad bought this condo for us, then what does that have to do with anyone else?"

"I don't know," Carina admitted. "I really thought we would find something of value to them or maybe some evidence against the illegal side of the family business. Nothing here has anything to do with that except for the stuff about Raymond. It must be someone on his side of the family who's still interested in us."

Jay appeared in the doorway leading to the hallway. "You're forgetting about the people who are on that list of Raymond's contacts. Maybe it's one of Raymond's friends from the FBI who is looking for you."

"Have you heard anything from Charlie about that yet?"

Jay shook his head. "But I think I may have found something else."

"What?"

He held up the file Carina had found in the desk. "According to this, when this condo was purchased, it was placed in a trust. Carina, once you turn twenty-five, you legally take control of the trust and all of the assets in it."

"I turn twenty-five next week."

"Exactly. Until your birthday, your father maintains control." Jay read further. "It says here that in the event that your father is not able to actively manage the trust, Raymond Alexander and your uncle Marciano would then take joint control."

"Why would they agree to that? According to Uncle Marciano, he and my father didn't want anything to do with Raymond."

"Yes, but we also know that when your grandfather started going senile, he split up the family assets. It looks like he's the one who created this trust. My guess is that he divided up the key parts of their business in an effort to force his sons to work together."

"That clearly didn't work," Bianca muttered.

"But why would my grandfather include us in this trust? If he wanted his sons to work together, he obviously wouldn't want me to take over as trustee only three years later. We haven't been involved with the family for years."

"I think that technically your father would still be a trustee," Jay told her. "I'm certainly not a legal expert, but it looks like either one of you can buy and sell assets as long as they remain in the trust."

"I still don't understand." Carina shook her head. "If they control the assets, then what do they want with me? If they want to take control of this condo and what's in it, they could do that without my permission, right?"

"They could . . ." Jay gave her a pointed look. "If they knew what the assets were. Your father sold off all of their cash-based companies. According to the documents I found with the trust, he bought this place a few weeks later. Your uncles didn't have any way of knowing where your father had put the proceeds from those sales."

"So in essence, my father bought this place so he could hide family money from the rest of the family?"

"Exactly."

Carina's eyes sharpened, and she asked, "Is there anything in those documents that says who would take over for Raymond if he wasn't able to? Maybe if we can figure that out, we'll know who is looking for us."

"If either Raymond or your father were unable to act as trustees, then a financial management company would take over until your twenty-fifth birthday. At that time, everything would be under your control."

"Could the financial management company be a front for one of my relatives?"

Jay shook his head. "It looks legitimate."

Bianca watched her sister and Jay try to make sense of what appeared to be a very confusing legal document. Finally, she asked, "Does it really matter who is looking for us? It sounds like none of this will matter after Carina's birthday."

"That's true," Jay conceded. "For now, we should be able to hang out here and enjoy the view."

Bianca looked out the kitchen window at the stunning colors of fall spread out beneath them. Then she looked at the stark white kitchen. "You do realize that I'm going to go absolutely stir crazy if I have to stay here for a whole week."

"Sorry, kid," Jay said apologetically, "but there isn't much we can do about that. We have the gym and pool downstairs. If you want, I can pick up a couple of DVDs when I go out to the store next."

"You also have homework to do, and you can talk to Jonah on the phone."

Sarcasm dripped from Bianca's voice. "Yeah, when he's not at school or practice."

"Maybe we can venture out to the museum across the street later," Carina offered.

Slightly mollified, she shrugged. "I guess that's better than nothing."

"Go check out the intercom system over there." Carina waved at the sleek panel on the wall. "I bet you can order some movies through that."

Bianca crossed the room and started punching buttons. Her eyes lit up. "This is so cool! We can order takeout, groceries, movies. Even concert tickets."

"Don't even think about it." Carina wagged a finger in her direction. "No McDonalds and no takeout without my permission."

"You aren't any fun," Bianca complained.

When Bianca's phone rang, her spirits instantly brightened. She saw Jonah's name illuminated on the screen, answered with a cheerful hello, and headed for her room to ensure a little privacy.

"How is everything going?" Jonah asked casually. "What's the place you're staying at like?"

"You should see it," Bianca told him. "The view of Central Park is amazing."

"It must be pretty close to my aunt and uncle's house."

"I think it's only about a mile away. I tried to get my sister to let me go hang out with Sara, but she didn't go for it. Carina doesn't want me leaving the condo, especially since she doesn't really know your aunt."

"Parents are funny like that."

"Carina isn't a parent."

"Close enough," Jonah said. "So what are you doing about practice? Is there a pool nearby?"

"Actually, the La Palestra fitness center is in this building, and they have a pool there where Jay and I will be working out."

"I know that place. Isn't it down on 67th Street?"

"I don't know. There might be one there too, but the one here is private. I guess it's only for the people who live in this building."

"Sounds like you've got it made, a lot better than we had it yesterday," Jonah told her. "Six people in one lane doesn't work when you're trying to work on different intervals."

"Why did you only have one lane?"

"The pool double booked again. I thought Pete was going to blow a gasket."

"I'm surprised he didn't," Bianca said. "I think it's been tough on him trying to work with these different pools. He pretty much had the run of the place when we were in Miami."

"Then why did he come up here?"

"I'm not sure. I think to be closer to Jay."

"Maybe he missed having you around too."

"I doubt that."

"I don't know. Practice definitely isn't the same without you there."

Bianca let the warmth of his comment spread through her, a smile forming on her lips. "I know I'm looking forward to getting back home so I can be with everyone again."

"We'll see each other again before you know it," Jonah told her before changing the subject to the unexciting topic of homework.

CHAPTER 34

HE'D ALWAYS KNOWN IT WAS just a matter of time. She thought she could hide. She thought she could use her heritage to her advantage when she wanted and ignore it when it didn't suit her. Now she would learn that she was wrong. Dead wrong.

He used the darkness of the back alley to approach the rear entrance. Personally, he loved these old buildings. It wasn't the charm and character that most people noticed that caused the sentiment. No, he appreciated the old-fashioned locks and the lack of security cameras.

He pulled a slim case out of his jacket pocket, retrieved his tools, and went to work on one of the outdated locks. Forty-five seconds later, the lock turned, and he made his way inside.

He located the stairwell and once again faced a locked door. It didn't stay locked for long.

Faced with a long climb up many flights of stairs, he took his time. After all, he didn't want to get too winded in case she wasn't alone in the top-floor unit.

He had come too far, had plotted for too long to let anyone get in his way. And the hardest part was over. The search was over.

When he finally reached the final barrier to her unit, he once again methodically picked the lock.

Adrenaline surfaced, and he fought it back. He couldn't let his emotions cloud his judgment. He couldn't think of the woman inside as family. She was in the way of what he wanted, and as long as she lived, she would continue to threaten his way of life.

He reached for the pistol he had holstered beneath his jacket and took the time to attach a silencer. Then he listened for any sign of life on the other side of the door.

At three in the morning, he assumed everyone would be in bed, but he couldn't take any chances. His gun at the ready, he turned the knob and soundlessly stepped inside.

He stopped and listened once more, not sure if he was relieved or disappointed that there wasn't a bodyguard waiting to add another challenge. This wasn't a game, he reminded himself. This was life. His life and his future.

He waited for a moment to let his eyes adjust to the darkness, and then he started along the edge of the living room and headed for the hall. He already knew the layout of the unit, previously studying the floor plans that were ridiculously easy to find on the Internet.

His heartbeat quickened when he reached the bedroom door he believed to be hers. This time, the doorknob turned smoothly in his hand. He made his way forward in the darkness, using the bit of moonlight splashing through the far window to guide him.

He reached the side of the bed and looked at the woman sleeping peacefully beneath the thick comforter, her dark hair contrasting against the ivory pillowcase.

He took a moment to see the family resemblance, but he didn't let himself feel any kinship. He and this woman might share the same blood, but she wasn't really one of them. Her choices had alienated her from the family, and now she would have to deal with the consequences.

Apparently sensing his presence, she stirred, and her eyes cracked open. The moment she realized she wasn't alone, her eyes went wide, and she scrambled to sit up.

He didn't give her time to reach for whatever gun she might have tucked away nearby. Without any regret, he aimed for her heart and squeezed the trigger.

* * *

She couldn't sleep. Carina reached for her cell phone on the bedside table to see that it was only five in the morning. She flipped on the lamp, squinting against the sudden brightness. Then she threw off the covers, padded across the thick rug, and made her way to the sitting room, where she had unpacked her clothing into a dresser.

After pulling a sweatshirt on over her pajamas to ward off the chill in the room, she made her way down the hall and headed for the main living area. She slowed when she reached the gallery area in front of the elevator.

The Cezanne hanging directly opposite the elevator looked vaguely familiar, making her wonder if she had seen it before in a museum.

She continued past the artwork and wandered into the main living room. The first fingers of sunlight were breaking through the clouds on the horizon. Crossing to the window, she rested a hand on the wide sill and stared out at the park below.

There had been a time during her childhood that she had thought everyone lived like this, enjoying spacious, beautiful homes, money being simply a means to gain whatever one desired. Now, after pinching pennies for the past few years, she felt indulgent to be standing here in a room that was larger than many New York apartments.

What had her father been thinking when he'd bought this place? And why hadn't he come out and told her what he wanted her to do if and when she found it?

"Hey," Jay's voice sounded behind her. "What are you doing up so early?"

Carina considered it a good sign that she hadn't jumped when she heard his voice. She glanced back at him and shrugged. "I couldn't sleep."

He stepped up behind her, wrapping his arms loosely around her waist as he rested his chin on her shoulder. "What are you so deep in thought about?"

"I was just thinking how weird it is to be living like this again after how difficult things have been for the past few years."

"Have you thought about what you're going to do with this place?"

She shook her head. "All I've been able to think about lately is what to expect after my birthday. Do you think everything will really end once I turn twenty-five?"

"I hope so." Jay moved his hands to her shoulders and turned her so she was facing him. His expression was so serious that for a moment Carina wondered if he had received bad news. "Assuming you really do have access to the assets and money in the trust, are you going to want to buy your own place instead of living with my parents?"

She keyed in on the term *your own place*. "Wherever we decide to live, it will be *our* place, not mine."

"You know what I mean." Jay slid his hands down her arms and linked his fingers with hers. "I guess I'm just uneasy about the idea of you and Bianca living alone when I deploy in March."

"I never expected to say this, but I kind of like living with your parents." Carina considered for a minute. "I know your dad rented the place we're in for a year. Maybe we could buy a place for all of us to live after his lease runs out. If we were to sell this condo, we could get something that would be big enough to give all of us our privacy, and we'd still have more money than we would know what to do with."

Jay's expression softened. "Are you sure?"

She nodded. "Your parents have been so great with Bianca. I love the way it feels like we're part of a family again."

"You *are* part of a family. You're my family." Jay leaned down, his lips touching hers in a sweet, simple kiss.

"I love you," Carina whispered.

"And I love you."

* * *

Jay flipped through the newspaper he'd picked up that morning, stunned to find the murder of Rosa Alexander in the headlines. He didn't know what to think about the report that someone had broken into her penthouse apartment and shot her in her bed. Had someone in Carina's family killed her to help protect Carina and her sisters, or was the person who murdered Rosa the same person who was looking for them?

Jay read through the entire article, discovering the mention of Rosa's relationship to Raymond Alexander, along with the speculation that she had taken over his illegal businesses after his death. He read the article a second time, hoping for some mention of the rest of Raymond's family, but the only reference to them was that they had not been available for comment.

Jay's phone rang, and he answered it to find Charlie on the other end. "Hey, Charlie. I was just reading about Rosa Alexander."

"Yeah. I just got the call on that this morning."

"Any idea who is behind it?"

"At this point, your guess is as good as mine, but there's something else," Charlie said. "We just had a hit on facial recognition for the guy who was at Bianca's school asking about her. His name is Nigel Rafferty."

"What do you know about him?" Jay asked. "Was he from Chicago?"

"Actually, he's from Las Vegas."

"That's odd. I thought for sure he would have some ties to either the Perelli or Alexander families."

"There's no guarantee that he doesn't. He was picked up three years ago and questioned about the disappearance of one of our informants." He paused for effect. "The informant had been feeding us information on the mob activity in the Vegas area."

"Does the Perelli family have holdings in Vegas?"

"According to our guy, they do. Unfortunately, the informant disappeared before he gave us any names, but Rafferty was sighted at a bar with him on the night he vanished."

"Sounds suspicious, for sure," Jay said. "Do you have anything that would tell us who within the family he was working for?"

"Unfortunately, no."

"How about that list of names I gave you?"

"Oh, we've been busy with that. The list was pretty much a roadmap of the Alexander crime organization."

"Was there any indication that Raymond Alexander's wife or son was involved?"

"Believe it or not, it actually looks like they may have been as clueless about Raymond's illegal activities as they said. When we originally questioned them, everyone in the immediate family said Raymond indicated that his father's family was very wealthy and that he had inherited his fortune."

"They thought he was independently wealthy but still worked for the FBI?"

"Supposedly they bought his story that he was working with the FBI because he liked the challenge."

"Wow."

"Yeah," Charlie said. "One more thing. Our finance guys here did track down the account that pays the maintenance fees for that condo."

"And?"

"And the money comes from a bank account in Monaco. The account is registered to a shell company called Tri-Star."

"Who owns the company?"

"You're not going to believe this, but the only name associated with the account is Carina's."

"What?"

"We were able to trace some of the deposits back to their origins. It looks like at least some of the funds were the proceeds when Giovanni sold off the companies his father left in his control."

"But why would he put the funds in Carina's name and not include his own?"

"My guess is that he was worried the government might be able to seize his accounts. With his half brother working for the FBI, he must have been worried that Raymond would figure out a way to get him arrested and then go after his money."

"That makes sense, but why only Carina?"

"When he opened the account, Carina was the only one of his daughters who was already a legal adult."

"That's a lot to take in," Jay said. "Any idea how much money is in the account?"

"Yeah. It's just over twenty-five million dollars."

"You've got to be kidding me."

"Nope. The interest alone is enough to pay for all of the fees and still have some left over, so the account has been growing steadily over the past few years," Charlie told him. "I think that's all I have for now, but I'll give you a call if I find out anything else."

"Thanks, Charlie."

Jay hung up the phone and set the newspaper he had been reading aside. Then he headed for the kitchen, where he had last seen Carina. He found her sitting at the kitchen table, a pen in one hand and a notepad in front of her.

She looked up when he entered. "Was that your phone I just heard?"

"Yeah. That was Charlie." Jay sat down across from her and told her what Charlie had told him.

"So you're telling me the aunt I didn't know I had was murdered and I have twenty-five million dollars in a foreign bank account."

Jay nodded. "Yeah. That's pretty much the news of the day."

"I can't believe this. I can't believe any of it." Carina stared at him, obviously stunned. "Every day my life keeps getting more surreal."

"You're telling me. I thought I was marrying a girl who was having a hard time keeping up with her rent, and now I find out you're a multimillionaire."

"It doesn't seem possible that the money is really mine. I keep expecting someone to walk in here and tell us this is all a big joke. Or worse, to have the government come seize everything and tell me it's all from blood money."

"Try not to think that way." Jay gave her hand a squeeze. "If you're okay for a while, I'm going to go downstairs to see if I can find any information on Tri-Star. Maybe that will give us a clue as to what your dad's intentions were when he juggled all of these assets."

"All right. Is there anything I can do to help?"

Jay could tell her thoughts were as much on the design book in front of her as they were on the news he had given her. Knowing he could go through the files just as easily with or without her, he gave her a slow smile. "Did you say you were going to send out for some more groceries today?"

"Yeah. I forgot how much milk you and Bianca can go through in a day."

"You could get the ingredients for Bianca to make chocolate chip cookies."

"You know your dad doesn't want her eating that stuff."

His smile widened to a grin. "Yeah, but if she thinks I'm letting her get away with it, she'll make us cookies too."

"You're impossible."

He just shrugged. "Yeah. I know."

CHAPTER 35

BIANCA CURLED UP IN THE TV room, a knit throw over her legs and a bowl of popcorn tucked beside her.

She had ordered several DVDs through the concierge service, but they had gone through all of them yesterday, since Jay didn't want to risk letting them go to church. Like anyone was going to hunt them down at an LDS church house.

Now here she was on a Monday morning, a holiday no less, watching this particular movie for the third time while she waited for a new batch to be delivered.

She and Jay had already gone downstairs to put in their first workout of the day. When they had returned, Carina and Jay had started talking about the trust and who might be looking for them. Watching a movie had been the easiest way for Bianca to make her escape.

It wasn't that she wasn't interested in what was going on, but listening to them talk about her family made her nervous. She didn't want to think about her family's business or the crimes they had supposedly committed. She was also afraid to let herself dream about what their lives might be like from now on if this condo and the money they had found was really theirs.

Bianca pushed those thoughts aside and glanced at her watch, estimating that Jonah would be home from practice in another fifteen minutes. When her phone rang less than five minutes later, she looked down, surprised to see his name on her caller ID.

"Hey, Jonah. Don't tell me Pete actually ended practice early."

"No, nothing like that," Jonah said. "So what are you doing right now?"

"Being bored. I'm watching the same movie for the third time."

"In that case, maybe we can hang out for a while."

"Um, that would be great, except you're in Virginia and I'm in New York."

"Actually, I'm standing outside your building."

"What?" Bianca rushed to the window to look down onto the street but couldn't identify anyone standing on the sidewalk below.

"I kept bugging my dad to let me take the bus up here to visit my aunt and uncle and surprise you, so he finally decided to bring the whole family up for a quick visit."

"Seriously?"

"Yeah. Your doorman said someone has to call down before I can come in."

"I'll just come downstairs." Bianca raced to her room and grabbed the elevator key Jay had given her. She poked her head into the kitchen to see that Carina was on the phone with someone and Jay was nowhere in sight, which likely meant he was still downstairs in the storage room. Without a second thought, she pushed the button for the elevator, grateful the doors slid open less than a minute later.

She hurried through the lobby, excitement jumping in her stomach when she looked through the glass doors to see Jonah standing beside the doorman on the busy sidewalk.

Bianca stepped outside and, without thinking, threw her arms open for a hug. Jonah embraced her, a grin on his face.

"I can't believe you're here."

"I can't believe I managed to figure out where you were staying so I could surprise you."

"How *did* you figure out my address?" Bianca asked curiously. "I never told it to you."

"No, but you told me the name of the fitness center, and I knew you were near Central Park. That made it easy."

"Impressive." Bianca's eyebrows lifted. "Come on. Let's go upstairs, and I'll show you around."

Bianca thanked the doorman as he opened the door for them, and she made her way inside and headed to the elevator. She put the key in to access her unit as Jonah followed her inside. The doors were sliding closed when a gloved hand reached out to keep it from closing.

Bianca looked up at the man briefly, noting that he looked like he was in his midtwenties. Living with Carina, she knew enough about fashion to recognize the cut of the designer Italian suit and to be aware that it probably cost more than six months' worth of rent at her old apartment. She imagined such expensive clothing was probably commonplace in this neighborhood.

Excitement still bubbling through her, she turned to Jonah. "I still can't believe your dad agreed to come up here for the day."

"We actually got here yesterday and spent the afternoon with my family."

"Did your dad drop you off here?"

"No, I walked. My aunt and uncle only live six blocks away."

"I didn't think it was that close." Bianca glanced up at the numbers on the elevator panel as the doors slid closed. She noticed for the first time that the only number illuminated on the control panel was for her unit, and an uneasy sensation overshadowed her excitement about seeing Jonah. She shifted to the side and turned to the man who was now standing behind her and motioned to the elevator control panel. "Did you need to access your floor?"

He shook his head. "I'm going to the same floor as you."

Bianca's heartbeat quickened. As far as she knew, the only person they were expecting was the delivery guy, but this man wasn't carrying any packages. Not to mention that the concierge would have called up rather than send him to the elevator unescorted.

Her eyes swept over him again, past experience causing her to look for any sign that he was carrying a weapon. She didn't notice anything unusual, but just the realization that this guy was trying to go somewhere he didn't belong was enough to dampen her palms and send a streak of panic through her.

She looked up to see they were passing the third floor, and her mind raced. She reached for her cell phone, her panic hiking up another notch when she realized she must have left it in the condo.

Jonah said something, but she couldn't quite make out the words. She couldn't just let this man walk into the condo, especially not without warning Carina.

Steeling her nerves, she shifted to speak to the man. "Do you live in this building?"

"I'm here to look at a unit for sale."

"There must be some mistake. No one on my floor is moving."

He didn't respond, causing Bianca's nerves to strain even further. The man beside her looked normal enough, but then, so had Raymond Alexander right before he tried to kill Carina and her.

Terror clawed through her at the possibility that she had literally opened the door to whoever was looking for them.

Jonah must have sensed her tension because he suddenly became quiet and gave her a questioning look.

"Hey, Jonah. Can I borrow your cell phone for a minute? I left mine upstairs."

"Sure." He pulled it out of his pocket, unlocked the screen, and handed it to her.

They passed the tenth floor.

Bianca took it with shaky hands and started dialing Carina's number. She already knew what to say, how to warn her.

Thirteen illuminated above her. The call took an indescribably long second to connect. Fourteen. Fifteen.

The elevator seemed to speed up as they approached her floor. The phone rang. The doors started sliding open. The second ring could be heard both through the phone and from inside the condo.

Jonah didn't make a move for the door, obviously waiting for Bianca to exit first. Not sure now what to do, she hesitated for a moment.

"Is this your floor?" Jonah asked.

The doors started to slide closed. Bianca grabbed Jonah's arm, yanking him forward with her free hand. Surprise lit Jonah's face, and he stumbled into the apartment right behind her. The sensor in the elevator caused the doors to open again.

A seed of hope burned inside of her that the man in the elevator was just lost, but then she looked back to see the steely-eyed stare as he slapped a hand on the elevator door to keep it open.

Jonah's phone was still in her hand, and she could hear Carina's hello coming from the kitchen. She had to warn Carina somehow that there was a stranger here, someone who wasn't supposed to be here.

She forced herself to voice her questions, praying that Carina would hear the answers and know what to do. "Who are you? What do you want?"

"You really don't know me." He said the words as a statement rather than a question. The subtle shake of his head added emphasis to his condescending tone. "You have been away from home for far too long."

"Just leave us alone!" Bianca reached out and slapped at his hand in an effort to get the elevator to close once more while Jonah looked on, alarmed.

"That's not going to happen." He stepped forward and grabbed for Bianca's arm.

"Hey!" Jonah's voice was filled with surprise and indignation. "Let her go!"

The man spoke authoritatively. "You stay out of this." He gave Jonah a derisive look before turning his attention back to Bianca. "Bianca, I think it's time you and I got reacquainted."

CHAPTER 36

CARINA NEARLY DROPPED THE PHONE when she heard Bianca's voice carry through the apartment at the same time it sounded through the phone. She heard the man's voice but didn't recognize it. All she knew was that it wasn't Jay.

She quickly ended the call that she assumed was from Bianca and hit speed dial for Jay.

As soon as she heard his voice on the other end, Carina spoke in a low, urgent whisper. "Someone's here in the apartment."

Carina could hear the tension in his voice when he responded immediately, "Do you have your gun?"

Her heart squeezed in her chest. "It's in my room."

"Can you get to it?"

"I think so." She peered out into the hall, and the sound of her sister's voice left her torn between wanting to use the element of surprise to go help her sister and go collect her weapon so she was in a position to defend herself and Bianca.

As though reading her mind, Jay said, "Don't do anything foolish. Go get the gun. I'll be there as soon as I can."

"Hurry." Carina pocketed her phone and kicked off her shoes to avoid making any sound as she started down the hall. As soon as she was sure she hadn't been seen, she raced into her bedroom.

* * *

"Who are you?" Bianca asked once again.

The man's grip tightened on her arm. "Let's go find your sister and see if she remembers me."

"Let go of her." Jonah moved forward again, pushing himself between the man and Bianca.

He reached out to shove Jonah aside, and to Bianca's surprise, the moment the man's hand made contact with Jonah, Jonah's hand bunched into a fist and he struck out.

The man tried to duck, but Jonah's fist connected with the side of his face and knocked him back a step. The man gave a quick counterpunch, and Jonah stumbled toward the now-empty elevator, his elbow knocking into the side before the doors had a chance to close. Another strike knocked Jonah down. He landed inside the elevator, his long legs sticking out into the entryway.

Jonah pulled his feet back and started to scramble up, but then he froze when the man reached into his jacket and drew a gun.

The sight of the gun once again flashed Bianca back to six months before, and for a moment, she couldn't move. She could barely breathe. Then she remembered. Carina had fought back to protect her. Now it was Bianca's turn. She took a step back and bumped into one of the padded stools along the wall and fell down onto it.

She wrapped her fingers around the top of the stool. Acting on instinct, she stood and swung it as hard as she could at the invader, slamming it into his back. The gun flew to the ground, the man falling down beside it.

The elevator doors slid closed with Jonah still inside. Before Bianca could decide whether to flee or continue to fight, the gun was once again in the man's hand. Only now it was aimed at her.

* * *

Jay raced down toward the elevator and gave an urgent wave toward the concierge. "Who went up to the sixteenth floor?"

His eyebrows drew together, clearly confused by the urgency of Jay's tone. "The young woman with you came down a moment ago to escort some friends upstairs."

"Describe them."

"Is there a problem?"

"Yes," Jay said but didn't give an explanation. Instead, he demanded again, "Describe them."

The elevator doors chimed open, and Jonah stepped out.

"There's one of them."

"Jonah! What's going on?"

"Some guy got into the elevator with Bianca and me. He pulled a gun."

The concierge picked up the phone, presumably to call the police.

Jay took a step toward the elevator and quickly reconsidered. If he went up that way, he would announce himself and could end up getting shot before he had time to analyze the situation.

He turned to the concierge. "I need to access the roof."

"Sir, the police are on their way."

"Look, I'm a Navy SEAL, and I'm not going to wait. Tell the cops to come in quiet, and let them know I'm up there." Jay grabbed a piece of paper and scribbled down his phone number. "As soon as the cops get here, have them call me on my cell phone."

"Sir, I really think you need to wait for the police."

"That's my fiancée up there," Jay said, trying to ignore the wave of panic that washed over him. "I'm not waiting."

The concierge stared at him for a brief moment and then retrieved another elevator key. "This is the master key. You can use it to access any floor." He held it out and then added, "The unit on the fifteenth floor is currently on the market. No one is living there right now."

Jay snatched the key and sprinted for the elevator. He heard Jonah's footsteps following behind him. "You stay here."

Jonah shook his head. "I want to help."

As a SEAL, Jay was used to working as part of a team, but Jonah was just a kid. The determination on his face, though, was enough to remind Jay that they didn't have time to argue. Jay gave him a curt nod and handed Jonah his cell phone. "For now, you answer that phone if it rings. You can be my liaison with the police."

As soon as the elevator doors opened, Jay used the master key to access the fifteenth floor. Jonah looked at him, confused. "I thought we were going up to the roof."

"It will be easier for me to climb up to a floor than to climb down."

"Can't you just use the stairs?"

Jay shook his head. "The stairs lead right into the living room. It's too likely whoever is up there would be able to take a shot at me before I could do anything to help the girls."

"How are you going to climb up the building? We don't have any ropes."

"I don't need any rope." Jay could tell the kid was confused, but he didn't elaborate further. He pulled his Swiss army knife out of his pocket and rushed into the apartment below Carina's. He took a quick glance around to see the floor plan was similar to the one upstairs. Considering his options, he headed for the nearest bedroom.

"What are you going to do?" Jonah asked, following behind him.

Jay hurried to the window to find it bolted shut. "Start checking windows. See if you can find one that will open."

Jay tried the library next to find its window also bolted. He was considering the best way to bypass the barrier when Jonah called out. "Jay! The kitchen window is open."

Jay sprinted for the kitchen and pushed the window open as wide as it would go and popped out the screen. "When the cops call, have them call Bianca's cell phone. Don't use Carina's."

"Okay." Jonah gulped. "Are you really going to try to climb up the building?"

"I'm not going to try. I *am* going to climb up there." Jay climbed onto the counter and slid his legs through the opening. Jonah was watching him as though he had stepped into the middle of an adventure movie and wasn't sure how he felt about his role as the superhero's sidekick. Under different circumstances, Jay might have enjoyed the idol worship, but at the moment, all he could think about was Carina.

"Tell the cops not to do anything unless they hear gunshots," Jay said with a nod toward his cell phone. "You got that?"

Jonah swallowed hard again. "Yeah."

Jay slid his body out the window, taking the time to make sure he had a good toehold before abandoning the safety of the window. "Hey, Jonah. Prayers would be helpful too."

"You got it."

Jay gripped the brick above the window, took a good look at the immediate challenge before him, and started his climb.

CHAPTER 37

BIANCA TRIED TO LOOK PAST THE gun, but she couldn't. All she could think was that she was too young to die. Deep inside, she knew this was all her fault. She had practically told Jonah how to find her. This guy must have followed Jonah or had somehow figured out how to listen in on their phone calls.

"That was very stupid." The cold, even words helped break her out of her stupor. The man rubbed his thumb along the corner of his mouth and then looked down at his hand, irritation visible on his face when he saw the bright red blood.

"Why are you here? What do you want?" Bianca asked. Then she forced herself to ask again, "Who are you?"

She heard movement behind her. Before she could even blink, the man grabbed her again, only this time he gripped her around her neck and anchored her in front of him. "Don't do it, Carina."

Bianca felt the familiar sensation of a gun barrel against her temple. She swallowed hard, panic filling her eyes as she looked up to see her sister standing in the doorway, a gun aimed in their direction.

* * *

Carina held the gun steady as she sized up the cousin she hadn't seen in nearly a decade. Silvio was barely a year younger than she, but since he was the only apparent male heir, his father, Uncle Marciano, had clearly started grooming him to someday take over the family business.

Carina had waited until there was some space between Bianca and Silvio before entering the gallery, but Silvio had recovered too quickly from seeing her for her to react. Now all she could do was stare as her sister once again became a pawn in the power play being staged by her family. "Leave her alone, Silvio."

"Well, well. It's nice to know at least one of you remembers your family."

"You're family?" Bianca managed to squeak out the words.

"We *were* family," Silvio corrected. "You haven't used the Perelli name for years."

Carina could see the disgust in his expression, but all she could think of was getting Bianca away from him. "Let Bianca go."

"Put the gun down."

Carina hesitated. If she put it down, they would be helpless against him. If she didn't, there was no telling what he might do. And the reality was that the gun was useless as long as Silvio was using Bianca as a shield. Trusting that Jay would find a way to get to them, she took a leap of faith. "I'll put it down if you let my sister go."

He considered and then slowly nodded. His grip loosened slightly on Bianca as Carina lowered the gun to the ground. As soon as she set it down, he shifted so he was only holding Bianca by the arm. He waved the gun in Carina's direction. "Aren't you going to ask me in? I think it's time we catch up."

Carina took a step back, watching cautiously as he waved them into the living room.

"What do you want?" Carina asked, her mind racing over all of the details Jay had given her over the past few weeks.

"You're a hard person to find," Silvio answered. He motioned them toward the couch. Bianca sat down, but Carina remained standing.

"You're working with Raymond Alexander's family," Carina accused. "Why? I thought our fathers were trying to push the Alexanders out of the business."

"I don't have anything to do with them," he spat back at her. "They're already self-destructing. They thought they could use drugs to build an empire, but all they did was enslave themselves to the cartels. Now that Rosa is dead, the family is free of those chains."

Her blood chilled at the knowledge his statement invoked. "You killed Rosa Alexander?"

He didn't answer.

"Obviously we don't have anything to do with the Alexander family, so why are you here pointing a gun at us?"

"You two and Gianna. You've done nothing but turn your backs on the family business. You gave up the Perelli name. You don't deserve any of the benefits. I'm not going to sit by and watch a third of my family's money get handed over to you while I spend the next thirty years trying to recover from our grandfather's mistakes."

"What mistakes?"

He seemed to debate a moment. Then one of his shoulders jerked up. "Grandfather knew Raymond Alexander couldn't be trusted, but he was so ingrained in tradition that he looked past the warning signs. By the time he realized what good old Uncle Ray was up to, it was too late. Raymond used his position at the FBI to convince Grandfather that it wouldn't be a good decision to hand over the reins to my father."

"He blackmailed his own father?"

"Grandfather became weak," Silvio sneered. "He wanted everyone to think he wasn't afraid of anything, but when he was faced with spending the rest of his life in prison, he rolled over, too afraid to fight back."

"Even if that's true, your father is the youngest son. Wouldn't my father have taken over first?"

"Not with everything he was trying to hide from us." Silvio shook his head. "We all knew he sent you away, that he didn't want you corrupted by the family. If he was too ashamed to have his own wife and children stand by his side, then he had no business being in charge."

"Your father is in charge now. And someday, you can take over. We aren't doing anything to stop that."

"I'm glad to hear you say that." He drew a folded paper out of the inside pocket of his coat. "Sign this, and then you can go back to your pathetic life in Virginia without any more interference from me."

"What is it?" Carina took the paper from him, skimming over the legal document.

Understanding dawned, and she looked up at him, stunned. "You want me to resign as trustee and appoint you in my place?"

He nodded. "It's simple. You don't want anything to do with the family. I'm just offering to take the burdens off your shoulders."

"You mean you're offering to take control of my father's money." Carina shook her head. Could it have been Silvio who had been looking for her all along? The expression on his face was cold, almost blank. It was a look she had seen reflected on Marciano's face before, usually when he made the decision that someone had to die.

His smile was steely. "Your father doesn't have any more right to the money than you do."

Terror closed over Carina as Silvio's intentions became clear. He truly didn't see them as part of the family anymore, and he was going to eliminate them as soon as he got what he wanted. Praying that she could stall him until Jay could find a way to help them, she tried to keep her voice steady. "It isn't my money to give."

"We both know better than that. In a few days, you basically inherit a hundred million dollars."

"The money's in trust," Carina said, hoping that by sharing some information she could dissuade her cousin and buy more time. "My father is a trustee too."

"Not for long."

Something in his expression confirmed her fears and made Carina suspect there was a solid basis for her father's paranoia. "What's that supposed to mean?"

He gave a casual shrug, and Carina got the distinct impression that he was backtracking when he said, "We both know your father can't act as a trustee while he's locked away."

"What does your father think about this plan of yours?"

He avoided the question. "Just sign the paper, Carina. No one has to get hurt."

"So I'm supposed to just sign this and walk away. Then you'll never bother us again?"

"That's right."

She debated for a brief moment. Her father's money certainly wasn't worth dying for, but everything inside of her told her there was more to Silvio's intention than just collecting a big payday.

"Tell you what," Carina began. "You let Bianca stay here, and I'll come with you to the nearest bank. You'll want this notarized anyway."

"Getting a document notarized won't be a problem," Silvio said arrogantly. He lifted the gun once more. "Just sign the paper and tell me where your father hid the money."

"I'll sign as soon as you let Bianca go."

He shook his head, not so much in answer to her request but more like he was silently scolding a small child. "We both know I can't let either of you go."

"Then you'll never get what you're looking for."

Anger spewed from him. In a quick move, he grabbed Carina and shoved the gun into the soft skin beneath her chin.

"Where's the money?"

"I don't know where he hid the money."

"Don't lie to me!"

"I'm not lying." Carina prayed that she could find the right words to say, some way to calm her cousin so no one would have to die today. "Please tell me you aren't really planning on killing your own cousins."

"I already told you. You aren't my cousins anymore."

Carina heard Bianca whimper behind her. "It wasn't our choice," Carina managed to say. "We didn't know it was our father who sent us away."

"I know my father came to see you. He told me you didn't want anything to do with us." Indignation filled Silvio's voice. "You think you're better than the rest of the family, but you're really nothing. You're just an obstacle your father put in our way."

"Why?"

"Why what?"

"Why is my father hiding money from you?"

He didn't answer. Instead, he shoved her down, forcing her to kneel beside the coffee table. Then he shoved the pen and paper in front of her once more and pressed the gun to her head. "Sign it. Now!"

Carina's hand shook when she lifted the pen. She was out of time. She looked up at Bianca's tear-streaked face, helplessness overwhelming her. She put the pen on the signature line and wrote her first name before the silence of the room was interrupted by the ringing of a cell phone.

CHAPTER 38

JAY HEARD THE DISTANT RINGING of the phone. It was time. Finally.

Traversing from the fifteenth-story apartment to the sixteenth had only taken a few minutes, thanks to his ability to use the windowsills to facilitate his climb. Popping the lock on the window in Carina's apartment had taken several precious more minutes, but as soon as he was ready, he had signaled Jonah to make the call. He needed the distraction.

He had chosen the dining room as his entry point, finding that window the easiest to access. Using the sound of the phone to mask any sound he might make, he now slid the window open and quietly crawled inside. He heard a man's shouted demand. "I said sign it!"

"Here." Carina's voice was shaky.

Through the doorway across the room, he could see Carina on her knees, a gun pressed against the side of her head and a paper in her hand. Jay quickly lowered himself off the window seat, but before he could retrieve the gun holstered at the small of his back, the wail of sirens rang through the open window.

The man's attention shifted immediately to Jay, and he fired a shot in his direction.

"No!" Carina screamed. The man reached for her with his left hand and sent another shot to keep Jay at bay.

Jay scrambled down behind the china cabinet and drew his weapon. He heard the man's voice demanding that Carina cooperate and Carina's pleas for him to let them go. Jay crouched down to peek around the edge of the hutch to see that the man now held Carina as a shield, the gun shoved into her side.

"I suggest you come out of there before someone gets hurt."

"Let them go," Jay called out.

"You're not in any position to make demands."

Recognizing the man's words to be uncomfortably true, Jay glanced at the doorway behind him, the one leading to the kitchen. Silently, he pressed himself against the wall and slipped into the kitchen.

He heard the man call out again, frustration in his voice. "Come out where I can see you. Now!"

Hoping to use his familiarity with the condo to his advantage, he quickly made his way into the hall and then circled to the gallery. Carina's gun lay on the ground, and he quickly scooped it up, considering. Moving to where he could see everyone clearly through the wide doorway, Jay tucked his own weapon into the back of his waistband and kept Carina's in his hand.

He took a good look at the intruder and tried to ignore the smell of fear in the room. The man was around Jay's age, and he was still focused on the dining room, with his arm wrapped around Carina and his weapon still pressed against her.

Knowing he couldn't get a clear shot, Jay looked for other options. From where she was sitting on the floor, Bianca looked around, clearly terrified. And she saw him.

Forced to use every tool at his disposal, Jay used his hands to signal Bianca, mouthing words as he tried to communicate his plan. He saw her surprise melt into acceptance.

When she gave him a shaky nod, he decided it was time to play his hand.

"You have until I count to three to come out, or I'll kill her."

Jay stepped into the wide doorway, his arms outstretched, Carina's gun held loosely in his hand. "Just let her go. No one has to get hurt."

The man whirled around to face Jay, pulling Carina with him. "Put the gun down."

"First let Carina go."

He shook his head and tightened his grip on Carina.

"Okay," Jay said, trying to keep his voice calm. "You win. I'm putting it down. Just don't hurt her."

Slowly, he lowered the gun to the floor, his eyes staying on the man's. As soon as he set the gun down and started to straighten, the grip on Carina loosened slightly, and Jay gave Bianca a slight nod.

From where she sat behind the man, Bianca used her feet to shove the coffee table into him. The table connected with the back of his knees, and the force of the impact knocked both him and Carina off balance.

Carina managed to scramble free and shouted at Bianca to run.

Jay heard Bianca's footsteps pounding toward the elevator, but his attention stayed on the intruder. He kicked out and knocked the man's gun from his hand. Jay struck out with his fist now, a shorthanded jab to the man's midsection. He groaned and dropped to his knees. Then he unexpectedly threw a hand out and grabbed Jay's leg, pulling him down to the ground beside him.

Jay yelled out to Carina, giving her the same instructions she had given her sister a moment before. "Run!"

The two men grappled, rolling over the ground, throwing punches, and the man kept trying to scramble back to where his weapon had fallen. Determined to end this fight, preferably without shooting anyone, Jay kicked out again to get himself clear. Then he sat up, drew his weapon, and took aim.

Jay's voice was low and even, annoyance humming through it. "Hold it, or I swear you're going to have a bullet in you."

Carina reemerged in the doorway, her gun in hand, and spoke to the man who was currently frozen in place, clearly considering his options. "Silvio, just stop. This money isn't worth dying over."

Jay quickly stood up and kicked the gun away from Silvio. Then he bent down to retrieve it. "Who is this guy?"

"He's my cousin."

Jay held up Silvio's gun and released the ammunition clip. He let out an exasperated breath. "Just once I'd like to meet someone in your family without them shooting at me."

Carina's shoulders relaxed slightly, and they heard the sound of a door opening. A moment later, two policemen entered, their guns drawn.

"We received a report of a disturbance."

"Yeah." Jay glared at Silvio. "I'd definitely call him a disturbance."

* * *

Carina stood in the living room and waited for the elevator doors to open. Jay had gone downstairs a few minutes ago to escort Charlie Whitmore up to their apartment.

The police had already come and gone, their statements recorded and Silvio now in custody. Before leaving the apartment, they had informed them that someone from the FBI would be arriving to speak to them in a few hours.

The local police had provided security downstairs to ensure they wouldn't have any more unexpected visitors.

The elevator dinged, the doors slid open, and Jay and Charlie stepped out of the elevator and moved into the living room.

Carina shook Charlie's outstretched hand. "Thanks for coming."

"I'm sorry it was under these circumstances," Charlie told her.

Jay motioned to Jonah. "Charlie, you remember Bianca's friend, Jonah?

"Of course."

Jonah shook Charlie's outstretched hand. "I'm so sorry. I had no idea that guy was following me."

"He wasn't exactly following you," Charlie told him. "We think he was actually following the GPS signal on your phone."

"But how did he even know about Jonah?" Bianca asked. "I thought my cell phone was set up so people couldn't trace it or anything."

"It is, but when Nigel Rafferty showed up at your school and pretended to be a reporter, he talked to some of the kids at school and must have figured out that you were friends."

"Have you found Rafferty yet?"

"It wasn't easy, but yeah, we found him," Charlie said. "He's been arrested for the murder of one of our informants from three years ago."

"I thought you said you didn't have enough evidence against him to get a conviction," Jay said.

"We didn't before, but now we have someone willing to testify against him."

"Who?" Carina asked.

"Your father."

"What?" She shook her head in disbelief. "My father would hardly talk to me when I went to visit him in prison. How in the world did you get him to agree to that?"

"We relocated him to another prison facility and explained the situation to him."

"I still can't believe he would agree to testify against anyone within the family business."

"He only agreed to testify against Rafferty," Charlie told her. "And that was only because he was threatening your safety."

"What about his safety?"

"We'll keep him hidden as part of our witness protection program. He also knows that by only testifying against the person who was threatening his daughters, he'll be sending a message to the rest of the family."

"How so?"

"Pretty much, they'll know that if they go after you again, he'll turn state's evidence against them."

"What will happen to Silvio?"

"His attorney is already on the way from Chicago, but there's no doubt he'll do some prison time. We're pretty sure we can strike a plea bargain, especially since it appears that Silvio was double crossing his own father," Charlie told them. "We believe Silvio was supposed to pressure you into signing the assets over to Marciano. He definitely didn't know the legal document had been changed to give Silvio control instead. Also, your uncle apparently didn't know anything about Silvio's intention to hurt you or about any threats against your father."

"How can you be so sure?"

Charlie gave her a smug look. "One of our sources called in right after Marciano found out about Silvio's arrest. He indicated that Marciano is very displeased with his son."

"Then you think Uncle Marciano will let his own son go to prison?"

"Oh yeah. I don't know if we'll be able to prove Silvio killed Rosa, but we have him cold on several charges. Besides multiple witnesses, we also have surveillance tapes and the potential testimony of Rafferty against him. Your uncle will undoubtedly tell their attorney to plea this one out for a reduced sentence. Silvio will take his punishment. Whether or not Marciano will forgive him enough to let him back into the family business when he gets out remains to be seen."

"What are the chances he'll come after Carina and Bianca again?" Jay asked.

"We don't have any guarantees, but we're quite certain Marciano will keep him on a tight leash from now on."

"So now we can just go back home and pretend none of this ever happened?" Bianca asked hopefully.

"We want you to stay here until after Carina's birthday. After that, we shouldn't have to worry about people trying to find you."

"Is it safe here?"

"We have assigned a protection detail to you for the rest of this week; they'll watch the lobby," Charlie said. He motioned to Jay. "I'm trusting that Jay can handle things inside your condo."

"Yeah. I actually just talked to Seth. He and his wife, Vanessa, should be here any minute. They're staying with us until we're ready to go back to Virginia."

"Sounds like you have everything covered from your end, then." Charlie motioned to Jonah. "As for you, when you go back to school tomorrow, you can't talk to anyone about any of this."

Jonah nodded somberly.

"What about this condo and the trust my grandfather set up?" Carina asked now. "What happens to all of these assets?"

"Whatever you want." Charlie shrugged. "From what the New York agents have been able to ascertain, the businesses your grandfather placed in your trust were all legitimate. They all paid taxes, and none of them has been implicated in any kind of criminal activity."

"I hate to sound skeptical, but I didn't think my family did anything that was legitimate."

"Actually, it isn't uncommon for criminal families to have some legitimate businesses so they have an explanation for where their money comes from."

"I thought maybe the government would seize my family's money."

"Like I said, none of these assets under your control has any ties to illegal activity." Charlie stood up. "I'm heading to Boston tonight to catch up with Kendra. She has a concert there tomorrow, but if you need anything, just give me a call."

Jay stood as well. "Thanks, Charlie. We really appreciate all of your help."

"I'm the one who should be thanking you. My superiors are grateful to finally have the pieces in place to shut down the rest of Alexander's business."

"Let's just hope that this time it's really over."

CHAPTER 39

THE WAIT WAS OVER. CARINA's birthday had come and gone. Along with it, the reward her cousin had offered for finding her had expired. Jay was still being overly cautious, insisting that she and Bianca stay in the condo until they were ready to head back to Virginia tomorrow, but for now, she was just grateful Jay and Seth had been in the condo to make her feel safe.

The FBI agents who had been assigned to keep an eye on the lobby area hadn't seen any activity since the day Silvio was taken into custody, and they already planned to end their surveillance today.

Last night, Jay had ordered in a nice dinner to celebrate Carina's twenty-fifth birthday. The quiet celebration had been perfect, complete with a phone call from her sister, Gianna. She had also received word from Charlie that her father's relocation had been successful.

Carina was hopeful that the FBI would allow her to see him again in an environment where he would be willing to speak freely with her, but for now, they weren't allowing anyone from his past to make contact with him.

Jay and Seth had spent the past few days scrubbing through the records her father had locked in the storage room. So far, they were convinced that Carina was aware of approximately half of the assets her father had hidden. The overseas bank account and the condominium accounted for approximately fifty-five million dollars. They believed another fifty million was hidden somewhere, but her father hadn't left any clues as to where.

Honestly, Carina wasn't terribly concerned with where the rest of the money was. Her father certainly knew where it was hidden, and she suspected it was stashed away somewhere for him in the event that he ever did succeed in leaving his old life of crime behind.

She stared out over Central Park. Under other circumstances, she might have enjoyed living here, but knowing that her cousin had discovered the condo, she and Jay had already decided it was time to sell this particular piece of real estate.

Though she hadn't discussed plans for what to do with the proceeds, she did have a few ideas that she thought both Jay and her father would approve of. She heard the elevator chime, and a ripple of anticipation pulsed through her. The sales agent for Sotheby's was due any minute. Since Jay wasn't anywhere in sight, Carina assumed he had gone down to meet her.

Carina crossed into the gallery and waited as the doors slid open. Sure enough, Jay was standing inside with a stylishly dressed woman.

"Carina, this is Marabelle from Sotheby's."

"Hello." Carina stepped forward and extended her hand as the woman stepped off of the elevator. "Thank you for fitting us into your schedule today."

"It's my pleasure." She stood in the gallery, her shrewd eyes looking past Carina to take in the view. Then her gaze landed on the painting behind Carina, and she stepped forward to take a closer look. With an expression of astonished delight, she turned back toward Carina. "Are you planning on auctioning off the artwork here as well as your condo?"

"I hadn't really thought about that."

Jay stepped forward and motioned to the painting that had caught Marabelle's interest. "I'm not really into art. How much would this collection go for?"

She pulled a notepad and pen from her oversized purse and made notes as she moved from painting to painting. "My suggestion would be to break up the collection. The individual pieces will sell for significantly more than they will if you try to keep them together. The most valuable of these would be the Cezanne, but the Monet shouldn't be far behind it. My guess would be that the entire collection would sell for somewhere between fifty and seventy-five million dollars."

Carina tried to hide her astonishment. She took a step closer to the Cezanne, for the first time taking the time to study it. She hadn't ever considered that these paintings were originals. Clearly understanding her surprise, Jay took Carina's hand and gave it a squeeze. "Carina, what do you think?"

Carina tried to hide the astonishment that was surely evident on her face before turning back to face Marabelle. "Do you think you could give us a list of the estimated values of the assets in this condo, including the condo itself?"

"Of course." The agent jotted down another quick note. "I have to say that you would probably be better off holding on to the condo for another few years if you can manage it. The real estate market still hasn't quite recovered from the downslide over the past few years. Selling the paintings would be the better source of liquid cash."

"We'll certainly consider that."

Marabelle moved into the living room. She looked around and then turned back to face Carina. "Is there any way you might consider renting this place out for the next year or two?"

"I guess that's an option," Carina told her. "I hadn't really thought about it."

"I have a client who is looking for something beginning in January. He's going to be starting rehearsals for a show on Broadway in late January and wants to move his family here for the duration of the show. This place would be perfect for him."

Carina tried not to show her excitement of having the condo produce some money. "I think we can probably work something out."

"Excellent." Marabelle motioned toward the kitchen. "Why don't you show me around, and then we'll sit down and get to work."

* * *

Jay walked into his parents' house, suitcases in each hand. He knew he should be exhausted, but the drive from New York to Virginia had been extremely productive. Carina's idea to find or build a house for his entire family was ample reason for the excitement he was feeling, but when he and Bianca had started talking about other dreams, so many pieces of their combined futures had fallen into place.

Jay set down Carina's suitcases in the living room and headed for the kitchen. Sure enough, his mother was standing at the kitchen sink, and his father was sitting at the counter with his workout logs spread out in front of him. "Hey, there."

"Jay!" Sandra dried her hands on the dish towel hanging off her shoulder and rushed around the counter to give him a hug. "Welcome home!"

"Thanks, Mom."

Carina and Bianca followed him into the kitchen and received their greetings and hugs in turn.

"How was the drive?" Pete asked, shuffling his papers into one messy stack.

"Not too bad." Jay grabbed a roll out of the bread basket his mother had yet to put away after dinner. "It took longer than we expected, but we had a lot of time to talk about what comes next and what we want to do now that we know about the money Carina's father set aside for his daughters."

Pete looked down at the counter and straightened his papers. "I guess now that you've come into all of this money, you'll be wanting to buy your own place."

Jay fought back a grin. "Actually, Carina and I wanted to talk to you about that."

Pete looked up. "You wanted to talk to me about what?"

Jay glanced at Carina and saw that she too was trying to keep a straight face. "We wanted to talk about our living situation."

"You know we'll support whatever you want," Pete said stiffly.

"Good." Carina grinned at him. "Because we wanted to start looking at some places closer to the beach this winter, and we really wanted both of you to help us look."

"Why do you want our help?"

Jay slipped his arm around Carina's waist. "Because we were hoping we could find a place big enough for all of us to live."

Pete's eyebrows drew together. "We already have a place for all of us to live."

"For now," Carina said. She and Jay went on to explain their plans to buy a house that was well suited for multiple families.

"Are you sure you really want us to combine households like that?" Pete asked skeptically.

Jay chuckled. "I think we already have."

The doorbell rang, and Bianca hurried to the front door. A moment later, she returned to the kitchen with Jonah following along behind her.

"Did you already tell him your plans?" Jonah asked with excitement in his voice.

"Not all of them." Jay shook his head.

"There's more?" Pete asked skeptically.

"Yeah, there's more." Bianca stepped forward and put her hand on Pete's arm. "You know how mad you get when you can't get enough pool space?"

Pete nodded. "What about it?"

"We found you a new pool."

"I've looked at every pool within thirty miles of here." Pete shook his head. "I doubt you found anything better than what we've got."

"It'll probably take a year or two," Jay said now, "but I think you'll be happy with the new place."

"A year or two. What are you talking about?"

"We're talking about helping you follow your dream while you help them follow theirs." Jay motioned at Jonah and Bianca. "Carina has decided to use part of the money to build an athletic complex, complete with a full aquatics facility. She and her sisters thought it would be nice to name it after their mother."

"What?" Pete's jaw dropped.

"And we want you to make sure it's done right," Carina said.

Pete's mind was clearly racing. "You're serious?"

"Definitely." Carina grinned. "So what do you think?"

"I think you two had better hurry up and finish with your wedding plans so we can get started."

Jay pulled Carina tighter against him and grinned. "Dad, I couldn't agree with you more."

ABOUT THE AUTHOR

ORIGINALLY FROM ARIZONA, TRACI HUNTER Abramson has spent most of her adult life living in Virginia. She is a graduate of Brigham Young University and a former employee of the Central Intelligence Agency. She enjoys writing what she knows and considers it a bonus when her research includes travel and attending sporting or cultural events.

Since leaving the CIA, Traci has written several novels, including the Undercurrents trilogy, *Obsession*, the Royal series, and the Saint Squad series.

When she's not writing, Traci enjoys spending time with her husband and four children. She also enjoys coaching North Stafford High School's swim team.